Novels of the Earth Witches

Viper Moon
Vengeance Moon

D0029293

Vicious Moon

A NOVEL OF THE EARTH WITCHES

Lee Roland

A SIGNET ECLIPSE BOOK

SIGNET ECLIPSE
Published by the Penguin Group
Penguin Group (USA) Inc., 375 Hudson Street,
New York, New York 10014, USA

USA | Canada | UK | Ireland | Australia | New Zealand | India | South Africa | China

Penguin Books Ltd., Registered Offices: 80 Strand, London WC2R 0RL, England
For more information about the Penguin Group visit penguin.com.

First published by Signet Eclipse, an imprint of New American Library,
a division of Penguin Group (USA) Inc.

First Printing, July 2013

ISBN 978-0-451-23826-9

Printed in the United States of America
10 9 8 7 6 5 4 3 2 1

ACKNOWLEDGMENTS

This book would not be possible without professional and personal aid from many individuals. A few, but certainly not all, are listed below. There is no particular order of listing. Each was the "most important" at certain times.

My family, whose love and support keep me going.

My editor, Jhanteigh Kupihea, who has guided me through the process of publishing.

Agent Caren Johnson Estesen, who made my stories reality instead of dreams.

My friends, fellow writers and critique partners—present and past—whose critical feedback and encouragement was, and will continue to be, invaluable.

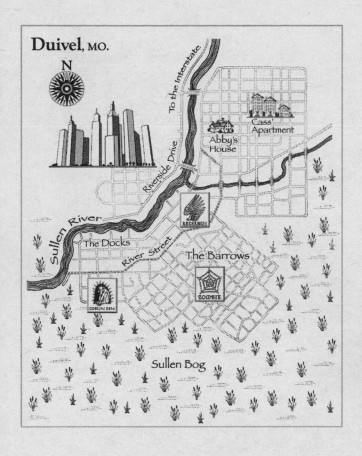

chapter 1

Disaster loomed like an earthquake-born tsunami. The moment the woman climbed into my car, that *watch your back* feeling kicked me in the ass and I wanted to hunch my shoulders and duck. I ignored it, as I had many times in the past. I based my decision on the often flawed theory that catastrophe wasn't so bad if you saw it coming.

She'd stood waiting in front of a convenience store, right where I'd been told to pick her up. She said her name was Mara, but she didn't offer a surname and refused to make eye contact.

I'm Nyx Ianira. I'm a licensed private investigator in San Francisco. I'm twenty-eight years old, a former soldier, armed guard, and an earth witch with magical powers that unfortunately didn't include the ability to discern lies. I stretched my legs, trying to ease the tension. Waiting is something every PI gets used to, but this time I couldn't relax. At least I'd had time to leave the office and change from my suit into more comfortable jeans and a T-shirt. I did wish this job was over with, though. I had a date with the owner of a dive shop later. He wanted to give me lessons. Actually, he wanted to take me to a beach in Mexico and talk me out of my bikini.

He wasn't a deep philosophical thinker, but he liked

what he saw. I have gold-brown hair with lighter blond streaks, nice perky breasts, and a tall, slim body that curves in the right places. There would be no great soul mate meeting of the minds, but it promised to be fun.

Harold, my erratic and occasionally inebriated partner at Single-Eye Investigations had called last night and asked that I take a pro bono case for him. I was to retrieve a child from a noncustodial father. While I'm always happy to help a kid in danger, the agency has firm rules against that kind of high-risk intervention. I helped write them when I became a partner in the firm. Those situations are best handled by the appropriate official authorities, the kind with warrants, guns, and badges. Harold said he'd made an exception for this one because the father was an abusive, drug-dealing fiend. Apparently he feels I'm more qualified to face abusive, drug-dealing fiends than he is. He's right, of course, but that didn't make it less dangerous or less a violation of the rules.

I had insisted that the mother—that would be Mara— come along. No way was I, a stranger, going to snatch a terrified seven-year-old by myself, even if it was legal. A kid in that kind of situation is usually traumatized enough. Now Mara and I were sitting in my car across the street from a modest three-story apartment building, waiting for our chance to get to the kid. It didn't look like the places usually associated with drug-dealing fiends. The building didn't have high security and the neighborhood appeared family oriented.

Mara didn't talk, which suited me. She might have been attractive at one time. Her drab clothes were clean, but she had the haggard look of a woman weather-beaten and aged beyond her actual years. Her hands twitched occasionally, fingers dancing across her thighs.

The early summer evening wasn't warm, but sweat trickled down the side of her face and neck. She was probably nervous and afraid of the ex, or afraid what I might have to do to get her kid back. Unfortunately, she had my discomfort level swelling like yeast bread in a warm bowl of water. Surely Harold had checked her out before he'd called me.

"What's your daughter's name?" I asked.

Mara didn't speak for a few seconds, as if she had to work to remember. Then she said, "Kate. Her name is Kate." Mara leaned forward. "That's him. He's leaving. See."

The man exiting the apartment house hurried down the sidewalk. He wasn't a substantial six-foot-seven bruiser, so I figured I could take him if I absolutely had to. Not that I wanted to get into a fight. Stealth was my method.

He continued down the sidewalk without getting into a car. Not good. That meant he might not be gone long. Timing would be critical on this little adventure.

Mara followed me as we hurried across the street and up the stairs to a second-floor apartment. I laid my hand on the apartment door and called on the powers of earth magic that were my birthright. The locks quietly opened.

"Hurry," Mara urged from behind me. Her whole body vibrated now.

Was this a mother anxious to see her child? Maybe. I knew nothing about being a mother—except that I personally never wanted to be one. I was not qualified for that.

I slowly opened the apartment door, then had to grab Mara to keep her from rushing inside. "Don't," I hissed in her ear. "You don't know who's in there." Drug dealers often had lots of guns on hand. I held her tight and she stopped struggling. She didn't stop shaking.

Fortunately, the apartment seemed empty. It was neat and smelled faintly of pine cleaner. Dishes washed and floors swept, it had none of the trash, beer cans, whiskey bottles, or paraphernalia I'd expect to see in the home of a drug dealer.

A girl's faint laugh came from the bedroom. I grabbed Mara's arm so she wouldn't run to the little girl. The kid might not be alone.

Not a problem. Mara stood frozen, gazing around the room with the intensity of a cat searching for a slow-moving mouse.

I dragged her toward the bedroom.

The little girl, Kate, was sitting on a bed with a pretty pink bedspread. She appeared quite content as she cradled a stuffed animal in her arms and hummed to a tune from the tiny headphone buds in her ears. She hadn't heard us come in. I glanced around. Again, a clean room decorated with pictures of animals and hand-drawn children's art.

I still held Mara, who by now struggled to escape. I released her.

Kate glanced up. Her eyes flew open in horror.

"No!" she shrieked. She jumped up and threw her small body away from us. We stood by the doorway and she had nowhere to go. She jammed herself tight into a corner. Her face twisted into a mask of terror, and all my uneasiness about the operation coalesced into a total rock in my chest.

"No!" Kate screamed again. "The judge said I didn't have to go with you! He told me. Daddy! Daddy!" She hunched down, sobbing, and covered her head with her little arms.

I turned to Mara. She'd better have a good excuse for this. But the bitch had disappeared.

Now what did I do? Leave the child I'd managed to terrify? Try to calm her? My mostly happy and fearless childhood had left me ill equipped to understand her panic. Other earth witches might have cast a spell to make her sleep and forget, but I had no training in such and feared I'd harm her.

Something crashed in the living room. A sick sense of impending doom I'd felt earlier descended like a massive, soul-chilling storm rolling in off the Pacific. I rushed back to the living room and found Mara on her knees on the floor. Pieces of broken ceramic surrounded her. She was scooping up loose bills. Not much, maybe a couple hundred dollars. "I knew it was here. He always hid it in the same place. I knew it. I knew." She puffed out breathless words.

Pure rage filled me. The father wasn't the addict here. Mara had totally conned my stupid partner and I'd fallen for her lie, too. This bitch wanted to steal money from her ex, not rescue her daughter. The cops would arrest me for attempted kidnapping and burglary. Worse, what horror had I inflicted on a little girl for no good reason?

I marched over, locked a hand in Mara's hair, and snatched her to her feet. The cash went flying everywhere as she clawed me, trying to escape. I caught one of her wrists and twisted her arm behind her back. We'd left the door open, so I muscled her out into the hallway. She struggled so hard I had to use magic to close the door behind us. I didn't dare release her. She'd go back in. I could comfort Kate best by getting her disgusting mother out of her sight.

By now, Mara was screaming something about needing the money. I mightily resisted the urge to throw her down the stairs.

As we emerged onto the sidewalk, Kate's father

rushed up. I didn't give him time to speak. I released Mara and she crumpled to the concrete, wailing and covering her head with her arms as if to ward off blows, just as her daughter had.

I glared at Kate's daddy. "You need better locks."

Then I marched across the street to my car. There'd be hell to pay later, but Harold, who had set me up for this disaster, would take the heat with me. I was fuming with anger. How could he not have investigated the custody battle? There must've been plenty of court documents that would reveal Mara's duplicity.

A movement down the block caught my eye.

Three tall women strode toward me. My still-simmering anger at being duped instantly vanished. I'd only seen women like those approach me once before in my life. I'd recognize that warrior's look anywhere.

The Sisters of Justice.

They belonged to a world I no longer inhabited. And they were scary as fuck. They had no magic in them, but they carried the power and authority to kill my kind. To kill me. The Sisters were the Earth Mother's official enforcers. Three of them together formed a Triad—an execution squad.

My mind raced with possibilities. I had committed no crimes, practiced no evil spells. The insignificant bits of power I used in my daily life and work were permissible—or so I thought.

So why were they stalking toward me? That meant an execution. No way had I done anything to deserve that. My well-honed fight-or-flight survival instinct surged. I had to escape so I'd have time to figure out why the bitches were after me.

I jumped in the car and raced away like I had demons on my heels.

chapter 2

Like most witches, I can see in the dark. Everything appeared in shades of gray as I sprinted through the woods of Northern California. I'd made my speedy exit from the Mara/drug dealer fiasco in San Francisco yesterday with nothing but what I carried. Summer had withheld its fickle blessing at this altitude, but I wasn't cold. I raced down the hill, leaped across a trickling stream, and started up the next one. With every breath I cursed my pursuers.

Sisters of Justice.

Three hours ago they had caught me on the highway north of Redding and run my car off into a ditch. I escaped into the Shasta National Forest on foot. I had no idea how they kept finding me. I was a better driver, but no matter what road I took, they were eventually right behind me. It was as if I had a GPS tracker on my ass. That couldn't be, because it was the first thing I checked. I'd thrown every hiding and cloaking spell I knew at them. Running away had often been an important facet of life. I had run away from my home in the southern Georgia swamp ten years ago when the leaders of my coven pressured me to take a bunch of vows and become a true certified witch. And they wanted me to find a suitable man and produce little witch babies. I didn't want to be a witch and I certainly wasn't then, or now, a high-quality candidate for motherhood.

I wanted more. I wanted the world. Anywhere I went though, they could probably find me. I solved the problem by joining the Army. Once I took the oath to serve, even witches would have difficulty extricating me from the military's clutches. Oaths and vows were impotant to them. After the Army, I'd lived and worked abroad until I returned to the States three years ago—to California, over two thousand miles from the swamp.

I still had no idea why the Sisters of Justice were after me.

I'd led them on an energetic chase. The only thing I carried was the backpack containing certain life essentials that I always kept in my car. I was battle trained by the army, and conflict trained by life—no one would take me down without a fight. Given the tenacity of their pursuit, I had a feeling it would eventually come down to that fight, using all my resources, magic, training, and anything else I could dig up. And given their official function, abilities, and numbers, I would probably lose.

I made another hill at a dead run. I could feel the power of the land in these mountains, draw upon it like fuel for a fire. It gave me the strength to run forever—or at least until I outlasted the Sisters. I was barely winded and pursuit fell farther behind with every step—until something massive slammed into my back. It rolled me over into some brush and banged my ribs across a rock. Then an enormous slimy mouth locked on my ankle and a large body plopped down on me. The body farted in my face.

"Herschel!"

The ridiculous canine that had been given to me as

my familiar when I was a baby had taken me down. I hadn't seen him in ten years. I didn't have time to think about how he got here. I pounded him with my fists. "Get off of me."

I wrestled with him, pushing and shoving, but he wouldn't budge. Since he was my familiar, I couldn't use magic on him without hurting myself. Some witches actually had familiars that helped them use magic, not pin them down for execution. I was so blessed.

It didn't take long. The Sisters of Justice were on me in minutes as I struggled.

I suddenly had my arms twisted behind my back, handcuffed, and a beaded necklace looped around my neck—a necklace infused with a powerful spell that would prevent me from using magic to escape. They'd come prepared. Worse, I'd been betrayed by a creature I thought was my friend.

The tallest of the women spoke. "Nyx Ianira, by command of the Earth Mother, you are ordered to come with us. If you resist, we are authorized to deliver you by any and all necessary means."

"Bitch. You can stick your 'any and all means' up your ass." What the hell did that mean, *If I resisted*? Of course I was going to resist. Adrenaline raced through my body, and I fought. "Dirty cowards, let me show you." I kicked one in the knee. She danced back, but not soon enough. I knew I hurt her.

It was a long difficult trek back to a highway, especially because I fought and cursed the whole way. Herschel trotted along behind us. The Sisters remained cold and stoic, though I had them breathing hard. The one I'd kicked in the knee balled up a fist and grabbed my hair once when I managed to trip her. She glared, fist drawn back, then relaxed. I had to admire her control.

The night didn't get any better when they shoved me in the car and drove to a cheap hotel. They chained me, hand and foot, to the bed. A prudent action on their part since I'd managed to get out of the handcuffs in the car. Before I could remove the necklace and form a spell, Herschel, now my seatmate, pinned me down again and stopped me.

Apparently my forcing them into a footrace had totally pissed the Sisters off. They refused to answer questions and accepted my curses with stoicism that befitted the nature of cold killers. One of them remained awake, watching me, at all times.

"I might be nicer if you tell me what's going on," I said softly to the Sister watching me. Not the one I'd kicked in the knee. They'd taken two rooms, so at least two of them could rest. "You know, a little info . . ."

"You fight good." The Sister had a lovely voice, one so totally out of sync with her rough appearance. "You should sleep. You can fight again tomorrow. I'll show you a little trick if you show me how you got out of those handcuffs." She closed her eyes. She wouldn't rest. She wasn't going to tell me anything either.

The morning after my capture I sat in the hotel lobby handcuffed and feet chained, with Herschel's massive head on my knee. His floppy jowls slimed my pants with slobber. Herschel's heritage seemed to be mostly bullmastiff crossed with a Great Dane. He weighed in at two hundred pounds, far larger than any domestic dog. Black as the inside of a deep mountain cave, he could be mistaken for a small pony at a distance. I did love him, in spite of my irritation. I'm told he arrived on my doorstep the day I was born. His primary functions in life were sleeping, eating, and farting. And there was the incessant drooling. Since I hadn't seen him in ten years and my captors, the Sisters, wouldn't speak, I had no idea how he got from Georgia to California.

"Traitor." I shoved his thick head off my knee.

Since my earthly demise at the hands of the Sisters didn't seem imminent, I had plotted an escape. The next hour was interesting. I'd managed to slip a piece of paper with the words "Help, Kidnapped" to one of the hotel maids. Someone kindly called the police.

Local law enforcement, a SWAT team even, arrived in force. The Sisters were immediately put on the defense, especially since these particular ones were really rough and well-armed characters. It came down to a gun-waving shouting match with me ready to jump behind the woefully inadequate shield of a worn couch and crawl away if bullets started to fly.

While everyone was busy deciding who had the most authority, I flirted with a really cute cop, hoping to get him to take off the spelled bead necklace. Unfortunately, every time the cute cop approached me, Herschel would growl and shove his substantial body between us.

Before long, things were settled—though not in my favor—and Herschel and I were in the backseat of a car. The Sisters had packed themselves up front. It had to be miserable, but obviously they'd been traveling with Herschel for some time and were aware of his habits. The immense canine had the backseat thoroughly slimed within the first hundred miles. As the miles passed, we drew closer and closer to my old hometown, Twitch Crossing, Georgia. Shit!

chapter 3

Twitch Crossing is not on any maps. Carefully hidden by spells, it lies down a long, winding, white limerock road to the southeast of Fargo, Georgia, and deep in the Okefenokee Swamp. The Native Americans had called the Okefenokee Land of Trembling Earth, and it was a formidable place, filled with earth magic and mystery. Alligators and snakes swam in water black from the tannic acid of rotting vegetation. Unless you were careful, it could swallow you without a trace.

As a child I paddled the waterways in my canoe and followed trails through the pinewoods and over the islands. I loved every square mile and feared nothing there. If the damned coven had left me alone, I might have stayed, or at least returned for a visit.

The white limerock road hadn't been graded in some time and rain had definitely cut ruts and holes big enough that the Sisters, crowded in the front seat, were quite uncomfortable. I was, too, but it was worth it to hear their grunts and curses fill the air.

We crossed Twitch Creek and rolled onto the two-hundred-foot blacktop that stretched through town. Founded in 1852, the town, population 169, consisted of a general store run by the coven, the barnlike structure of the meetinghouse, the school—there were six of us in our graduating senior class—and various houses of every style you could imagine.

From early childhood, I expressed no interest in becoming a full earth witch. The coven considered me a disgrace to witches everywhere. I considered them a bunch of inbred idiots. Then there was the parentage issue. Witches often had children without marrying, but usually those children knew their dads. Certainly my younger sister, Marisol, knew hers. My father remained unnamed and undiscussed by anyone. I'd long since recovered from that emotional trauma.

To my amazement, the Sisters didn't stop. Odd. I thought they were delivering me to the coven. The brief stretch of pavement passed and we were back on the bumpy limerock. Three more miles and the road widened in a place where a car could turn around. Turn around they did, and one of the Sisters said, "Get out."

Surely they hadn't brought me all this way to kill me now. A Sister climbed out with me. She stood a lofty six feet, towering above even my five-ten. "Will you go home from here?"

"Yeah, I'll go." I knew she didn't want to drive deeper into the swamp. This was a witch's place. She feared it. Were it not my home, so would I.

She removed my cuffs and chains, lifted the spelled beads off my neck, and handed me my backpack. She gave the briefest of smiles and said, "Too bad you're a witch. You'd have made a good Sister."

No problem with that. They had dumped me within a quarter mile of the house where I was born and raised. My grandmother would be there, as would some other friends. My sister, Marisol, might be home, too. Unlike me, she did quite well with the coven and her magic lessons. My Gran raised Marisol and me after our mother died. I was six and Marisol was barely three. I shouldered my pack and headed home. Herschel ambled along beside me.

The Okefenokee is many things. Deep woods and pine forests covered some of the land, but watery swamp surrounded the raised road to my grandmother's house. Cypress trees draped in veils of Spanish moss cast a cool shade over land and water. Birds sang from trees, and frogs occasionally croaked while a feeding fish rippled the black liquid.

This beautiful wild place, filled with an incredible variety of life, was home. I wiped tears from my eyes. Why had I allowed the coven to keep me away so long? Suddenly I was filled with guilt at having abandoned Gran and my sister.

I walked onto the thirty-foot-long solid wooden bridge that spanned a deeper section of open water. At the center of the span I leaned against the railing.

"Pen, are you there?" I didn't shout. He'd know I was there. He would choose to come or not.

The water remained calm for a moment, then rippled at the approach of the immense black water dragon. Penrod had been my friend from the time I learned to walk. His long slender snakelike body stretched fifty feet. He had no wings, but when he lifted his massive head from the water, it was pure picture-book dragon. He gently swayed in front of me, water dripping from his scales like fine rain.

Missed you, his words slid into my mind.

I missed you, too. I was blessed with the ability to communicate with him the same way.

I reached out my hand and he lowered his head so I could touch him. Then he slid away into the deep. There were stories of all sorts of dragons in ancient lore. At one time they flew, swam, and crawled across the earth. Only when the Earth Mother, the deity the earth witches worshipped and I long mistrusted, allowed men to become so numerous did they leave. It's said she found a place for them deep within the earth. I had no idea why she allowed Penrod to make the swamp his home.

My grandmother's house sat on a small natural island. There was enough land cleared for a frame, shotgun-style house set on tall concrete pillars in case of occasional high water. It had porches on the front and back and a metal roof that roared when it rained. Like the barn that stood a hundred feet away, the house was made of heart pine and oak, weathered gray, and never painted.

Gran sat on the front porch in her rocking chair. No sign of Marisol, but she had probably long since moved away. Beautiful and silver haired, Gran smiled at me. "Well, well, the wanderer has returned."

I started to say *Under duress*. But I didn't want to disturb her. I just wanted to drop to my knees beside her, lay my head in her lap, and wallow in the love I hadn't known I'd missed. She stroked my head and kissed me and completely destroyed me by crying. It was a while before either of us could talk. I drew another chair up and sat close beside her. My heart ached.

"Gran, I'm so sorry . . ." I swiped at tears tickling my cheeks.

"Don't be, love." Her voice, if not her appearance, was young as a girl's. "You had to leave. I told the Council that. I wanted more for you than Twitch Crossing. You simply weren't born to be a conventional witch. I wanted the world for you, and I hope you found it."

"Oh, I found the world, Gran. It wasn't what I thought it would be, but I found it."

After the army I'd entered the dark realm of private guard services that stretched across Africa and Asia. It suited me, that multiplicity of cultures in the places I traveled. I had a good memory for languages and could pick up one quickly, at least enough to get by. With the skill I learned in the army and a bit of simple magic occasionally, I survived. The Earth Mother's power drenched the land in some places, and I'd marveled at the wonder of some of the ancient hollows where men first walked. I also made a fair sum of money, which I carefully deposited in a bank in the islands.

When I'd returned to the States, I'd taken a job as a secretary for Single-Eye Investigations, a firm in San Francisco. I worked hard and eventually received my PI license. Last year, I'd let Harold talk me into investing in the firm. I had a nice condo, a good job, and a life. I couldn't get rid of the feeling that such a comfortable life was now gone forever.

chapter 4

Gran ordered me inside to eat. She'd considered me too thin all my life and made it her mission to feed me well. Apparently she'd expected me, so everything was already prepared. The Sisters had probably kept her apprised of my location. Though she seemed troubled, she spoke very little. I'd long since learned that Gran would speak in her own time. She'd tell me why I was here when she was ready. I ate heartily for her sake, and after I finished the dishes, she brewed tea for us. Insects began their evening chorus outside, and the occasional grunt of an alligator thrummed through the night. Alligators rarely came close here. Penrod usually swallowed them whole.

We sat at the table, and oh, it felt good to be there. Stupid, I was totally stupid. But I had to get to the reason I'd been kidnapped.

"Gran, why did you send the Sisters of Justice after me? That's pretty drastic. You must have pulled in some favors. Especially if you got them to put up with Herschel."

"There is one Sister I call a friend. A powerful Sister. I asked her to find you and to take Herschel so you wouldn't be frightened and run from them. They probably shouldn't have sent three, but I'm told if they hadn't, you would have escaped them." I heard pride in her voice, not admonition. It didn't last long. "Nyx, if you had stayed in touch . . ."

Ouch. She was right. I wasn't a great communicator. I could have written her from San Francisco at any time. And if I'd actually *seen* Herschel with the Sisters, I might not have been so quick to run.

Gran sighed as she sat in her chair. "I suppose I could have had the coven find you, but this problem is none of their business. They're the reason you ran away in the first place. I'll never forgive them for that." She sat quietly, hands wrapped around her teacup. The fine wrinkles on those hands were overlaid with brown spots of age. One finger twitched ever so slightly. "Nyx, I fear something has happened to your sister."

"Marisol? Where is she?" Marisol had always been the darling of the family. Jealousy did rear its head occasionally, but since I was a loner by nature, it didn't plague me a lot. When Mama died, it fell to me to help care for her and keep her from toddling off and drowning in the swamp. She was a good girl, always loving and loved in return, even by me. She also had the makings of a powerful witch, something I would never be.

Tears formed in Gran's eyes, and her small body shook. I wanted to soothe her, but I didn't think anything I could say or do would help. When she stilled, she said, "Marisol went to Duivel. Now she's disappeared."

My sister had, even in her youth, quickly surpassed Gran and her other teachers. What kind of trouble required her magically incompetent sister to help? My use of magic often compounded problems, rather than solved them. Nevertheless, I did love my sister and I'd do anything for Gran.

"Duivel. Missouri? That's where the High Witch Abigail lives. Right?"

"Yes, but Marisol went to study with a witch named Laudine, who also lives there. Two weeks ago, Laudine sent me a letter saying Marisol was missing. But she asked that I not contact Abigail." Her voice quavered. "She said that if I'd come as soon as possible, she'd tell me why. I've grown too old for that kind of journey. I immediately contacted my friend, the Sister, not the High Witch."

Gran didn't look at me. She stared across the room where Marisol's picture hung on the wall by Mama's and mine. I knew about Duivel. Most witches did. It was the center of earth magic in this part of the world.

"Gran, that sounds seriously . . . wrong. A witch disappears, but you shouldn't talk to the Earth Mother's High Witch? Do you have the letter?"

"No. It was spelled. It crumbled after I read it. And I feel that the word *wrong* does not even begin to cover the situation."

"I know Marisol would have written you, Gran. She say anything about trouble?" My tea finally cooled, so I sipped. I would have preferred coffee.

"She did write, but it's been over two months since I heard from her. I am worried, and I want you to go to Duivel. To find her."

"Okay, Gran, I'll go." Instant decision. She had only to ask. While I wasn't the perfect granddaughter, Gran and Marisol were my only family, and if they needed anything from me, they would have it.

Of course, a simple phone call would have worked, too. Witches, the Sisters of Justice and all closely associated with the Earth Mother lived archaic lives, steeped in history and tradition. I had lived in a modern world where mysticism and magic had been shed for electronics. It simply didn't occur to Gran or even the Sisters to do an Internet search to find me and pick up the telephone.

Gran stood. She grabbed the back of the chair to hold herself steady. When she carefully walked to the stove for more tea, I could see pain in every movement. An ache formed in me. Witches like Gran live for a very long time, but I didn't know exactly how old she was. "Gran, are you okay?"

"I'm fine." She poured more tea. "You need to take Herschel with you, though, just in case the Mother calls me to return to her cauldron before you come back. I won't be able to take care of him. And you may need him."

The cauldron was, of course, the place of life, death and rebirth. I jumped to my feet and drew her into my arms. I fought not to pull her frail body too tight, too close. "Don't you go anywhere. I'm not ready to be an orphan." I wanted to hold her, make sure she remained. She was all I had except for Marisol. Guilt edged its way into my fear. I was the one who left, not her.

Gran hugged me back. "Very well, darling. I promise I will remain until you return."

We talked longer and laughed as she reminded me of some of my more spectacular failures when I practiced magic. I could see her concern for Marisol even as she smiled. My strength finally gave out around ten. My back ached from sitting in a car so long, and my eyes burned from lack of sleep.

I left the kitchen, showered, and crawled into my bed, the one I'd left behind so many years ago. My room remained the same as when I left it. My old pajamas were still in the drawer, so I snuggled in, allowing the familiar scents of home to comfort me. The pillow smelled like the pots of rosemary on the porch, and the sheets slid under my skin like silk and not the well-worn cotton I knew. I didn't regret leaving Twitch Crossing when I had, but now I regretted not coming home occasionally.

Once, during the night, someone came into the room. Trained as I was, I should have wakened instantly. I remained in that foggy half-sleep area where dreams and reality occasionally meet. Vague voices came from the kitchen, but I fell back to sleep before I could determine whom they belonged to. When I opened my eyes in the morning, the sense of a presence, the presence of a stranger, remained in the air like low fog over the swamp. The fragrance of breakfast coming from the kitchen moved me to put my concern aside for a while. Gran had, magically I'm sure, cleaned my clothes. They were folded and lying across the foot of the bed. I'd been wearing the same ones for many days and they were far from aromatic.

After I ate breakfast, Gran called me into her bedroom, one she rarely occupied. The older a witch gets, the less she sleeps. I'd always loved that bedroom, even if I never wanted one like it. Lace curtains covered the windows, and a pink floral bedspread draped over the white cast-iron bed. Just the smell of it had fascinated me as a child. Gran and everything about her carried the scent of summer roses, even in a dark swamp of rotting vegetation.

I sat beside her on the bed. She handed me the thick, solid bronze band Mama had called the Dragon's Tears. A bracelet of sorts, it was worn on the upper arm rather than the wrist. I'd seen Mama wear it occasionally, but when she died, Gran had hidden it away. Though Marisol had clamored for it, Mama had promised it would be mine one day. Gran had been pretty firm about that, too, and Marisol finally stopped begging.

The bracelet tingled in my hand when I accepted it from Gran. As she released it, she said, "I've kept this thing from you as long as possible. I don't know exactly what it is. My heart tells me it is a dangerous thing for someone with little training in magic. But it is yours. Your mother called it a birthright, though she never said why."

I turned the heavy metal in my hand, my fingers tracing the three teardrop-shaped symbols cast into it when it was forged. I could feel them shift slightly under my fingers. The metal warmed, too. Gran shuddered and hunched her shoulders. "Your mother said it belonged to a warrior queen from an ancient time."

I set the Dragon's Tears down and wrapped an arm around her.

I'd probably pay attention to her warning of danger. Danger had fascinated me once, until people started shooting at me on my first job. I still loved the adrenaline rush, but I'd learned to be a lot more careful.

"My only regret," Gran said, "was that we never could find anyone to teach you about your affinity with fire."

Oh, yes. Fire. I'm really good with calling, manipulating, and throwing fire—except when I'm not. The fire thing gets out of hand occasionally, especially when I throw it. My fire sometimes acts like an out-of-control rubber ball carelessly tossed by a three-year-old.

chapter 5

Gran insisted that I take her car to Duivel. I'd need the car because no way would any respectable driver allow Herschel on a bus, and I didn't have enough money to pay for damages to a rental car. Gran's vehicle had been parked in the barn for many years. It truly surprised me when the mechanical beast actually started—and had a current tag and registration. The shit-colored behemoth of an Oldsmobile she bought in the 1970s roared down the highway, sucking in gasoline at ten miles to the gallon. She told me gas was fifty-five cents a gallon when she bought it.

She offered me money, but I declined. She had a whole trunk full of the stuff. I wasn't poor, though, and some of her bills, Federal Reserve notes, were so old they would attract attention. And the silver dollars. Marisol and I used to count and stack a fortune in pure silver, minted long before it was cut with copper. The magnificent gold coins made a priceless pile, too.

It was almost noon when I finally kissed her good-bye and drove away. I would have loved to stay another night, but her worry for Marisol probably wouldn't let her or me sleep. Maybe she would rest if she knew I was on the way. I decided I didn't need to discuss someone coming in my room. No point in upsetting her. She had wards that would tell her if someone came onto the property and Penrod as a guard. Given that protection, I wasn't entirely sure I hadn't dreamed the intrusions, anyway.

I'd left my cell phone in my car when I ran from the Sisters, so the first thing I did after I left the swamp was buy a new one. I also purchased some jeans, shirts, socks, and underwear. Then I called Single-Eye in San Francisco.

"Where the hell are you?" Karen, my computer genius of an assistant at Single-Eye, screamed into the phone. "Do you know how worried—" She stopped speaking to suck in deep breaths.

"Listen," I yelled back. "I'm okay."

Karen sputtered for a while, then settled down as she always did. I liked her from the minute I met her. She'd explode in all directions at the slightest problem, then cool off and begin a complete detailed resolution.

"What's been happening?" I asked.

"We've been trying to reach you. I went to your condo. Your car is in your parking lot. I checked inside. None of your clothes are missing. Harold is scared that he might actually have to do some work with you gone. He says he knows he did wrong. That Mara woman came up to him while he was drunk and begged him. He swears he has it all straightened out with the police. He—we— want you to come home." She drew another deep breath. "And your plants are dead."

The only thing that surprised me was the fact that my car was in the condo lot. The Sisters must have arranged for its return. My plants had died months ago.

I gave Karen her instructions. "I'm on vacation. Give all my open cases to MacLellen." MacLellen was the newest detective we'd hired several months ago. He wasn't ready for a full load, but he was smart and he'd learn. "Tell Harold to chill. I'll get back when I can. And throw my plants in the Dumpster."

My life had taken a number of sharp turns, including the one that drew me out of African and Asian firefights and into a San Francisco office. Now it appeared I was on my way to something new. I promised Karen I'd keep in touch.

I drove west on I-10, north on I-55, and on into eastern Missouri. Gran had given me a crude map of Duivel.

Herschel hung his head out the window most of the way, even at seventy miles an hour. That way, he slimed only the side of the car and the drivers who foolishly drove too close behind me. I'd gotten a late start, so I pulled into a rest stop for the night. The Olds had a monstrous backseat, so I stretched out with the pillow and blanket Gran had provided. I'd slept under far worse conditions.

Herschel, of his own free will, stayed outside at night. I had no idea what he did, but maybe he wouldn't eat anything inappropriate and puke it up in the car. He was always there when I woke in the morning.

We ate mostly at fast-food restaurants—ten burgers for him and one with fries for me. It was okay except for the time some woman chewed me out for feeding a dog "people food." I ignored her, but Herschel thanked her for her concern by sticking his nose up her crotch and sliming her legs.

The first blush of morning had already passed when I entered Duivel. Unlike in the mountains of Northern California, summer had not withheld her blessing here. A substantial city with a few high-rise downtown buildings, surrounded by expansive suburbs, it looked like average Middle America. My directions led me across the deepwater Sullen River. The blue green of the river was far from my black-water swamp.

Drive to the end of River Street, Gran had said. *Laudine will be on the right.*

I turned onto River Street at midmorning. The day promised to be clear-skied and balmy. I left the main part of the city, crossed the river, and headed south, feeling good about my journey until I punched through a ward, a mighty ward, one that could only have been created by the Earth Mother herself. Wards are a magical barrier designed to keep something out—or in. The magical obstruction slid over me like an ethereal waterfall, causing my muscles to quiver for an instant.

Herschel barked, as if he had the same sensation. Incompetent witch I might be, but I recognized energy of that magnitude. Something that powerful had to mean trouble.

It had been a long time since anything other than minor witchcraft in self-defense had interested me. This ward spoke to major events. What kind of trouble could sweet little Marisol be in? I had skills, though, skills that had nothing to do with witchcraft. Gun, knife, and high explosives might not beat or break a spell, but when used correctly, they could do serious damage to the spell caster. A powerful witch might live a long time, but a single well-placed bullet could change that. While my preferred weapon was magic, I was not averse to shooting at anyone or anything offering my sister or me harm.

River Street beyond the ward looked innocuous enough. It had repair shops, gas stations, a couple of fast-food places, and a grocery store with empty carts scattered through the parking lot.

On my left was a surprising block of new construction

in various stages of completion. It appeared so out of place, I had to slow the car and stare. Apartment houses went up three to five stories there, and retail shops faced the street. It was as if the God of Urban Renewal closed his eyes and stabbed a random location on a map. One masterpiece of steel and glass had a sign proclaiming it to be the Archangel. It had a parking lot full of high-end cars that appeared as out of place here as the buildings towering over them. Once I passed construction sites, the architecture went back to being slightly depressed and in need of its neighboring block's good fortune.

The road split and River Street continued to the left, descending on a gentle slope. The stylish business atmosphere significantly declined into a more neglected state. I passed a couple of boardinghouses, and a place called the Armory. Then everything deteriorated into bars and strip clubs. A few blocks more and most of the buildings were boarded and closed.

River Street ended in a cul-de-sac with a sign that read SULLEN BOG. Sullen Bog appeared to be expansive acreage of wretched mud and lumpy tufts of grass. It looked like plugs of hair on a bald man with an inferior transplant procedure. A bit of deeper water glimmered in the distance, surrounding a few more formidable islands. A pathetic sight for a woman who grew up in the mighty Okefenokee and waded through Asian jungles. It smelled of mud and water, but lacked the musky fragrance of home, probably because it froze in winter.

On my right as I faced the Bog was a stand-alone storefront with a sign painted on the window in brilliant lime green. *Laudine.* In smaller letters, passion-purple letters, it said *Psychic Readings, Spells, and Potions.* Most witches preferred anonymity rather than discuss spells, usually because it opened them to ridicule.

"I guess this is the place, Herschel."

Herschel grunted, then farted, prompting me to park at the curb and quickly exit the car. He followed me. As I closed my car door, a gray sedan drew up behind me. The door opened and a man climbed out. A big man, over six feet, he wore black fatigues, sharply pressed like a soldier's uniform. From the way he stalked toward me and the snarl on his face, he might as well have had the word *bully* tattooed on his forehead. I knew the type very well, having worked with them for many years. I also knew not to take any crap from him. I could see another man in black driving the car.

I stood, feet apart, hands loose, ready for action. I drew a little magic from the earth and let it shimmer around me. It brushed my skin like fairy kisses and feathers. I am the Mistress of Small Magic. I am also the Mistress of Massive Magic Disaster when I try anything bigger and stronger. Not that I let that stop me when I needed it.

Black fatigues stopped. He didn't appear armed.

"Where you going?" he snarled into my face. His voice was one that saw little use, I'd bet, other than to bellow for another drink.

"That's enough, Ralph." The driver had exited his car and hurried up to me and Ralph. A smaller man with a pinched, worried face, he stood beside his larger companion, but at a careful distance. He clasped his hands together in front of him. "Sorry, ma'am. We're trying to discourage people from patronizing that woman." He nodded at Laudine's.

A little worm of amusement wiggled in me. "Why? Is it illegal?"

"No ma'am." He hooked his thumbs in his pockets and puffed up his chest. "She claims to be a witch, and that's not the type of establishment we want for the area. I'm Johan Parker. We provide security services down here in the Barrows."

Oh, this was good. Laws were different state to state, but didn't they know that kind of intimidation was illegal?

"Tell me, Mr. Parker, how do you discourage people from using the strip bars up the street? Surely they're a better type of target for moral purification than a mere psychic. You sic Ralph on their patrons?" I choked down my laughter but couldn't stop a silly grin.

Parker glared at me. "I have my orders. No one is to go in there."

Ralph puffed his chest up and loomed over me. Oh, oh. Big buffoon on the job.

I didn't know Laudine, so I didn't feel compelled to defend her. What I would defend was my right to go where I pleased.

"Well, I appreciate your warning, Mr. Parker, but I will go where I need to go, and right now I need to see Laudine."

Ralph suddenly grabbed me by the upper arm. He jerked me toward my car. I stared at his hand, my mind forming an image. My most adept image. *Fire*. The magic responded, correctly this time, and burned his palm where it touched me. Not a deep debilitating burn, but certainly painful. He screamed and released me, staggering backward. Holding his wrist with his other hand, he stood wide-eyed, staring at it. With a howl, Ralph ran for the Bog, probably seeking water.

There are two kinds of fire. Physical fire that can burn the body, and witch fire that can burn other more personal things, like memory and emotion. Both kinds of fire were in my blood and my soul. I used fire in what I considered minor ways, but I did not delve deeply into the heart of a thing I didn't understand. I feared that, should I give in to it, it would destroy me. It might also cause me to commit a crime that would truly earn a visit from the Sisters.

Parker stood with his mouth gaping open. Using magic on Ralph was overkill, but I really don't like to get into a fistfight first thing in the morning. It tended to ruin the day, even when I won.

I decided I was done with them.

"Let's go, Herschel."

I turned to go into Laudine's. Herschel walked behind me.

The first thing I noticed when I entered was a small round table in the corner with a crystal ball plopped in the middle. The robust odor of sandalwood brushed my nose.

Hundreds of jars of liquid and powders lined shelves on the wall, all sizes, all shapes, all colors, none labeled. Either they were props for a witch's shop, or Laudine had a fantastic memory. Bunches of dried herbs hung from the ceiling, and glass cases were filled with an odd assortment of things: mirrors large and small, feathers, tiny metal boxes, each enameled and etched with colorful designs, and other objects I couldn't identify.

The witch standing behind the counter, staring at me, stood on guard; she had probably felt a strange witch's magic on her doorstep. I held out my hands, palms up. It was a universal gesture to imply I offered no aggression. It wasn't a promise that I wouldn't strike in the future, but it was an offer to talk first.

"I'm Nyx," I said, keeping my voice calm. "Marisol's sister. Are you Laudine? You sent my grandmother a letter."

"I asked your grandmother to come." I heard the immediate accusation and irritation in her deep voice.

"And she sent me. She's not well enough to make the journey." I tried not to frown. She started it, but I wanted to keep this meeting nonconfrontational at least until I was sure Marisol was safe.

Laudine, long and lanky at six feet, wore an ankle-length multihued skirt worthy of a Gypsy fortune-teller. Her hair, obviously dyed jet-black, was secured in a bun at the nape of her neck. She had an angular face, but it was smooth, regal. That face formed an expression of distaste aimed directly at me. The thing I noticed most was her eyes. Dark as her hair, they gave the impression of power. Impression being the key word. I'm not an expert at determining the power of other witches, but years of observation told me she had no more, maybe even less, power than I did. Or she was exceptionally successful at hiding it.

"I don't approve of what you did out there." She nodded toward the window. Her mouth pinched into a sour line. "It will cause me more problems."

"I don't approve of men grabbing me. Why did he try to stop me from coming in here?"

"Certain people have determined that my business is somehow out of character for the area. Redevelopment! That's what they call it." She sneered. "The Barrows is evil. And that evil will win out, whether or not I'm here."

Now I was confused. "And the Barrows is . . . ?"

Laudine studied me for a moment, then suddenly relaxed. Too suddenly. "Let me make some tea and I'll explain."

Damn witches and their tea. With the exception of Gran's, I usually avoided the stuff. I could have used coffee. I hadn't had any since dawn, and something told me that I'd need to stay alert in Laudine's presence.

chapter 6

I followed Laudine through the back of the store to a sizable kitchen. It didn't have the homey feel of Gran's place. This witch obviously didn't spend much time here. It held the basics, a few cabinets, small stove, and a small refrigerator. All had a look of disuse. A round table with four chairs sat in the corner. At least the cloyingly sweet odor of incense and herbs didn't reach here.

"Please sit down." Laudine spoke with her back to me as she prepared the tea.

I sat in one of the chairs and Herschel went to lie in a patch of sun by the open back door. Laudine hadn't commented on him, but seemed to have automatically accepted him as my familiar. She worked in silence until she brought two steaming cups to the table. Her preparations had taken long enough to put me on edge. I wanted to start demanding answers, not sit guzzling tea.

Laudine took a slow sip of her brew. I didn't touch mine. Was she trying to piss me off? The arrogant tone of her next words confirmed that she was indeed spoiling for a fight.

"Marisol was a delightful little witch." She gave a light flip of her fingers. "But she was a bit frivolous at times.

She would often go off for days at a time. I figured she had a lover."

I sat silent, trying to show no emotion. Marisol had a sunny disposition, but was as far from frivolous as the Arctic Circle was from the equator. I had no clue about lovers. I'd been gone too long for that.

Laudine continued. "This last time, a month ago, when she didn't come back—"

"A month!"

Laudine jerked. I realized I had shouted.

Laudine raised her nose in a completely arrogant gesture. "Yes. She's not helpless. I understand you are something of a nomad. I've heard you called a vagrant."

"Vagrant? I move around, but I can assure you that wherever I am, I have a serious reason to be there. And this isn't about me." I fought the anger curling inside.

Laudine's jaw clenched so tight I doubted she could swallow tea then if she wanted to. She relaxed, as if sensing she had pushed me too far. "You don't understand. I need to tell you from the beginning, about this place. About the Barrows."

The front door slammed. The sound of heavy footsteps marched through the store. Fear flashed across Laudine's face.

Herschel raised his head and growled. Something dangerous approached.

I'd brought my backpack in with me, but extracting my gun or the knife I always carried there would be difficult. That left only magic to deal with a threat.

A man stepped through the doorway. He stood over six feet and had a rugged body, slim and lean but at the same time well muscled. Jet-black hair curled slightly against his neck and around his ears, and his eyes . . . oh, those eyes . . . cold, dark, and dangerous as black ice on a frozen highway. He had copper-colored skin with sharply defined black tattoos down his taut forearms. Not pretty colored tattoos or pictures, but inked midnight curved like pieces of a puzzle. His jeans fit that impressive body well, as did the gun he wore openly in a shoulder holster over his T-shirt. There are places in the world where that might be done, but this was Middle America. Most everyone owned a gun of some sort—they usually kept it out of sight. He obviously didn't give a shit.

I'd met men like him before—powerful, dangerous. They were usually lovers or enemies. The look on this one's face said he didn't have love on his mind.

"Didn't I warn you about using magic, Laudine?" His voice was as deep and dark as the rest of him. This was a man who got what he wanted, when he wanted it. A man used to being obeyed.

Laudine sat hunched in her chair; her posture said she was ready to jump and run. Witches are not supposed to run—ever. At least that's what Gran taught me. Well, if she wouldn't take charge ... I stood, drawing his attention. I spoke firmly. "If you're referring to those two dogs who tried to bully me when I arrived, I will defend myself as necessary."

He looked me up and down for a long time, then obviously dismissed me as a lightweight. I'd basically told him I was a witch and he dismissed me like a servant. I'd teach him to pay attention.

Laudine stirred. She'd apparently gained some strength from my defiance. She still would not meet his eyes. "You think I should not have visitors?"

Why was a witch cringing before this man? Explaining herself?

He crossed his arms over an impressive chest. "I've

told you before. You need to leave the Barrows. Go find another place to sell your petty magic. And you." He nodded at me. "You need to leave right now."

I stared into those dark eyes . . . and laughed.

He drew an almost inaudible breath, nothing more.

Jumping into battle without knowledge of your opponent's true strength usually did not end well, even for a witch. Not that such a consideration ever stopped me.

"Nyx, don't . . . ," Laudine pleaded. "You don't understand. Let it go." She turned to the man. "Etienne, why can't you leave me alone? You've driven off all my customers. This is my friend's daughter."

She pleaded with him. He had challenged both of us. I was ready to fight and she begged. I clamped my teeth, holding my rage. It was her house. Etienne, she'd called him. Where had I heard that name?

He stood for a moment; then some fleeting emotion passed over his face. "Laudine, this isn't personal and you know it. Your time is running out here."

Laudine stared at the wall.

Etienne turned abruptly and walked to the front door. Oh, no. It wasn't going to end like this. I followed him.

When we got outside on the sidewalk, he abruptly turned to face me.

"Who are you?" he demanded, but once away from Laudine some of his edge had dissipated, replaced by curiosity.

I watched him for a few seconds. His face was a bit worn, but not hard to look at. It would be quite handsome if he smiled. I doubted he was older than his late thirties. Deep underneath I could sense an earthy wildness, something tightly controlled but ready to strike like a stalking leopard.

"My name is Nyx."

He raised an eyebrow, obviously speculating. "And you're a witch?"

"If you say so."

"The man you burned said so."

"He shouldn't have grabbed me."

He frowned slightly. "Why are you here?"

"My business."

"Not entirely." He left me and climbed in a black SUV and drove away. I stared after him. He had disturbed me on a level I didn't understand. There had been men in my life, but this one . . . I shrugged the thought away. I'd deal with it later.

When I returned to the kitchen, Laudine stood in the middle of the floor, shivering.

"What in the Earth Mother's name is wrong with you?" I threw up my hands in disgust. "You're a witch and you can defend yourself. Why are you afraid of him?"

Laudine staggered to her chair and plopped down. I sat and waited for her to calm. When finally relaxed, she picked up her teacup with both hands and drank. She set it down on the saucer and laid her hands flat on the table. "It's a long story. It involves the Earth Mother, magic, and a demon hiding in the ruins." She let out a long sigh. "And that Etienne is more dangerous than any of those." She closed her eyes. "He's immune to magic."

chapter 7

"Immune to magic? How?" I'd never met a person who was immune to magic, though I'd heard it was possible under rare and specific instances. A string of spelled beads from the Sisters had certainly kept me from using magic to escape.

Laudine leaned back in her chair, her eyes filled with tears. "He's more than immune. If you hit him with a spell, it bounces back tenfold. I know. The spell I used almost killed me when I tried." She lowered her head. "To protect myself, of course. He terrifies me."

"That's not immune. If it bounces back, it's a shield of some sort." She should have known that.

She shook her head. "Did you see a spell around him?"

"No." She was right. I'd have felt it if he'd been spelled. If he was immune, it was for some other reason.

Laudine wiped her eyes on her sleeve. "Come with me. I need to show you something."

I followed her out the front door. Herschel groaned, but he came at my heels. He hadn't slimed her house, but slobber began to drip as soon as he hit the sidewalk. Laudine didn't bother to lock up behind her. I suspect any trespasser would get a surprise, though.

The pink morning through which I'd driven had morphed into a sunny day, and a clear sky promised it would remain that way. For a brief second, I wondered about the weather in SF, but the thought drifted away in the warm air.

Laudine set a ground-eating pace as we walked across the cul-de-sac to a big boxy building that might have been a warehouse at one time. The doors were boarded with plywood and it had no signs, except an orange one taped by the door that said DEMOLITION PERMIT followed by a lot of fine print.

Laudine didn't hesitate as she went around to the back of the building. Like good puppies, Herschel and I followed. When I rounded the corner of the building, I stopped. Before me stood a long, narrow street in ruins. So many buildings had crumbled into that simple roadway it was impassable by car.

I walked closer, threading my way around piles of glass and debris. It was as if time had suddenly turned malevolent, overcome its human keepers, and crushed their dwellings.

Laudine flung out a hand. "This is the Barrows. From here north are square miles of ruins, some like this, some better, some completely collapsed. Near the center is the heart of evil—the Zombie Zone, they call it. That's where the demon hides."

The demon. My lessons in earth magic involved the Earth Mother, her power, and living in the natural world around me. There were no angels, no demons to cloud things. Had I missed something?

I didn't know what to say. I'd seen ruins before. I'd walked through many from the Middle East to Southeast Asia, some ancient, some blasted to rubble by modern warfare.

"What caused this?" I demanded.

"Earthquake. Mass exodus sixty or seventy years ago. Followed by a slow decline. Some witches say the Earth Mother drove people out. I know the Mother deliberately hides the ruins from people living uptown with a spell. Beyond that . . ." She shrugged.

Laudine's face became a mask of pure hatred. "And the demon!" She spit out the word. "He's not really a demon. He's just a creature, a monster from another world. Brought here and held prisoner by the Earth Mother. The Earth Mother who betrayed us, her witches, her daughters . . ." Her face crumpled and she gave one sob. "And I believe that demon has killed Marisol. I am little threat to him, but she . . ." She drew herself up and headed back to her shop.

I stared down the wrecked street a minute longer. Mostly I wanted to know what Laudine based her claim on. She seemed like a pretty unreliable witness. Her words and actions so far were so unwitchlike they raised suspicions. I really needed to investigate the claim that the Earth Mother hid the ruins stretching before me with a spell, too. That was beyond anything I'd ever heard. Herschel came to stand beside me.

"What do you think, buddy? Is there a killer demon down there?"

Herschel growled low in his throat.

"I'll take that as a yes." I'd reserve judgment about other things. The Barrows, a demon, Marisol—there was more to this story than the few words she'd given me.

For the first time in my life, I regretted the excuses, bogus illnesses, and outright blatant lies I used to skip every class on witchcraft I could. The geography and history of the nonmagical world brought me straight-A grades. Math? Piece of cake. I'd been told by Gran my desire not to be a witch, not to play by the rules, would hurt me someday.

I followed Laudine back to her place.

When we returned to her kitchen, she seemed calmer and made more tea. I wondered if she'd let me buy her a coffeepot. When she sat again, she began her tale.

"I don't know all the details of the Barrows ruins and the collapse. That's history. More current is that the Earth Mother herself brought the demon here several years ago for unknown reasons. Aiakós is his name. He is hers. Her toy. She plays games we cannot comprehend. She protects him.

"There were two other witches like myself living in the Barrows and now they are gone. Last year when the pressure to leave began, I appealed to the High Witch Abigail. She, too, very politely told me I should go away. I will not."

"Why?" I asked. I'd grown uncomfortable with this. One of the reasons I'd left Georgia was coven politics. If Laudine's statements were true and involved the High Witch, it went far beyond political scheming.

"This is my home. I've been here for over forty years."

That seemed a simple enough reason. In her place, I'd fight, too. Experience made me cautious. I'm not a truth-sayer, a witch who can discern lies, but Laudine wasn't telling me everything.

She continued. "You saw that warehouse across the cul-de-sac? That was once a bar called the Goblin Den. Then it was a fancy restaurant."

"People would come all the way down here for a restaurant?"

"The demon Aiakós has a son who was born in this world. They call him Michael. People, his followers, his worshippers, would come down here for the demon's son. You will understand when you see him."

"What does it all have to do with Marisol? Why do you believe the demon has killed her?"

"He feared her. Marisol was the only one here in the Barrows with the power to defy him. Other than the High Witch—and she will not."

A tiny breeze brought the odor of rotting vegetation through the open back door. It didn't smell clean and natural like in the swamp.

"Marisol had your reaction to my harassment," Laudine continued. "She chased off any who came and bothered me. She stood up to Etienne, even though I warned her about him. They had words. She even went to Michael, the demon's son, and asked for help. He seemed appalled that it was happening, but she went missing shortly after that."

I smiled inside. I could picture beautiful, powerful Marisol on a righteous crusade. "I'll ask again, Laudine, why not go to Abigail, the High Witch?"

"Because"—she lowered her voice to a bare whisper—"I believe Abigail is protecting the demon. I believe—I fear—she has betrayed her witches."

I remained quiet, absorbing the information. I had difficulty believing the High Witch, who I was told had direct access to the Earth Mother, would overlook the murder of one of her own. Other than that, Laudine's story *seemed* plausible enough. Still, I'd heard the hesitation in her voice at times. She'd paused too often, as if trying to decide what to tell me.

Laudine had an apartment upstairs on the second floor, where she lived, but she led me to what had been Marisol's room beside the kitchen. She told me I could stay there. It was cozy, had a small bathroom attached, and reeked of my sister. Her personal scent clung to everything. Her penchant for light colors, blues, and whites were evident in the curtains, bedspread, and rugs on the floor. Clearly, she found something of value in Laudine's lessons—or something else she found here—and planned to stay a while. Her clothing hanging in the closet was comfortable but very fashionable—as I remembered her. I searched her things, trying to find her Grimoire, her witch's diary. It would contain an account of what she'd been doing in Duivel. It would be locked and spelled, but knowing Marisol, she might have left me a key. She loved and trusted me. But it wasn't there. Either she'd hidden it well or someone had taken it.

I had stopped at a discount store on the way to Duivel, but my bag of things, jeans, T-shirts, and personal items, took very little space. I had a whole closet of clothes in San Francisco anyway.

On the table by the bed was a photo of me and Gran, taken before I began my walk on the wilder side of life. I looked so young, barely a teen, even though I had thought myself grown. I don't usually dwell on things I can't change or life as it might have been. I'd watched friends die and I'd killed to protect them and myself. I had had lovers, though none could be called the love of my life. Given my nature, I didn't have much hope for finding a Prince Charming who would tolerate my eccentric habits. I had part ownership in a profitable California business that would remain profitable if I could get back to it. I was satisfied with my life as it unfolded—if I could only find Marisol unharmed.

Laudine had come to stand in the doorway. "What's that?"

She nodded at the soft cloth that wrapped my gun to keep it clean. I'd laid it on the bed as I emptied my bag.

"That's a Smith & Wesson nine-millimeter." I liked my gun a lot, even if I hadn't used it in a while. I practiced regularly so I wouldn't lose my touch.

"A gun?" Laudine sounded shocked. "You're a witch."

"I've been too many places where magic alone wouldn't be enough to protect me. Look at the bright side. I can always shoot Etienne if magic doesn't work." I unwrapped the gun.

"You think Etienne can be shot?" I heard hope in her voice.

I had to stifle that quickly. "I'm not here to kill anyone. I'm here to find Marisol. But he probably shouldn't get in my way."

She stared for a moment, then turned away. "I've made some lunch," she called behind her. "Come and eat."

I'd hoped she'd give me some clues over lunch, but she remained quiet. Herschel wanted out and I let him go. He could take care of himself.

"Who was the last person to see Marisol?" I asked, breaking the silence.

"Michael. As far as I know." She sounded dismissive. "The day after she talked to him, she went out and never came back."

That sounded like this Michael, supposedly a demon's son, was a good place to begin. Over lunch, I asked Laudine more about the politics of the Barrows and specifically who the most powerful players were.

She looked annoyed but answered anyway. "The black troops, as I call them, are under Etienne's charge. Some are weak clowns like the ones you saw this morning. He hires them out as security for businesses. The ones you *see* are always the weak ones. The ones you don't see are well trained and far more dangerous. Etienne has a small army hidden in the ruins. You won't see them until they strike.

"Michael is powerful, simply by being the demon's son. He's the one doing the so-called redevelopment here. Michael's only companion is a witch's daughter who is not a witch herself, but the Mother has given her certain . . . powers. I'm told Etienne works for Aiakós. There are a few street gangs called the Bastinados. They are vile, but disorganized and not as prominent as they once were. They have a leader of sorts. I know nothing about him."

"The police?"

"Virtually no presence down here, except for the tax cash cow of the docks. They come if there is something they are forced to notice. A big fire, explosion, things like that. If you call them, they sometimes forget to come before they even hang up the phone. It is an unfortunate consequence of the Earth Mother's spell to keep attention off the Barrows. To keep attention away from the demon.

"All other policing is private—or nonexistent. I will admit that Etienne has done a good job of keeping River Street viable. His security team patrols and protects legitimate business so people who do come from town are safe—except my customers." She stopped for a moment and again, I had the cavernous feeling in my gut that she wasn't telling me everything.

"That's all?"

"No. There are the Sisters of Justice."

"Here?" That stunned me.

"Two of them. Retired, I believe. They run the Armory, a women's defense school. And I'm told they occasionally persuade pimps to leave town. Bastinados aren't safe when they're around."

This was a thing I would never have expected: Sisters of Justice, the Big Brother of witches, doing community service.

"Okay, Laudine, we have private security, gangs, and Sisters of Justice. Is that all?"

"There is the demon himself, but he's never been seen as far as I know. Etienne does his evil for him."

"Have *you* ever seen the demon?"

"Only once. If you ever do see him, you will understand. You will understand that he is quite capable of killing a witch."

A confusing array of players lived here, it seemed. And I could not be sure who ruled and who served. I believed Laudine's picture, while it might be accurate on the surface, did not tell me the whole story of a very complex place.

After lunch I left Herschel to his own pursuits and headed up the gentle hill that made River Street. An easy journey since I had walked many miles up and down the hills of San Francisco. Laudine had told me where to find Michael. She said it was safe to walk as long as I got back before dark, so I set out at a steady pace for the glass and steel palace called the Archangel.

chapter 8

I walked past the boarded buildings, stretching my legs along the low rise of the ascending sidewalk. Broken sidewalks required careful steps at times. The faint whisper of a breeze kept the car and truck exhausts to a minimum. That same breeze glided across the storefronts in soft waves.

Cities intimidated me when I first left the swamp. In my desperation to escape, I'd traded the Okefenokee's deep natural silence for the babble and roar of human and mechanical chaos. In time, I'd come to respect the power of chaos and human activity, but I would probably never favor it over the solitary peace of nature. That's why I often left the towers of San Francisco for the woods and more natural places.

It didn't take long to reach the line of bars. Only those that offered food were open; the others remained locked until the coming night. They had few customers. I'd had a lot of fun in bars during my soldiering years. I could drink but had enough control not to get dangerously drunk—except when I wanted to.

A few early prostitutes stood outside, leaning against the buildings. Their faces held bored and somewhat hopeless expressions. They didn't know or care, but their sisters in Africa and Asia were treated far worse. They were often prisoners, slaves by day and forced onto the streets at night.

Farther up the hill I passed the small and forlorn businesses, those that seemed to be hanging from the proverbial thread. A grocery store, a rooming house, and across the street the place called the Armory, supposedly run by the Sisters of Justice.

My first and only actual experience with the Sisters had not been positive. I carried a witch's wariness of them, hence my hesitance to seek them out. I needed to learn about this place, though, and the Sisters would have their own take on things. I crossed the street.

A silent door opened and closed behind me, shutting off the grumble of traffic outside. I'd entered a room completely empty except for a plastic-covered foam mat spread over half the floor space. The place had a sense of energy—a very human energy that had nothing to do with earth magic.

A woman stepped into a doorway that apparently led to other rooms in the back. She had to be at least six feet tall. Sister of Justice indeed. Like all of her kind, she stood balanced on the edge of instant violence. She had tan skin that spoke to heritage rather than baking under a hot sun. Her tank top and shorts covered a healthy, muscled body. A woman that tall, with that kind of bulk, could look coarse and masculine. This one didn't. Just the same, she wasn't someone you'd expect to meet at a garden party.

"Good morning, Sister." I wanted to stay on neutral ground with her.

"Good morning, witch." Her voice was deep but smooth.

"How do you know . . . ?"

She grinned. "You have a tattoo on your forehead that's only visible to Sisters."

"Well, damn." She'd stunned me. Sisters of Justice weren't supposed to have any power like that.

The Sister broke out in peals of laughter. She clapped her large hands in delight.

Okay, I'd been had. "Well, I'm glad I provided your laugh for today."

"Yeah, you did. I'm Eunice. I was going to go looking for you. Got a call wanting to know if you arrived. Couple of Sisters said they left you in Georgia. Apparently you didn't provide any laughs for them."

"That's because they were transporting me under duress. I did my very best to make the journey as miserable as possible for them."

That got me another laugh. I guess she approved of the challenge I gave her fellow warriors. Then she sobered. "I've been ordered to help you. If you need it."

The surprises kept coming. She was ordered to help me. Ordered. Not volunteering. "I'll remember that, Sister. Thank you."

A group of four girls—teenagers—walked into the place.

"Go get changed," Eunice said to them. "Gonna work harder today 'cause you were so pissy last time."

They didn't speak. Pretty girls and not so pretty girls, with the hard defiant eyes of juvenile delinquents. They walked with the wariness of the abused. Abused, but learning to fight back. I'd seen that look in young eyes in Africa where children were forced into sexual slavery or to carry guns they could barely lift.

"I teach them not to be victims," Eunice said.

I'd stared at the girls long enough that she noticed.

"That's good, unless they use their skill to become better aggressors themselves."

Eunice shrugged. "It happens."

I left her there and continued my journey.

The Archangel came up on my right. I wondered who thought up such an inappropriate name. The parking lot was filled with high-end vehicles, most running in the fifty- to a hundred-thousand-dollar range. I know because I'd considered buying one last year. Given the state of traffic on the streets of San Francisco, I had decided that I could put my sixty thousand dollars to better uses, so I made a down payment on an upscale condo with an excellent view of the city and the bridge.

Glass and steel made nice modern buildings. and through the clear windows I could see two floors of exercise machines, all filled with huffing and puffing patrons. When I entered, the chilly hush of an air-conditioned breeze brushed my skin. How much electricity did it take to cool a place that massive? Through multiple glass interior walls, a blue swimming pool reflected light around the room. The whole place reeked of a surplus of money, freely spent by management and patrons.

The first person I met was a receptionist in a pink stretchy outfit that left nothing to the imagination. She not so politely demanded to know if I had an appointment. Her pretty face scrunched into a mask of disgust and she looked at me like I was a derelict, maybe the vagrant Laudine called me. She figured I was going to beg for money from her wealthy patrons. There must be a universal job description for barely dressed girls in places like spas and exclusive clothing stores. Wanted: egotistical young bimbo to dump shit on customers who don't meet a narrow perception of affluence. My jeans were almost new and while my white shirt was a bit rumpled, it was clean and definitely acceptable. So what was her problem?

"I want to look around," I said.

"I'm sorry. No one is permitted to do that without an appointment." She didn't sound the least bit sorry.

"So make me one." I shrugged and gave her a go-to-hell grin.

She frowned, clearly annoyed, but tapped keys on her computer. "Well, how about next week . . . ?"

"How about now."

I'd no more than spoken the words when a woman approached. Long black hair streamed around her shoulders and her stance said she could fight if necessary. I'd seen the posture of course, very recently. It appeared out of place here. Sister of Justice. Although I have to admit I'd never thought to see one in a really sharp, tailored suit. The creamy fabric enhanced her darker skin.

"Is there a problem here?" the woman asked. She sounded genuinely concerned.

I shrugged. "No. I just wanted to look around before I signed up."

The woman nodded politely. "My name is Madeline. I'm the manager here. I'll be happy to show you everything." She turned and I followed.

When we were out of the receptionist's hearing, she gave me a formal greeting for a witch. "How may I help you, Innana's daughter?" She wasn't a witch, but she knew I was.

I smiled. I really wanted to keep things friendly. "You look like a Sister, talk like a witch."

"I am neither," Madeline acknowledged my statement, still playing the polite game.

I'd bet hers was an interesting story, but I didn't have time. I had to start somewhere.

"I'm here about my sister, Marisol. She came here a month or so ago and talked to someone named Michael. She had a complaint about some men harassing her mentor, Laudine."

"I remember her. She . . ." Her voice trailed off as two men in black fatigues approached, obviously intent on me. My old buddies from yesterday morning, Ralph and Parker. Ralph had a bandage around his hand. I gave him a warm smile.

Madeline stepped between me and the men. Her rigid stance shouted, *Don't screw with me.* "What is it? There's no problem here."

They stopped, glared at me, then turned and left without protest.

Madeline turned back. "Come, we can talk to Michael."

I followed her around the machines and their sweaty, struggling occupants to a long silent hallway toward the back of the building. On my left was a room with a multitude of computer screens monitoring every inch of the pool and exercise floor. We went into an office and I was again reminded of the many bizarre things I didn't know about the world. It seemed like an inordinate number of them were in the Barrows.

"Michael," Madeline said.

Michael. He was stunning. Blond, beautiful, wholly masculine, he was the most spectacular creature I had ever seen. Oh, he looked like a man, but when I slipped my vision to witch sight, he blazed like a golden statue — a statue that screamed danger. There was something not quite human about him. I'd heard nonhumans existed in the world, but I had never seen one.

But I now knew why they'd named the place the Archangel.

A chill settled over me, prickling my skin like nettles. I gathered my magic close and Madeline stepped between me and him. Incredible. She'd felt my gathering power. She assumed the posture of a Sister of Justice ready to do battle. "He will not harm you," Madeline warned. "And you cannot use magic to harm me."

"Okay." I didn't relax. I only had her word that he wouldn't attack. "What is he?"

"My husband."

Michael smiled, clearly amused and unperturbed by being referred to as a *what*, though there was a cloud of tension gathering around him.

"And he's the one who talked to Marisol?"

Madeline relaxed—slightly. "Let's start this over again. I'm Madeline, this is Michael, my husband, and you are . . ."

"Worried. My name is Nyx Ianira. I'm looking for my sister, Marisol. She's missing and I'm told you were the last person to see her."

"I remember her," Michael said. His voice was low and soft as fog on a swamp. "She was concerned about Laudine, the witch at the end of River Street, being harassed. I spoke to Etienne, but . . . is there a problem?"

"Only that Marisol has disappeared and Laudine is still getting harassed."

chapter 9

Michael and Madeline stared at each other with eyes obviously communicating a vast amount more than they were going to say to me. When they looked back, they had locked emotion down completely and were acting as one person.

"How long has your sister been missing?" Madeline asked.

"A month . . . I'm told."

"And Laudine?"

"Doesn't know anything." I cocked my head a little to show some skepticism about the truth of Laudine's words. "Except that she's gone."

Michael laid a hand on Madeline's shoulder, asserting control of the situation. She bared her teeth, obviously objecting, but said nothing. There would be words between them later.

"I will speak to Etienne again and inquire about your sister." Michael gave me a brilliant smile that said I didn't have to worry about anything. "I'm sure everything will be fine." His voice was like a spell. I could feel it tugging at me—not earth magic but charisma that he apparently thought would work to keep me placated. I laughed softly to show my amusement at the thought he could charm me with his voice.

Madeline nodded at me. Her expression seemed to acknowledge that I hadn't fallen for his benevolent Prince Charming ruse—and it amused her, too. "I'm going to talk to some people, too," she said. "Including Etienne. He has good reasons to intensely dislike witches, but he's going too far. Laudine is harmless."

"I met Etienne. And the fact that some witch busted his—" I stopped myself before swearing. ". . . abused him is not my problem. My sister is." The assertion that Laudine was harmless was a bit of a stretch, too. The lack of actual power did not always coincide with the lack of the ability to do harm. Even a weak witch could create chaos at times.

Madeline came toward me, seemingly urging me to leave. She offered consoling and meaningless words as she escorted me toward the door.

I nodded politely and did as she wished. I'd bet there were going to be fireworks between them before I got out the front door. Laudine was right about one thing. They were power players here. I just wasn't sure of their actual role.

A yellow sun had settled on the horizon when I walked back to Laudine's place. It was that time of day just before afternoon reached its peak and fell silently into evening. Traffic quieted as day people went home to families and supper, and night dwellers prepared for their time to howl. An SUV, similar to the one Etienne drove, rolled by and slowed, on pace with me. The windows were tinted so dark I couldn't see who it was. It turned off after I went a few blocks.

When I reached the cul-de-sac, I was surprised to find several cars parked there, ordinary cars, sedans in no-color grays and whites. One taxicab waited with them, happily running his clock. I stepped into Laudine's shop and found six middle-aged and elderly ladies standing frozen, staring at me. Their bodies were hunched, purses clutched to their bosoms and eyes widened in fear.

I held my hands up in mock surrender. "I'm harmless. I swear."

"That's most assuredly a lie," Laudine said from her place behind her counter. "But she won't hurt us."

The ladies relaxed, but kept an eye on me. I went to Laudine.

"These are customers," she said. "They need my herbs and potions. I called them to come while it was quiet."

I grinned at her. "You mean while I'm here to kick ass."

She acknowledged the fact with a brief nod. She went back to her deft measuring of dried leaves and powders.

It was fine with me. In trying to drive Laudine out, someone had frightened these relatively helpless women without just cause, much as I had frightened little Kate in San Francisco only days ago. That was not acceptable. I almost wished some bully would come so I could do a little more ass-kicking.

More women came, and for the next hour I helped Laudine package her herbs, teas, and lotions. She did, indeed, know every one of them without labels on the jars. By the time the last customers left, a deeper darkness had drifted from Sullen Bog, bringing a less than fragrant odor of rotting vegetation.

"What did we sell those women?" I asked as she went to lock the door against the darkness. I didn't care, but what she sold would tell me something about her.

"Mostly herbs for hot flashes. There were some for arthritis and sleep. They've been my customers for years—and their mothers before them."

The sound of an approaching vehicle—a heavy vehicle—

came from outside. When I looked out the store's front window, I saw a set of headlights aimed at the place. A truck, maybe a ten-wheeler, approached the store. This could not be good.

Laudine's face paled and her eyes widened.

I *disliked* violence in general. I'd lived with and participated in too much of it. *I hated* the fear I saw in Laudine's face, and that made contemplating a little carnage easier. There was also the matter of her helpless, but fortunately departed, customers. "You better go out the back and hide," I told Laudine. "I'll deal with this." I'd certainly been attacked before, but I usually had backup. Laudine didn't count, because she was so weak, she'd probably only interfere with whatever I needed to do. "Have you seen Herschel?"

"No." She quickly left out the back door.

Herschel wasn't exactly the best familiar. I hadn't fought in a long time, and never like this. I always had comrades, fellow fighters. At least I could fight and use magic without worrying about accidently injuring my friends.

The truck stopped. In an instant, high-beam headlights and spotlights illuminated the store like a cloudless noon. They needed light. I didn't. I shot a thread of magic toward them, trying to skim the electrical wiring behind the lights. It worked. Sort of. The headlights and spotlights exploded, plunging everything into darkness.

Damn. Often when I tried magic, it went wrong. Sometimes it was my lack of training, but sometimes I just felt incompetent. I had to go on, though. I used my attackers' momentary confusion to step out back and run to the side of the building. I dropped to the ground. I didn't think they could see me, but there was some light from a few streetlights and they did have flashlights.

Ralph and Parker, the guys in black fatigues I'd bested earlier in the day, hadn't had guns, nor did they have weapons at the Archangel. I could see the shapes of men milling around—and yes, these ones were armed. I counted eight, but there might have been more. They were not dressed in Etienne's black fatigues, either. I saw the flash of a lighter and spied a bottle with its rag fuse being set ablaze. They planned to burn us out.

One of them threw it at Laudine's glass window.

Amateurs. A single spike of sharp hard magic from me flipped it back and slammed it through the truck's windshield.

Oops! I'd meant to toss it in the Bog.

It exploded in flame. Now there was plenty of light. A whole burning truck full. Which was bad because they had no way to leave—and they could clearly see me.

One of them fired into Laudine's store. A single shot and her fancy glass window burst and glass shards flew everywhere. I didn't know if she was inside. I immediately threw up a shield. Several others drew and started firing—at least until the bullets bounced back at them. They only had handguns, no automatic rifles, but what came my way was deadly.

Using magic to toss things around is easy. The fire, too. The shield I used to stop bullets was something else. I'd rarely tried it before. Unskilled and unpracticed in that area as I was, I'd inadvertently drawn too much earth magic power. It surged through my body like electricity, holding the shield, but drawing most of my physical strength like water down an open drain.

Any witch can use magic, but there is always a physical price. The purpose of potions, spells, pentagrams, and training with an experienced witch is to reduce the corporeal drain on the body. Since I never learned the actual craft, I had to manipulate magic with my own personal strength and will. I made do with my small magic in the outside world, but when I entered the Barrows, a place steeped in earth magic and other mystical powers, I quickly realized the price was too high.

The shield held, but it drove me down. Dirt and small rocks bit into my hands and knees as I tried to crawl away. I had to get farther from the battle. I'd never had the patience to learn my lessons on how to draw major magic slowly and safely, and I was paying now. Where the hell was Laudine? Even a little of her magic would help me. I'd been drained trying to save her damned store.

I heard the shouts behind me, but they were suddenly silenced by a terrific howling from the Bog. The sound rolled and undulated like a pack of wolves, but was cut off by the grunt of a giant alligator. I'd heard nothing like it in my life. I had bigger problems, though.

The beam of a flashlight found me lying on the ground, and I was suddenly surrounded by men and guns. One of them kicked me in the ribs. I rolled away, but another boot—steel-toed—caught me on the hip. The kick in the ribs was a warning tap, but the one on my hip sent brilliant pain searing through my body. They were just getting warmed up.

The howl from the Bog came again, only closer.

My attackers stopped paying attention to me. They stared around, wide-eyed, guns pointed everywhere. There was no specific focal point. They flashed the lights around, but the pitiful beams could not possibly illuminate much.

Something black flashed over me. The thing was the size of an elephant—or it seemed that way. A man screamed. I could see nothing but four thick legs the size of trees and a bulk of black covering my body. Some unknown creature, some monstrous darkness, hovered over me, protected me. At the same time, it crushed me with the claustrophobic sensation of being trapped in a coffin. For one awful moment, my mind went blank with terror. Inches above me was this blinding mass, a living body of some creature beyond my comprehension.

More screams came, shots fired, and all sound condensed into a roaring in my ears. Chunks of dirt shot up where bullets slammed into the ground beside me. None touched me. I lay upon the Mother's body, the earth.

Lying prone on the ground, listening to the sound of its magic, I desperately willed the power to rise, to come to me. It didn't. I'd gone too far. My misjudgment would cost my life. The world faded. I would never find Marisol.

chapter 10

Awareness came with a pure white light blasting through my eyelids. I slapped my hand over them and got dirt all over my face. I kept my eyes closed tight and flailed around only to encounter Herschel, who was apparently lying by my side.

Herschel grunted, farted, and moved. Oh, damn. Using my arms to force my body into a sitting position, I brushed the dirt away. I sat where I'd fallen the night before.

Laudine approached. She had a broom in her hand. "Your familiar wouldn't let me touch you to bring you inside." She spoke in a monotone and stared up the hill toward Duivel. "She even came from her throne up there." She nodded toward Duivel. "She felt what you did last night. But even she didn't challenge the dog. Why is that?"

"Who came?" My body throbbed like an impacted wisdom tooth and my legs didn't want to work right.

"The High Witch Abigail, of course. I understand she is very angry." Detached, seemingly uncaring of a stranger, she stared down at me. "You should come in, shower and dress. There are probably going to be consequences today." She turned and walked away.

What in the Earth Mother's name was going on here? I'd grown up with a bunch of inbred witches and seen a lot of insanity in the world, but this reached the top of the pile. And what was the Earth Mother's High Witch angry about? Laudine being attacked, or me defending her?

I managed to rise with a minimum of moaning. I stared around me. The only sign of last night's battle was a large patch of scorched and pitted asphalt and the missing store window. I knew the burned truck did not roll away under its own power.

When I staggered inside, Laudine had most of the glass from the single bullet swept up. Other than the window itself, damage seemed minimal.

I held on to the walls as I tottered to my room— Marisol's room. Laudine said, "I'll have some healing tea that will make you feel better after you clean up. You'll probably need food, too." She didn't look at me. At least she didn't complain that I'd let a single bullet through.

My body ached as I limped into the room. Muscles twitched with little sparks of fire, and bones creaked like arthritis consumed them. The only time I'd ever lost control since before Gran was there to help me. Since that single time, I'd stuck to my small magic. What I could do, I did very well. The other stuff like throwing up shields . . . shit, I'd screwed up.

After I showered, I dressed in a pair of clean jeans and a T-shirt. When I entered the kitchen, I found Etienne sitting at the table. He stared at me without expression. Had he forced his way in? No, he came and went from this place as he pleased. I knew she couldn't, or maybe wouldn't, have stopped him. She'd raised no objection when he came in yesterday.

I sat at the table across from him because I could no

longer stand. Laudine set a cup of tea in front of me. It smelled of oranges and spice and I could feel the tiny healing potion surrounding it. I immediately picked up the cup with both hands so I wouldn't drop it. I swallowed the lukewarm liquid. The potion slid through my veins and eased my hangover from indulging in too much magic last night—then the hunger began.

Magic consumes a lot of physical and psychic energy. It depletes the body, but for me, it can be cured with rest and food. I didn't have time to rest.

Laudine presented me with another cup of healing tea, a knife, a whole loaf of unsliced bread, a couple of bananas, and a large chunk of cheese. Not exactly a gourmet lunch, but I didn't care. I ignored everything while I acted like a ravenous pig. When I was finally full, I leaned back and nodded my thanks to my master chef. Then I turned my attention to the man across the table.

Etienne wore a T-shirt, but this time he wore a leather vest over it that obviously covered his gun and shoulder holster. He hadn't spoken during my meal, as if he knew what I'd done to need nourishment. I considered his attractiveness a curse. Those arms looked strong, and if he were to smile . . . ah, no. I had to stop thinking about him. Lean, tough, and he could take care of himself. I still didn't like him.

"Did you come to complain or apologize?" I asked.

"Neither. I didn't send the men who attacked you last night. I want to know what happened." He leaned back and smiled, warm, friendly—and a complete lie. I could see it in his eyes.

"You want to hear my side of the story. But you don't like witches, so I'm sure you think it's always the witch's fault." I glanced at Laudine. She looked away. I gave a casual shrug. "Men with guns came. I sent them away."

"Maybe they only meant to frighten you."

"Possibly. Maybe I did misunderstand. Maybe the firebomb was a peace offering. It did brighten things up."

He raised an eyebrow at that. Had he not known? Or had he thought I started the blaze? I wanted to ask Laudine what she saw before I answered any of his questions. She, in the meantime, was doing her usual stone statue impersonation.

"Come outside. I want to show you something." He stood.

"Nyxx?" Laudine jerked as she became animated. She spoke with desperation in her voice. "You shouldn't . . ."

I stood. I held up a hand to stop her comments. She'd lost all credibility with me. "I'll be okay. And we need to have a talk when I get back." I wanted to know what she knew about the terrifying creature that loomed over me last night.

I followed him out the door, pretending I didn't hurt. Recovery was going to take more than herbal tea and food this time. Herschel was lying on the sidewalk. He growled deep and low in his throat as Etienne walked by. I smiled my approval at my familiar, but his enmity didn't seem to bother the man. Etienne led me to the side of the building to the spot where I'd made my deplorable "bed" last night.

"Look here." He pointed at the dirt. I followed his lead. There, punched into the dirt, were the impressions of clawed feet. They were the size of platters. "What do you think that is? A grizzly bear doesn't make prints that big."

"What am I? A Boy Scout with a tracking badge?"

I didn't know the prints, but unfortunately I'd seen them before. My swampy homeland had many creatures living in its depths, some I'd never seen. We'd relied on

Penrod to patrol around where we lived and Herschel to warn us of impending danger. Prints like the ones Etienne pointed out had appeared occasionally on a path or trail I followed. As a child I was totally fearless. I'd followed the tracks, heedless of the consequences. By luck, or the Earth Mother's blessing, I never found the creature that made them.

Etienne simply stared with expressionless eyes, then asked, "Why are you here? This isn't a social visit."

"I'm looking for my sister. Laudine seems to have lost her. Marisol. Little witch, about five-four." I held out my hand, palm down at that approximate height. "Dark hair, brown eyes, really pretty when she smiles." I saw no point in not telling him. Michael and Madeline knew her, and he obviously had some contact with them. His antagonism toward witches made it highly unlikely he would not have seen her or spoken to her. She would never have feared him—and Laudine said he had met her and she had defied him.

Oddly enough, I could see a bit of curiosity form on his face. "Lost?"

He didn't deny he knew her.

Another vehicle arrived in the cul-de-sac. This one a van. The man in black fatigues who stepped out was not like the others. He walked like a soldier, and I knew him. He was older, dark-skinned, with gray streaks in his hair. He had a powerful, stocky body and intelligent eyes set in a smooth face. His hands still had evidence of the arthritis that had plagued him for years.

"Nicky!" he shouted with a laugh. "What in the hell are you doing in this garbage heap?" He rushed up, grabbed me, and lifted me off my feet and swung me around. I hugged him back. Darrow, once my boss and partner, and a good friend. Darrow appeared to be about forty, but I knew he was pushing fifty. He still looked good.

I hadn't seen him since I left Africa, looking for a different life. I loved him and I wasn't really happy to see him here, associating with Etienne. I had few friends, few people I trusted, and I didn't want Darrow as an enemy—or to put him in danger.

I slapped him on the chest. "What do you mean *garbage heap*? It has running water, electricity, and grocery stores; what else could I ask for?"

Darrow grimaced. "A lot."

I glanced at Etienne, who was seeing the potential to learn more about me than I wanted him to know. Darrow added to the uncomfortable situation. "Hey, boss," he said to Etienne. "You need to hire her. She's the best. Good to have at your back. And she can sneak in anywhere."

"Really." Etienne looked even more interested.

"Oh, yeah." Darrow hugged me tighter. "Yeah, one time in Mali . . ." His voice trailed off. He acted like he'd said too much, spoken too casually. Darrow never did that. Darrow said exactly what he meant to say and his words were a warning to me.

Etienne did what Darrow wanted him to do. He raised an eyebrow. "What happened in Mali?"

I pulled away from Darrow. "A mistake. Nothing worth talking about."

"Right," Darrow said. Still grinning, he handed Etienne a piece of paper. "Carpenter said you should see this."

Etienne accepted the paper without looking at it.

Darrow turned back. "Listen, Nicky, there's a bar two blocks east of River Street on Eighteenth Ave. called Larry's Place. Me and the boys go there on Friday and

Saturday if we're off. Rocky and Salvatore are here, too. Come by if you can. Be like old times."

"I will." I pulled out my cell phone and held it up so he could see the number. "Memorize that. Call me."

Darrow had been the leader of the troop of guards I worked with for six years before I returned to the States. Rough but intelligent men, I liked them all. I was just out of the army and surprised when Darrow hired me. As a woman, I had to prove myself. I used my army training and a little bit of magic to remain as gender neutral as possible. I proved that I was physically tough enough. But they instinctively knew something odd had occurred when I used a bit of magic to help us in our duties. I became their good-luck charm. Excellent things happened when I was around—except when I created a disaster.

Darrow hugged me again before he climbed back in the van and drove away. Etienne again asked, "What happened in Mali?"

He annoyed me, but because of Darrow, I remained polite. "The usual. A convoy. We were guards. Mostly goods, arms, ammunition. But there were passengers and I was guarding a rich widow and her female servants. Bandits started a nasty firefight. We barely escaped. It wasn't a stellar moment in our careers."

Actually, we'd screwed up badly. We'd jumped into a situation without enough information and had lost everything but our lives. It took a year to recover. I think Darrow had mentioned it as a warning. Not to take action until I knew all the facts.

Etienne and I stood there in the warm summer air and I realized that, because of Darrow, we'd made a tenuous connection. I had made none with Laudine, even though we were considered sisters serving the Earth Mother. That connection did not mean I could trust him.

Given Darrow's working for him, he was probably the Etienne I'd heard about, the leader of mercenary soldiers, and I was . . . well, I had a certain reputation, too. He and I had walked in the world of war-torn countries, guards and thieves, and lots of guns. A world where often your only loyalty was to your comrades of the moment and the man who paid you. If Etienne paid Darrow, Darrow's loyalty would be to him. If I were Etienne's enemy . . . ? No, I would not put Darrow in that position. I'd find another way to get to Marisol.

Etienne watched me with grave intensity. He'd know every pore of my skin before he was done. Somehow, he'd also physically moved closer than I usually allowed anyone to come. I hadn't realized it was happening. I stepped back.

Etienne smiled. It was as if he'd made a decision or believed he knew something I didn't know. He nodded politely and walked toward his SUV.

chapter 11

I went back inside to deal with Laudine. She sat at the kitchen table, sipping a cup of the inevitable tea, but she lifted a finger and pointed at a coffeepot and a cup on the counter. There was sugar and cream there, but I wanted mine pure, potent, and black.

"Okay, Laudine. What happened after I passed out last night?"

"A ... creature came out of the swamp." She rubbed her hands over her face. "A massive ... thing. I've lived here a long time. I'd never seen it before. I couldn't tell exactly what it was." She laid her hands flat on the table to still their trembling. "I'm sorry. I'm such a coward. I ran away. I hid in an alley until just before daylight."

I remembered the tree trunk legs surrounding me and the sense of a massive body hanging over me like an elephant. I would probably have run, too, if I could have moved.

I drained my coffee cup and rose to get another. "Who scraped up the burned truck and took it away?"

"I don't know. I heard noises before daylight. I stayed hidden."

And I had slept through it all. "Do you believe Etienne? That he didn't send them?" I returned to the table.

"I don't know."

"What did Abigail say when she came?"

"Not much." Laudine sneered. Her shame for being a coward had smoothly morphed into irritation. "Oh, she acted all concerned, and angry that it happened, but she didn't offer to help. She just stared at you a while, then left."

I finished my coffee and decided I'd better spend the day exploring. I loaded my backpack with a few essential items. I stuffed the gun in, deciding not to carry it on me. Magic and my knife should be sufficient. Very carefully applied magic. I did take Marisol's picture and my cell phone.

Once in the car, I called Karen in San Francisco. She answered without enthusiasm and I realized it was a little earlier out there. While I basked in the warm Missouri sun, it was probably a bit less temperate on the bay.

"Good morning, Ms. K. What's happening?"

"Oh, it's you. Finally. And we're just peachy, thank you. MacLellen is sitting at his desk, crying. I think he's been there all night. Harold called and said he could work better on the golf course. We wrote our aggrieved custodial father a significant check for the trouble we caused him and the little girl. Harold was drunk when he promised that despicable woman he'd get the kid. And I brought your plants in here to see if I could save them. What do you want?"

I laughed. "Ah, and I love you, too. Go give MacLellen a hug and a pep talk. Get him food and coffee if he needs it. Tell Harold to stick to his golf game. The business will be better for it. And the plants don't need saving, they need resurrection. I need some information ASAP."

"All right, let me get my notepad."

The business wasn't really in bad shape. Thanks to my controlling the money and giving Harold a generous allowance to stay away, we had solid cash backup and an accountant. The bills would get paid.

"I want you to research some things. Start with Duivel, Missouri. Look into the Archangel, Bastinados, Zombie Zone, and Abigail. You might find some weird stuff, but just record it. Look for the name Etienne with a connection to Africa and mercenaries. Spell it different ways so you don't miss anything."

I told Karen I'd call her back later in the day or tomorrow. I got the feeling she was really interested in my research. She was so competent she often got bored. She stayed with the firm because we paid her an exorbitant amount of money and she really cared for us, even Harold.

I doubted if any traditional witch would resort to using the Internet. The average witch fundamentally worked with nature and didn't deal with electronic data. Magic and spells aside, I'd take the chance that younger witches would be savvy in the newest trends, and they might be spreading things they shouldn't share with the world.

I parked close to the one street where I'd seen a little cross traffic and locked and spelled the car against the improbable chance that some thief would decide he needed a gas-guzzling antique. I had a good idea of River Street, but I wanted to see more. I started walking east, leaving the relative noise of traffic behind.

Some of the buildings I passed were abandoned. Others were obviously used, but I couldn't determine for what. They had clean facades and numbers above each door. Across the street was a clean, well-marked parking lot. Fresh oil drips from cars staining the asphalt told of recent activity. People had come here in significant numbers at times.

I passed Larry's Place, the bar where Darrow said he and the others hung out. It was Thursday, so I'd try it out on Friday if I could. I walked on. Silence reigned this far from River Street. I walked past storefronts with shattered glass windows. The chunks that had fallen on the sidewalk crunched under my shoes and made a sound like popcorn in a popper. It looked like apartments stacked above the storefronts, but I had no way of verifying that. A sense of despair filled this place. A thin breeze sliding through narrow alleys between buildings carried that desperation, even if no one remained here to feel it. It gave the sense of going on forever, a rubble-filled wasteland with no end.

Four blocks down, a ragged van drew up beside me. I'd heard it coming, of course, but the streets here were clear, so it wasn't an improbable occurrence. Doors popped open and men poured out. I was suddenly surrounded by what could only be Bastinados, the gangs that Laudine had said united under a new leader. They all wore chains and baggy clothes that I was sure covered weapons. Some were black, some white, others of a more indeterminate race. A few glanced over their shoulders, eyes darting to cover every inch of the area behind them.

"You come with us," one of them said.

"Why?"

They closed in on me, grabbed my arms, and forced me toward the van. I let them shove me inside. They did so with little effort, so obviously they weren't trying to hurt me. Yet. It seemed crazy, but I didn't really feel threatened. They didn't take my knife, probably seeing it as not much of a weapon against their masculine might. I realized that I could use magic here and no one would pay attention. It wouldn't be like the burning truck in the middle of the street—which actually hadn't attracted any outside notice, either. Deep in these ruins I didn't have to hide or excuse my power as I so often did on the outside. If I could release my magic without consequence, I could take care of things, maybe with a bit more finesse than I had last night. Well, except for the thing that came out of the Bog and saved my life. That might be a bit of a challenge if it turned on me.

The van drove three or four blocks, then turned south. It wove through piles of debris and ruined buildings, none that appeared to have been occupied in many years. Atrophy had this area firmly in its grip. We passed row houses set close to the sidewalk with shreds of curtains hung in some windows. A forlorn rusting tricycle sat on one tiny front porch, as if waiting for its owner, now probably an adult, or maybe even a senior citizen, to return. It had all the appearances of a terrifying mass exodus. What had been so alarming that it caused the desertion of square miles of a city?

The van finally stopped in front of what might have once been a grocery store. I was again surrounded and carefully escorted inside. As we entered the building, my guards spread out. A man stood there, apparently waiting for me.

At first I mistook him for a boy, a tall teenager. He wore a shapeless unfitted gray suit, and had brown hair, brown eyes, and a face that could only be described as pretty enough to be a girl's. Somehow, he reminded me of someone, but I couldn't say who. This was the leader of the armed thugs who had kidnapped me? I knew perfectly well that size or appearance didn't dictate any kind of power, but it seemed that this guy would have to constantly prove himself.

The gang members quickly scuttled out of the building, leaving us alone.

"Good afternoon," he said. He spoke in the voice of a man raised in the upper ranges of polite society. "Please pardon my methods, but I wanted to speak to you."

"Ever think of sending a note?"

"No. I'm often rejected when I do that. I don't like rejection. I am Anton Dervick."

My kidnapper wanted to be pleasant. I could do that. "And I'm Nyx."

"Nyx. Well, Nyx, you *look* harmless enough."

"I am. As long as no one attacks me."

"As they did last night." Dervick sounded a little too smug, especially since my attackers had the shit beat out of them.

I nodded. Dervick was still smiling, and his body language—hands carefully clasped in front of him—seemed innocent. Again, that sense of recognition came over me. For a moment, he seemed to shimmer at the edges before settling into his unremarkable shape again.

"Do you know what this place is?" He held out his hands in a grand gesture.

"A fairy-tale palace in disguise?"

A frown wrinkled his pretty face. He dropped his hands. Apparently I didn't amuse him.

"I mean the Barrows. As a whole." His voice tightened, became clipped, annoyed.

I wasn't sure what answer he was looking for. "Streets, buildings, businesses, miles of patchwork ruins, traffic."

"I have a wider vision." This time he went for a lofty tone, as if he possessed an all-knowing eye. This guy enjoyed acting, role playing. I was not impressed. "I see it as a fortress. A fortress of what might be called paranormal energy."

I nodded. Dervick's fortress was probably everything contained by the Earth Mother's ward, constructed to keep Aiakós the demon in check. I wondered how he knew about it.

He clasped his hands behind his back. "Last night, inside this fortress, someone, specifically you, set off a lightning storm of energy. No one who feels that paranormal energy could help but be disturbed by it."

I shrugged. What he called paranormal energy I called earth magic. Interesting. He'd just told me he could feel earth magic. Not impossible, but rare in a man.

"I will defend myself, Dervick. What do you want with me?"

He stepped closer and I pulled a little bit of his so-called "paranormal energy" from the earth. It tickled my feet and rose like bubbles of laughter. His body tensed and he stared as if he were trying to hypnotize me. He leaned forward, eager for something. His eyes had turned from brown to gold. "How did you do it? Can you do it again? Where did the thing, the creature that slaughtered men, come from? Can you summon it?"

Oh no. I did not answer questions about magic from this guy. "How about you tell me why you attacked?"

"To destroy that woman, of course. That devil witch." Dervick's fingers suddenly twitched as if playing the piano. This guy had serious issues.

"Devil witch? Why?"

"Because I gave her the opportunity. I invited her. Offered her great riches in exchange for a few minor things. She laughed at me. Then she killed my men."

"That was downright rude of her." I raised an eyebrow. "You kidnap her? Like you did me? Try to hold her prisoner?" Laudine feared Etienne, but she obviously didn't fear this little man.

Dervick's face reddened. His dancing fingers clenched into fists. "Do not mock me. She needed to know who had the real power in the situation."

The sounds of shots suddenly erupted. Men shouting, more shots.

I smiled at him. "Sounds like the cavalry has arrived. Did you send for them?"

"You come." He waved his hand, summoning me.

"No thanks. But it's been fun and maybe we can talk again sometime." I had a lot of questions for him, but I preferred not to get caught in the middle of a battle. I turned to go and a circle of fire flared around me. Now that was a surprise. The flames burned higher, closer.

"Come with me," Dervick threatened. "Or you'll burn."

I understood part of the recognition I felt with him. He was not a witch, but he carried one of the powers I called my own. Fire. He was weak, though, and I was certainly more proficient in that area. His little ploy wouldn't work with me. I simply snatched control of his flame. I broke the circle and sent it dancing across the room at him, flashing it up in his face. He staggered backward. Oops! I think I singed his eyebrows. The fire quickly died as I released the power holding it.

I caught a glimpse of pure shock on Dervick's pretty boyish face before he turned and ran. Oh, this was good. I was still laughing when Darrow raced up to me.

"Nicky? Are you . . ." He was fully armed with automatic rifle, vest, helmet, as were the men surrounding him. They looked like a SWAT team, only there were no white letters identifying them printed on their black outfits. What in the Earth Mother's name were they doing dressed like that?

Etienne came marching in behind them. He didn't go for the fancy armament and looked just fine in his jeans,

T-shirt, and leather vest. He carried that significant pistol in his hand, ready to aim and fire.

Darrow and the others surrounded me, but Etienne came close. His face was grim and those really dark eyes were full of fury as he glared at me. "What happened?"

"And good afternoon to you, too." I was in no mood to answer his questions. If I'd have had more time with Dervick, I might have gotten some information from the little twerp.

After a few moments of furious silent face-off, Etienne drew a hissing breath through his teeth. "You're a problem. I told you—"

"I'm a problem? Well, I've found that if you ignore a problem long enough, it resolves itself. You could try to ignore me. I can live with that."

I offered him a small bit of advice that I wouldn't take myself, simply because my problems took grave pains to bite me in the ass while I practiced ignorance.

"And who made you king of this place, anyway?" A dark temper rose in me as I made that demand.

He stepped closer, probably to intimidate me. I didn't intimidate easily. I had had a few deadly confrontations that darkened my path through life. I'd won, or at least escaped, all of them.

Etienne glared at me. "My men, my guns. That puts me in charge. I told you to leave the Barrows and you wouldn't. Now you do as I tell you." He whirled and stalked toward the door. "Bring her," he ordered without looking back.

The sudden pronouncement astonished me. He wanted me a prisoner? I hadn't expected it. Etienne's leadership couldn't be faulted, but I wasn't one of his men and he needed a lesson in manners. And a witch's power. He might, as Laudine said, be immune to witch-craft, but I had other weapons.

"Hey!" I shouted just as he reached the door. He stopped and turned. "Check this out, Mr. Immunity."

A rock the size of a football lay by his foot. It jumped in the air and stopped at eye level. He backed away from it. For all the good it would do him, he raised his gun. The room grew still with anticipation of violence. The men around me remained quiet. There were no gasps of sur-prise at the sudden show. With all the power I could draw without draining myself, I flung the rock toward a far wall. It punched through the wall like a cannonball—and probably through the wall of the next building. The impact came sharp as a rifle shot that reverberated through the empty building. An echo of thunder rolled around the room.

Darrow stepped close. He'd be in the line of fire if the men started shooting at me, but my friend's first instinct rose to protect me. How completely gratifying.

Etienne stared at the wall where the rock had punched a three-foot hole. He had in no way lost his composure. "That was good. Behave yourself and I'll let you do a magic show after dinner." He walked out.

"Son of a bitch," one of the troops said.

I figured his words pretty much summed up every-thing. Good men, though. I'd startled them, but they hadn't panicked.

Darrow sighed. "Nyx?"

Darrow only called me Nyx when something was wrong. Until then I was always Nicky. His loyalty was supposed to be to the man who hired him. He didn't want to force me, but he did as he was told or his reputa-tion was shot. He might actually *be* shot along with it.

The situation had placed him in a precarious position, and I would accomplish little by fighting him here.

Under different circumstances I'd have contested Etienne's domineering order. He had no right to take me or order me taken anywhere. I loved Darrow and for Darrow's sake, I went along. And, yes, Etienne and the men around me, their lack of reaction to a violent paranormal event, made me very curious.

They surrounded me as we walked out. Darrow stayed close, walking beside me. Again, he'd be in the line of fire if I tried to escape—and he knew me. He knew I'd chosen to come. Of all those I'd worked for and with over the years, he knew me best. I had missed him.

Etienne's men had arrived in two large black vans. I followed Darrow in—only when he sat, I plopped down on his lap and hugged him, ratcheting his uncomfortable situation to a damned high level.

"Thanks for the rescue," I said softly in his ear, even though I knew everyone could hear.

"Did you need rescuing?" He sounded doubtful.

"No. But I truly appreciate the concern for my welfare."

Darrow sighed. "I told him you'd be okay. He didn't believe me. He saw you pushed into the van."

He had to be Etienne.

"He's watching me? Or he just happened to be driving by?"

Darrow wouldn't meet my eyes. "You'll have to ask him."

Oh, yes. I had a lot of questions for Etienne.

chapter 12

Darrow introduced me to his men as an old companion, which obviously made them uncomfortable. They'd heard Etienne's orders to forcibly take me. My easy compliance and friendship with Darrow confused them. Was I a friend or an enemy prisoner?

I couldn't see much, but the van moved easily through the streets. It came to a halt and a door rolled up, allowing it inside a massive warehouse. More hardware filled the space, including trucks, armored and transport vehicles. Etienne had enough equipment for a small army. I'd presume he had the men and firepower to back it up. This I hadn't expected. While I'd come to recognize that the Barrows was strange, what was here that required such armament?

Darrow led me out across a parking lot to another warehouse building. All I could see around me was more tall warehouses and empty streets. There were no vehicles parked outside and they appeared abandoned.

Etienne stood by one building, waiting. "Leave her here," he ordered Darrow.

Darrow stared at him for a moment, then glanced down at me.

I kissed him on the cheek. "Don't worry, buddy. I

promise I won't hurt him *too* bad. And if I do, I'll wait until after he signs the checks on payday."

Darrow flashed a quick grin at Etienne. Then he laughed. Darrow knew my ability to defend myself. Immune to magic? I could still take him on. I'd bet his immunity wouldn't work if I picked up another rock and lobbed it at his head. The back of his head. If he saw it coming, he might shoot me first. I have little pride if I'm fighting for my life—or my freedom. Life and real bullets coming my way had taught me to fight dirty.

Etienne led me inside the building and into a simply furnished office. Desk, chairs, couple of filing cabinets, the place looked and smelled like it was rarely used.

Etienne didn't relax. His face remained grim and his voice deep and angry. "You can't just go wandering around in the Barrows."

I raised my chin and gave him my sweetest smile. "Yes, Daddy. I've been a really bad girl."

"Darrow tells me the word *dangerous* doesn't mean anything to you. He says you don't know how to be afraid." His expression softened a bit. Trying to make friends? I doubted it.

"Danger is subjective." I wandered over to a small window, attempting to do a better job of spotting where I was and how I could get back to River Street. "I told you, I'm looking for my sister. I will find her." The view from the window was another warehouse.

"I don't have time to babysit a witch."

Oh, we were back to restrain the witch again.

"Babysit! Arrogant ass. You think you rescued me, don't you? I had the situation under control."

Etienne stood with his arms crossed, glaring at me. Yes, he was attractive. Could I possibly use him? I suppose I could seduce him. I wondered . . .

I moved closer to him. With my arms at my sides, I tried to look as harmless as possible. I drew a deep breath, drawing the clean scent of masculinity, brushed with a hint of citrus.

He stepped back. Stepped away from me fast. For a brief moment I saw something in his eyes that shocked me. Fear.

"Keep your distance, witch." His hand went to the hilt of his gun.

This was not the reaction I expected. I knew I was desirable on a level that appealed to strong men like him. What was wrong with him?

"Sure." I smiled what I hoped was a wicked smile. It did, however, surprise me to find myself a little disappointed. "I'll just be on my way. How far is it to River Street?"

"No. You'll either leave the Barrows or you'll stay here. I can't have a rogue witch wandering around."

This little piss-off would not end well. "You think you can hold me?"

He studied me long enough I actually became self-conscious. I even flinched when the AC unit stuck in a window kicked on. Finally he said, "Maybe we can come to an agreement."

"Such as . . ."

"You leave Laudine's. Stay here in this compound. You have one friend here, with me. I'll have everyone start looking for your sister. You have a picture, don't you?"

"I have a picture. I don't want or need your help." This offer was unexpected and definitely unwelcome. No way would I allow a man who so obviously hated witches to take over my search. I edged toward the door. I didn't want to fight, but I would if I had to, especially now that Darrow had gone. He wouldn't get in the way.

I agreed that I could use help. I wasn't likely to find Marisol wandering aimlessly through this place, trusting luck to bless me with her location. I just didn't want *his* help. "I need to see Abigail, too. You know where she lives?"

"Abigail. She's . . ."

He stopped and I held out a hand and gave a *Come on, spill it* gesture. What a confusing man. Yes, all men are confusing, but his mixed signals and body language added to his complexity. His face suddenly relaxed. Obviously, he'd decided on a plan to deal with me. "I'll take you to Abigail."

Again, he'd surprised me. I could live with that one, though. Live with extreme caution. In minutes we were in an SUV and on our way out of the Barrows. The sun had dropped behind a black bank of clouds in the west, clouds that promised rain before midnight. Etienne didn't speak, but occasionally glanced over at me.

I watched him as we drove north through that invisible barrier, the Earth Mother's ward. He didn't flinch or give any other indication that it existed. I didn't know a way to test his immunity to magic other than to touch him with magic. I had no reason to do that. I'd been taught that magic used out of curiosity was considered offensive, if not illegal.

It was almost dark when we reached our destination. Abigail's house, a painted white wood frame structure with porches much like my grandmother's, seemed a safe and pleasant place. A multihued carpet of flowers spread across the front yard, and substantial trees clumped in a thick forest behind the house.

The flowers remained perky in the last rays of sunlight, but inky blackness spread under those trees, which seemed more like an ancient, primeval forest. A fortress of a forest where man's axes had never been allowed to kill or maim bark or trunk. The house sat lower to the ground than Gran's. Abigail probably didn't have to deal with floods, alligators, snakes, and other things that stalked or slid through the darkest swampy night.

The woman who walked around the house from the backyard to greet us looked like the picture-perfect grandmother. When she came closer, though, I could see that her hair was truly silver, not gray called silver to take away the sting of age. She wasn't large, but she was solid. Her head came up to my shoulder and her face looked as smooth as a young girl's. I'd heard of her, of course, but never met her. This was Abigail. As far as I knew, she'd been the Earth Mother's High Witch, High Priestess, long before I was born.

"Nyx, welcome to my home." Abigail held out a welcoming hand. I accepted it. The sudden surge of earth magic rolling through her staggered me. My knees almost gave way before I locked them in place. Seeing my distress, she quickly shielded me from her power.

"Oh, I beg your pardon," she said softly. "I sometimes forget how my aura affects young witches. I came to see you early this morning, but your familiar wouldn't let me near."

"Herschel is a bit protective. Sorry. I'll talk to him." Not that it would do any good. Herschel did what he wanted to do and ignored me.

Abigail blasted Etienne with a warm, welcoming smile I doubted he could possibly deserve. "Etienne, it's been a while. You better come in before anyone notices you."

Now, that was interesting. Having recovered from meeting the High Witch, I stepped beside him. "You don't want to be seen?"

Etienne shrugged. "Who is Herschel?"

"My dog. My familiar. You saw him."

"You mean that ugly mutt at Laudine's?"

"Hey. He may be ugly, but he has a sensitive soul. If you want to keep all your limbs intact, I suggest you not call him names." He hadn't asked me what a familiar was, so I figured he knew.

Abigail's kitchen was fantastic, a farmhouse room that smelled of fresh-baked bread and other delicious edibles. Like Gran, she had pots of herbs in the windows. Best of all, her table was set for three.

"Sit down, please," she said. "All conversations are more pleasant over food."

Etienne appeared a bit uncomfortable, but he did sit. Abigail placed a large tureen of soup on a trivet in the middle of the table, and a plate of sliced homemade bread by it. Big chunks of vegetables in broth swam in the soup. There was butter and jam, too. Yum.

When a witch offers you a meal for no explicit reason, it is considered an offering of peace and friendship, to be accepted without question. As soon as Abigail asked a blessing from the Great Master of the Universe and the Earth Mother, I dug in. The thrown-together meal I'd received at Laudine's that morning was long gone.

Etienne stared at the food for a minute. Then he ate.

"Thank you for trusting me, Etienne," Abigail said.

Etienne nodded.

Abigail smiled. "Nyx, I'm told you don't follow the traditional path of service to the Earth Mother. I hear nothing unseemly about you, though."

I almost choked on a piece of bread. "You probably weren't listening. Been out of the country for a few years."

"And you live in California now."

I nodded, but I wondered how she came about that little piece of information. I didn't want to talk about me, so I changed the subject. "You thanked Etienne for trusting you. Why shouldn't he?"

Abigail hesitated, then said, "The question is, *why should he?* You are not the first witch to cross his path, Nyx. Not all witches are as benign as you."

"Benign? Her?" Etienne sounded shocked.

Abigail gave him a beaming smile. "Don't be facetious, Etienne. There is nothing wrong with a good defense. A soldier like you should know that. I'm told Nyx excels in defense. She defended herself, Laudine, and Laudine's property." She frowned. "Though not against you, I'm told."

Abigail continued speaking directly to him. "I can see how her power would concern you, though. Do you think she harbors some malicious intent towards you? Why would that be?"

I didn't laugh. It took strength to remain solemn and steady. Malicious intent toward Etienne? He'd made me a semi-prisoner. The fact that I knew I could escape that prison made no difference. He'd used his men to contain me and used Darrow to suppress my anger.

Etienne glanced at me. He didn't answer Abigail's question. "I remember once I was chasing some thieves in Nigeria. I remember a bridge that collapsed under my truck. The wooden supports had been almost completely burned through—underwater."

I stuck out my chin to show how little I cared. "Or maybe *you* were the thief chasing a perfectly legitimate convoy. Defense depends on who's the pursuer and who's the pursued."

Abigail laughed, a warm and mellowing sound that tinkled like little bells. The tension left the room and we finished a nice meal in peace. And wonder of wonders, she presented us with coffee and cake for desert. Then it was back to business.

"Did Laudine tell you why I'm here?" I asked Abigail.

"No. Only that you were the daughter of a friend. Laudine was once a competent witch. She was, and still is, kind when those who sought her needed her help. Something changed a couple of years ago. She's become deeply disturbed. She isn't one to confide in me. I am not a tyrant, so I accept her decision."

"Etienne is trying to drive Laudine out of the Barrows. If I were her, I'd fight, too."

"I agree. That situation is very complicated and unfortunately, I cannot interfere at this time. But I don't think that's why you came here. How may I help *you*?"

"Information about the Barrows would be nice. Etienne isn't a talkative man. Laudine tells me things, but I'm not sure she's reliable. You've been here a while." I hadn't said anything about Marisol, and thought maybe I should keep it to myself for a while. Etienne could tell her, but as usual, he didn't seem inclined to talk.

Abigail leaned back and smiled, seeming willing to give me a lesson. "I should explain one thing first. Something incredibly important to your safety here. There is a singular and dangerous place, a spot in the Barrows that allows travel between worlds under certain circumstances. Locals call it the Zombie Zone. Circumstances in that place are often dictated by our moon—or its absence in the sky. There are other considerations.

"The Earth Mother has placed her ward around the Barrows to protect the rest of the world from things that have happened, and continue to happen, here. Almost all major events in the Barrows are directly or often indirectly connected to the Zombie Zone."

"I felt the ward around the Barrows." I sipped my coffee. A door between worlds. How interesting. Like most adults, I now wished I'd at least paid attention to the lectures in school, even if I didn't do the homework.

Abigail nodded. "Now a bit of history. About seventy years ago, the Barrows was a thriving community. There was an earthquake and infrastructure collapse. The Mother placed a spell over the ruins to keep the average person from seeing it, or if they did see, they soon forgot. That's why it hasn't been redeveloped in all this time.

"About fifty years ago, a . . . being . . . established an incorporeal presence in the Barrows. That's the only way to describe it. It was a powerful presence and it corrupted men to do its bidding. For many years, it was simply referred to as the Darkness.

"Six years ago, through a rather complicated plot, the Darkness was brought physically into this world. It was the Earth Mother's plan. He lost significant power over the Barrows, and men in general, during that event. He is called Aiakós. The ward that contained him in his incorporeal form then physically contains him today. The Barrows is his prison. The Earth Mother's ward is the protection for the Zombie, but it is also his cage."

Now we were getting down to some information. Even Etienne seemed interested. He leaned forward, eyes wide. "He was more powerful? Before he came here?"

"Oh, yes. He had a wide sphere of influence. He could whisper in men's minds and they would obey. Now he must speak to them one-on-one to charm them, get them to do his bidding."

"Laudino calls him a demon." I watched her carefully. She showed no surprise.

Abigail nodded. "And so have many others. Though,

he is not a supernatural being. I will tell you, I think it was a mistake for the Mother to bring him here."

"Laudine says you protect him. The demon."

"Not I." Abigail gracefully shook her head. "It is Etienne who has that rather unpleasant duty."

I glanced at Etienne, but he sat very still, watching us.

Abigail sighed. "Aiakós is virtually invulnerable to all but massive trauma—and witchcraft. For his employer's safety, Etienne has encouraged all witches to leave the Barrows. Most left easily enough. They simply wanted to be left alone. There were the generous offers of money, too. I don't know why Laudine clings to the place."

"What about Michael? He's Aiakós's son, I'm told. I met him yesterday."

Abigail stood and refilled our coffee. "Michael is Aiakós's son by a witch. He is, and always will be, a bit of a wild card. His loyalty is to Aiakós, at least for now. Though I doubt he or his wife would tolerate any atrocities."

"And Dervick?"

"Who?" She cocked her head and frowned.

"The guy who says he's in charge of the Bastinados. He's a feeble little magical fire starter with a massive inferiority complex. Or at least he appears to be."

"I know nothing about him. That's interesting, though. I will look into it. There are so few males that can use earth magic. Regarding the Bastinados, there are two Sisters of Justice in the Barrows who make it a habit to eliminate them virtually on sight. They've been known to chase them down an alley in broad daylight. I disapprove of that kind of vigilantism, but they are the Mother's direct charge, not mine."

As a witch, I had to place credence in the Earth Mother and her choices. Certainly, in spite of Laudine's warning, it seemed appropriate to speak honestly to the High Witch.

"Abigail, my sister, Marisol, came to Laudine's place a few months ago. She's disappeared. Laudine believes Aiakós has killed her."

Abigail's face took on a look of dismay. "I had not heard this. Why did Laudine not come here when it happened?"

"She thinks that you've betrayed the witches by protecting the demon."

Abigail stared at me, tears forming in her eyes. She'd reacted with hurt, not anger. She lifted her cup of tea. Her hands shook slightly. "As I said, I'm not protecting him. I think bringing Aiakós here was a grave mistake. I've told the Mother so. She tells me she has plans. But somehow, in some way I don't understand, he is drawing more evil to Duivel."

Etienne abruptly stood. "Plans? The Earth Mother has plans. Like the last one?"

Abigail studied him. "You mean the one that ended in a pitch battle that very nearly destroyed us all. Yes. I am concerned. But I rarely question. I have served her all my life.

"The Earth Mother loves us, Etienne. How frustrating it must be for her to send us into battle in a place where she cannot and will not intervene. I would say it is both a blessing and a curse."

Etienne clenched his fists. "I'll go for the curse." As a very strong man, he might, given certain circumstances, actually challenge the role the Mother had given him.

chapter 13

Before we left Abigail's, she gave me a promise that she would search for Marisol with all the resources she had at hand. We climbed in the SUV and headed south.

"What's this about Dervick and fire?" Etienne asked. "He seems pretty useless to me."

"He can call and manipulate fire."

"Can you? Call fire. You burned my man."

"I burned your idiot. A little burn. Probably didn't even blister. I told you, I won't be bullied. But yes, I can create and control fire." Except when it escaped my clutches and raced off like a runaway horse.

"And this Dervick can do that?" He sounded skeptical. "He's a . . . witch?"

"No. Technically, guys can't be witches. But some, a very few of them, can use earth magic. You heard Abigail."

I agreed with the confusing part. I felt a little sorry for him. "Etienne, earth magic and the people who use it can't be defined. Some can do things, have powers; others, witches' children who should have been born with them, can't do anything at all. You don't get to place us in little boxes, sorted by our power. It comes and goes at the Earth Mother's rather erratic will. It's like all of nature. Underneath seeming chaos is perfect order—even if we don't see the pattern. Or so I'm told."

"And you believe everything you're told?"

"No. I guess my life would be less complicated if I did." Life would be so boring without some adventure. The practice and study Marisol loved so much burned my soul. I created my own chaos and I lived with it.

Drops of water spattered on the windshield and the sound of thunder rumbled in the distance. It was a nice steady ride through light and dark until we came upon a bunch of cars with flashing blue lights.

"Shit!" Etienne hit the steering wheel with his hand. He stared around, looking for an escape. There was none. There were no side streets and driving over the sidewalk was bound to attract attention.

"It's only a license check," I said. "You forget to renew?"

He'd stopped the SUV and a car behind us honked, urging us to continue. It also caused the police officers to pay attention. There was nothing we could do.

A uniformed officer approached the driver's window. He looked young, handsome, more like a Boy Scout than a cop. He wore a sharp neat uniform, now wet on the shoulders from the misty rain, and carried a gun: a big, black gun strapped in a holster at his waist. I suppose that defined him in spite of his youthful appearance. Etienne handed him a driver's license and the registration for the vehicle he'd pulled from behind a visor. He hadn't pulled the license from his wallet as most men would have. Trouble was at hand.

The officer frowned and stared at it a long time. He glanced at me once, then went back to his study of the license.

"Sir!" The young cop spoke forcefully with the crisp

authoritative air that he'd obviously been trained to use to control the general populace. "Would you pull over onto the side of the road?"

"Sure," Etienne said. He complied with the order and pulled over.

The rain created a misty sheen on the windshield and had grown to a soft steady hiss on the trees and pavement. Lightning flashed in the distance, followed by low rumbling thunder. At that point, it seemed like the police should abandon their roadblock and head for some drier place. A few moved to do just that. Damn, the timing. The car behind us was waved on through without a check.

Etienne's body radiated tension like a stealthy cat ready to spring on its prey. Everything about him said he was prepared to explode into action. Action that would have a deadly purpose — and possibly deadly results.

I could see the officer with Etienne's driver's license calling his fellow officer's attention to it. Etienne's nervousness had infected me. I flinched when another officer tapped on my window. I powered the window down and he demanded my license. I handed him my narrow wallet and instantly realized my mistake. My wallet also contained my California PI license, something I hadn't planned to flash around. The officer walked away. He took my wallet with him.

"Are we in trouble?" I asked Etienne.

"There are warrants out on me." His voice was terse. "The name on the driver's license is fake, but someone may have seen my photos. I've been told I'm popular on posters in the post office." He popped his seat belt. "I'm going to run. They'll probably shoot at me, so don't you follow. Tell them I'm just a stranger who offered you a ride. You should be okay."

I grabbed his arm. "Wait. I'll create a diversion and we can both leave."

Etienne had taken me to Abigail and that had placed him in danger with the authorities. Having been in that position several times, albeit not in the US, I could empathize. I gathered my magic, a bit too quickly, and sent it out to fry the vehicle wiring as I had last night when under attack. And it had the same effect—on everything. Streetlights, vehicle lights, headlights, and flashing blue lights blasted into brilliance they'd never been intended to provide. One second, for a hundred yards around me, they lit up the area like old-time flashbulbs. Then all burst like balloons and plunged the area into darkness filled with shattered glass. Unfortunately, the burned-out lights and wiring included those of our own vehicle. We weren't going to drive away. Shit!

"Now we run." I opened my door and dropped to the ground. Etienne climbed over the console and landed beside me. He was clumsy, feeling his way around. I grabbed his hand. "Let me lead you," I whispered. "I can see in the dark."

Unfortunately, my little fireworks show again didn't include flashlights. One beam flashed over us and someone shouted, "Halt." We were quickly surrounded by menacing men who pointed flashlights *and* guns.

I stood on the earth, though, and still carried the magic.

"Get down on the ground!" multiple voices shouted, forceful, demanding, as if the hostile reverberation would force us off our feet.

My rational brain said to let them take Etienne. I could not. He was one of us. The Earth Mother's special children. The High Witch accepted him on that level, so I was obligated to do the same.

I could, if I chose, set every vehicle around us on fire. I would not. The flame, once sparked, would consume everything around. It could trap people.

Controlling the weather is a skill learned after many years with a powerful witch standing over you. Not my thing. But when you have nothing else ... All I could do was grab part of the storm and let it crash down upon us. At the same time, I built a small, carefully constructed shield over Etienne and me.

Lightning leaped to a massive blinding strike on a power pole not far away. The enormous sound blasted our eardrums and shook the ground. I flinched and ducked, along with everyone else. We were too close to unpredictable violence. Earth magic picked up some of the energy. In a rare display, it danced around the vehicles, skimming their metal skins, crackling, snapping like fire imps on a rampage.

Great Mother, what had I done?

Water came next. A *Look, I'm standing under Niagara Falls* flood poured down and spread across the land.

I *did not* have that kind or amount of power.

Etienne and I stood frozen. Stupid!

"Let's go," I shouted over the cyclonic deluge. He probably didn't hear me. I grabbed his hand. I carried the small shield I'd formed over us as we bolted, dashing through the prostrate struggling bodies of the police. The flood had forced them to their knees. The shield kept the pounding from above from flattening us to the pavement like everyone else, but the wind swirled under and around, lashing us with whips of water. We made little progress at first, having to battle the wind and water, but soon we were free of the clump of vehicles and racing away.

The area around us consisted of homes with the occasional shop. Residential yard fences could be a problem if we cut too far off the main street. Etienne slowed me down considerably as I guided him in the darkness. At least I'd managed to take out the streetlights for a good distance. I had to search for a reasonable path in the night, one where he could move freely along, directed only by my hand. He squeezed it too tight at times, crushing my fingers. He followed, though, blind in the dark, but without hesitation.

We slowed to a fast walk and made our way around closed businesses, open convenience stores, and through a residential alley where the occasional yard dog barked to mark our passage. If we actually had pursuers, we left them far behind. It would take time to send for patrols to track us. We were soaked, of course, since it still rained and I'd dropped the shield as soon as we left the maelstrom. That rain slowed to a cold drizzle.

"How far are we from the Barrows?" I asked.

"Half a mile." He didn't sound winded. He did pull out his phone and make a call. He told the person answering to report the SUV stolen as of earlier that afternoon. "You know it's a myth," he said to me. "That the cops don't go into the Barrows. They patrol the docks on a regular basis and occasionally River Street. They just don't go into the ruins."

"Is that how you hide a small army there?"

"It is. I'm told there's a spell. Some people don't see some things. I've been told that the police are prone to forgetting crimes that happen down here."

"I guess I understand that. I sort of burned a big truck in front of Laudine's last night. Nobody came to investigate." I had no idea how that particular magic worked nor did I need to know. I really did want to know who moved the truck carcass before I woke.

Etienne caught my arm and jerked me to a stop. "Are you usually so stupid?"

"What?" I twisted my arm from his hand.

"Why didn't you let it be? They have your ID now. You ran with me. If you hadn't, there would be questions, but they'd probably let you go."

"I don't do probably. Let's keep moving. I'll try to explain."

He followed me without a word. How *did* I explain the dynamic of my life? "Look, I don't know how much you know about witches, but—"

"I know entirely too much about witches." Rage filled his voice as he spit out the words. He walked beside me at a steady pace, even in the semidarkness.

"Okay, it's obvious you know too much about *some* witches. Can you compare that to Abigail? To me?"

He said nothing, so I continued. "When I was a guard, I worked for Darrow. He and I were part of a team. I know you understand that. When one of us got into trouble, the others were there. Witches, Sisters of Justice, and certain people involved with them are singled out and drawn together by the Earth Mother. We belong to her. Team Earth Mother." I laughed too loud, and heard the bitterness in my voice. I punched my fist into the air. "Go Team."

"I don't want—"

"You don't have a choice. Neither did I. I was born, you were chosen. It's not negotiable." *Chosen* sounded good. More likely *he'd* been caught up in a trap set by the witch who caused him to hate all of us. That set him in the Mother's sights and she claimed him. It made no difference.

"We're stuck with it, Etienne." I chuckled. "You're really on wanted posters in the post office?"

"Oh, yeah. For all you know, I'm a serial killer who buries his bodies in the ruins."

That seemed a sensible statement, but I had an answer. "No, Abigail would have spotted a serial killer in an instant. And I'd give good odds that she would bury anyone of that kind in her backyard so he wouldn't kill again. She likes you." I didn't want to encourage his ego. "Of course, Abigail hasn't had to put up with your control-freak shit like I have."

He didn't reply and gave no hint of what he was thinking.

I noted when we passed through the ward around the Barrows, but I kept us to the darker areas. My clothes were wet and clammy, clinging to my body, and my shoes squished out bubbles of water as I walked. The wind coming off the Bog chilled what should have been a warm evening. I wanted clean dry clothes, but I had something else to do.

I still wasn't tired. While I had used some magic to draw the storm down and hold a shield over us, that magnitude of weather control didn't come from me. Had Abigail sensed our need and aided us? This was a mystery I wouldn't solve immediately.

Etienne had relaxed considerably after we passed the ward. He probably felt it unconsciously. When he spoke again, his voice was calm, almost playful. "Darrow told me about a couple of your adventures. He said he understands *now* how they might have happened. The Barrows taught him . . . things."

"Darrow exaggerates." I kicked a beer can out of the way. "My car is parked in a few more blocks. I'll take you to your place."

"No. I'm sticking with you. I'm having too much fun." He smiled. He may not have intended me to see that smile since we stood shrouded in darkness and he was virtually blind. "Besides"—he slid an arm around my shoulders—"I now owe you a favor. I pay my debts."

I stopped and twisted from under his arm. I could say I'd developed a tiny bit of fondness for him, but I wasn't ready for that kind of intimacy. Especially since he'd so rudely rejected me earlier.

"I'm going to Laudine's," I said. "I need to find my dog."

"Then you and your dog come back to the compound with me."

The firm tone in his voice sounded like an order, not a request. While I didn't like that, I didn't like the other immediately available options. Stay with Laudine or leave the Barrows. Neither suited me. Laudine had done nothing other than scald me with irritation that Gran sent me and hadn't come herself. At least Etienne had taken me to Abigail, apparently at considerable risk to himself. All Laudine had done was warn me away from the High Witch. I'd finish with my plan for the next hour, then decide where to stay. Getting a room would be difficult without my wallet, money, and credit cards.

The sidewalks where we made our way were empty and only an occasional car passed by, tires hissing on the wet streets.

"Where is everyone?" I asked.

"Probably hiding. That storm you stirred up back there had to be felt. Crazy things happen in the Barrows sometimes," Etienne said. "People who live here feel it and stay inside. Safe. Or so I'm told."

"By Madeline?"

"And others."

We continued on in silence until we came to the block where my car was parked. I released the spell I'd placed on it. The spell whispered that more than one person had tried to touch it. My trusty backpack lay on the floor of the backseat where I'd stowed it. There was still little traffic as we climbed in and drove toward Laudine's. At least the rain had stopped.

"Nice car," Etienne said. I'd actually seen him smile when the engine rumbled to life. He ran his hand over the still immaculate leather.

The hour approached midnight and I wanted to try something. I wanted to use Herschel as my familiar, too. I hadn't had him around for the past ten years, but it seemed right to make up for lost time. That's what a witch's familiar was for, right? To be used. To help me out? Besides, he owed me for conspiring with the Sisters on my capture. He was standing on the sidewalk in front of the store. He growled at Etienne when we climbed out.

"I know," I told him. "I don't like him, either. I'll let you chase him off when we're done with him." I patted him on his substantial head. "Did you get something to eat?"

Herschel farted. I took that as a yes.

I stared around, looking for the best place to try my experiment. The city had decided that the mostly unused cul-de-sac required streetlights, probably to help keep cars from plunging through the pathetic rail fence and into the Bog. I didn't need the light, but I expected it comforted a fighter like Etienne. Clouds boiled low here, just above the lights, heavy and poised to descend and mask everything. The usual fresh clean air that often followed a rainstorm didn't come this time.

I wanted to be on the earth, not asphalt. I moved to the edge of the Bog where the pavement ended. "You should stand away," I told Etienne. "I'm probably going to set off some fireworks."

He moved about twenty feet and crouched and leaned against the fence. He broadcast suspicion and wariness with each movement and kept his eyes on me. I wondered if I could ever get him to tell his story. Witches could be evil. That's why the Sisters of Justice existed.

The hours of the day, the cycle of sun and moon, actually did have an effect on earth magic. Midnight, noon, full moon, dark moon, the solstice, counted as peaks, optimal times. Every witch knew that. Since I lived a life with little ritual, I usually ignored them. Now I wanted to use midnight. Since my clothes were already soaked, I sat cross-legged on the very icky wet dirt with a reluctant Herschel beside me. I'd had to grab him by the scruff of the neck and drag him across the asphalt to the correct place. My ass would be coated in mud before I rose. So would Herschel's. I understood his reluctance.

I'd done witchcraft in the past with Herschel, but only minor stuff. It had made me as uncomfortable as it did him and while it amplified my power, it often produced unpredictable results. The last time I tried using him, every bird within a few miles of Gran's house landed on the roof—thousands of them. Gran made me take a hose and ladder, chase them away, and wash all the shit off. All I wanted was a better TV signal. I laid a hand on Herschel's head and one on the earth.

"Fire," I said. This was my thing, something that ran in my blood. A circle of fire sprang up around me, much as it had at my rendezvous with Dervick earlier in the day. Other witches would draw a pentagram. This was my fire, my version of a pentagram and circle. It was my witch's magic, and would protect and aid me. It wouldn't burn me, but I'd cautioned Etienne to move farther away.

I turned my attention to Herschel. I became aware of

him, aware in a way I'd never known before. Oh, I had been away too long. I had never met this Herschel. He carried his own power, which didn't surprise me, but I'd never seen him as he was when I stroked my hand over his skin. His aura was not that of the wolf that might be expected, but that of a substantial beast who breathed flame and roared like a thousand lions in the savanna. Was this because of the Barrows?

I wanted to stop, talk to him, explore him, but I was already committed to another path. I closed my eyes and reached out to the magic. I'd been taught that the world itself was the Earth Mother's corporeal form. Her heart was at its molten core. The magic was the blood coursing through her veins. It ran through all humanity, though only the witches and a few select others could touch it.

I wanted to do a *sending*, a magical form of communication. I'd only tried it once before when I was fourteen. It caused me a four-day sick headache and Herschel puked everything he ate for a week. Herschel puking is far worse than farting.

"Please, Mother, let me do this right." I whispered a prayer into the night. I willed the flames higher and drew the magic into my mind and body. When I did the sending, I would add something of myself so all who could hear it would know who I was.

With my hand on Herschel's head, I asked for his power, his will, to aid my call. Something both strange and terrifying happened then. Herschel suddenly drew something from me. Some obscure part of me I didn't know existed. I thought I knew fire, but the fire that burst out at that moment soared beyond my comprehension.

Brilliance surrounded me, streaked through me, and spread. It seemed it could illuminate the impenetrable darkness in the void and race away through an unending universe. It faded but continued to flicker in my mind. I had no time to explore this strange new thing. I flung my calling out across the world of earth magic with all the energy I could muster.

Marisol.

Magic thrummed like a low note on a giant bass fiddle. It thumped with the heartbeat of a deeper drum. It rattled like windows in a massive storm and roared like a tornado. A tornado not of wind and rain, but of fire and ash. I called again.

Marisol.

Silence fell, a silence deeper than any I'd ever known.

Through magic, the blood of the Earth Mother, came my answer. Soft, dreamy, barely a whisper, it caressed me.

Nyx.

That single trembling thought touched me—and was gone. Marisol remained upon this earth, though I did not know where.

My body jerked. The fire dissipated, the magic vanished—and all hell descended upon me.

Herschel howled.

I stuck my fingers in my ears. That howl, so loud it hammered my eardrums to the point I thought I'd be deaf. Etienne knelt on the ground, his face twisted in pain and his hands over his ears.

It stopped.

I'd barely drawn a breath of relief when Laudine came rushing out of her front door shrieking undecipherable words. The words weren't important. The significant ax she held drew all my attention. She chopped at the air, her focus on me and her intention quite clear. She wanted me in pieces—immediately.

Etienne suddenly stood between us, gun drawn. Feet

planted, body tense, he aimed directly at her heart. He would not hesitate.

Laudine stopped. Her body swayed. She stood, poised, teeth bared like an animal, ax ready to strike. Her hair, released from its binding, flew wildly around her head and shoulders. The frozen mask of a madwoman twisted her face. She stepped to the side, trying to get past Etienne. Silent as a stalking tiger, he moved with her, covering me the entire time.

I tried to stand. Didn't make it. Herschel hauled himself to his feet, shook his heavy body, and yawned. I grabbed his back and used it as leverage. He grunted, but let me struggle until I made it.

I didn't know what had happened. I did know I had never before had the power to use magic the way I had here and at the traffic stop. This was shaping up as a night for great revelation, though the exact significance escaped me at the moment. The boost Herschel gave me through magic bordered on incredible.

Incredible, too, was the stink of burning asphalt. Where my circle of fire touched it, it bubbled and boiled. Part of the fence protecting the Bog was missing, probably burned away. Witch fire had become a true burning, something I had not thought possible.

I wobbled over to stand by Etienne. Not too close, in case he needed room.

Laudine still stood on guard with her ax. She'd stopped moving, but she kept the ax ready. It really seemed a pitiful weapon for an earth witch. Sadly, she seemed pitiful for an earth witch.

"I was only doing a sending," I said to her. "I know it was loud, but don't you think you're overreacting here? What's going on?"

Laudine lowered the ax. Like the average witch, she'd

never had any need to learn to use a weapon. Magic usually sufficed for defense. Tonight, she'd grabbed the only thing she had. She couldn't match the power of my sending, my magic. She'd known, or maybe just anticipated, I'd be vulnerable to physical attack when it was over. She hadn't counted on Etienne being there to defend me.

"Witch." Laudine snarled the word at me. "You have misused earth magic to such an extent that you will probably find a Triad of Sisters seeking you tomorrow. Sacrilege, a curse on the Earth Mother's name."

Okay, the aggressor was going to excuse her aggression by blaming her intended victim—me. It was all bullshit.

"I was only trying to find Marisol," I said. I wanted to sound defensive, to placate her. I had more important things than to start a war with another witch—even if she seemed to have already begun one with me. And I really didn't believe I'd done anything wrong.

Laudine raised an eyebrow. "And did you? Find her?"

"No." Something deep inside ordered me to lie.

"Very well." She shrugged as if I'd merely dropped one of her teacups on the floor. "Come in and let's see if we can repair the damage."

"What damage?" What the hell?

Laudine stared at me. "I don't know, but there's bound to be some." She softened and bowed her head. "I ask your pardon for my rash actions. I would not have harmed you."

"Rash actions, my ass." Etienne shoved his gun in his holster. He stared straight at me, his face a mask of implacable anger. "Want some advice?"

"Sure. I can always ignore it."

"Never, *ever* trust a witch." He spoke softly, but with such force I knew it truly came from his heart. "This bitch would have diced you like a carrot if I hadn't been here."

It was good advice. Never trust a witch. And this particular witch had disliked me from the moment I walked into her world. The carrot analogy wasn't quite bloody enough, though. I was thinking along the lines of a slaughterhouse pig. A least I knew Marisol was alive somewhere.

I would eventually have to rest tonight and did not wish to leave myself vulnerable to Laudine. Of course, that meant I'd be leaving myself vulnerable to someone else — a man about whom I knew virtually nothing except his hatred of witches. Thus far, Laudine hadn't offered me anything but cowardly indifference and swift violence. Etienne's intentions, other than control of me, were unclear. Etienne had one shining thing in his favor. Darrow.

To Laudine I said, "I've got somewhere to go, Laudine. I'll be back tomorrow."

"As you wish." Laudine marched off like a queen.

Etienne laid a hand on my shoulder. It surprised me how steady it made me feel.

"What happened earlier?" I asked. "What did you see?"

"Fire. It covered you. I thought you were dead. Then it went away. Your dog howled. No dog is that loud."

My sentiments exactly. Herschel's howl could be heard across miles of the swamp. "Maybe he swallowed a stereo speaker. He eats some weird stuff."

A smile twitched at the corner of Etienne's mouth. "Come on. Darrow can watch over you if you like." Interesting. He'd known to offer me something, someone I would trust. He glanced down at Herschel. "And there's always the mutt."

The easy way wasn't always the best way. Etienne had taken me to Abigail at some risk to himself. He'd stood between me and Laudine's ax. I'd rather have gone somewhere I could be alone, but my strength rapidly faded. I didn't have that option.

"Why didn't you shoot her?" I asked. Given his enmity toward witches, it would seem the logical thing to do. She believed she couldn't hurt him with magic.

He shrugged. "There was no real threat. I would have if she'd gotten too close. Is that what you would have wanted?"

"No. I've never wanted to kill anyone. There are always greater consequences for killing a witch, no matter your reason. My grandmother told me it sets up an imbalance in nature." He'd shown some reluctance to killing. That didn't necessarily make him a good guy, but it helped.

I nodded and headed for Gran's car. "Come on, Herschel."

The police still had my wallet with my ID, credit cards, and all my cash. They would be looking for me as an associate of a wanted man. I just hoped that, in contrast to what had happened to Etienne, the Barrows would not become my prison.

chapter 14

I had little reason to trust Etienne, to go with him, but if he hadn't been there when I finished my sending, Laudine might have been hiding my various body parts in the Bog. Or maybe not if Herschel had actually decided to take action in my defense. Laudine had apologized, but offered no rational explanation for her violent reaction to my magical melee. I had no doubt she was right that there would be consequences.

While I drove toward Etienne's compound, I realized how easily I'd fallen back into a life I thought I'd left behind. I didn't really miss it, the life where danger and death walked beside me within easy pouncing distance. In San Francisco I did my work, met with friends for drinks or dinner, and shopped for frivolous things. Occasionally violence was required, but most cases in SF were an easy *find this person* or *find this object*. A sudden sadness came over me. Why hadn't I ever invited Marisol? Or Gran. Gran wasn't a city girl, but she would have enjoyed some things I could show her, like the museums, art galleries, the ocean and the bridge. I'd screwed up big-time in my desire to stay away from the Twitch Crossing witches.

I pulled into a parking space in the empty lot that

Etienne specified. As soon as I turned off the engine, the vast weariness I'd been expecting gripped my body and mind. Overuse of magic two nights in a row demanded physical payment. I'd spent the night before unconscious on the ground at Laudine's. Tonight I'd also walked and run a number of miles after setting off a lightning storm of a spell. The sending required more strength. Even if, as I suspected, I had help with the magic, it drained me.

Etienne led me up some stairs. I stumbled halfway. He came back, grabbed my arm, and held me steady as I made what had become an incredible effort to place one foot after the other.

"What's wrong?" he asked.

"Spell catching up with me." My words came out a bit slurred. "Need rest." By that time I couldn't even see the room around me.

He lowered me onto a bed. I felt him removing my still wet shoes. I was in desperate need of a bath and dry, clean clothes, but it seemed unimportant just then. I needed to say something else. I had to force the words out. "Tell Herschel to drool outside. He can understand you." I couldn't say more. I'd hit the wall when it came to energy. Nothing remained. I had to rest.

Darkness descended, but it didn't last long. At least I knew I was dreaming and my body resting. I found myself suddenly standing in a forest of trees taller than any I'd ever seen. I wasn't afraid—there didn't seem to be any point. Dreaming. Right?

When she came drifting toward me, I knew her instantly. The Earth Mother. Beautiful beyond anything I'd ever seen, she looked a bit like Abigail, and probably me, but a bit like my own mother, whose face I'd often seen in my dreams. She was the essence of all witches, some of whom lived their whole lives without being blessed with actually seeing her.

"Mother." I bowed low to her.

"Nyx. You have surprised me, daughter. I do enjoy it when my children . . . to use a modern phrase, *step outside of the box*. Your search, your sending, was mighty and powered by your love for your sister." I basked in her attention, her love and approval. Whatever my actions, I had never wavered in my loyalty to her.

"Did I screw up too bad?"

"No. You did no wrong."

"You helped me, didn't you? With the rain."

"A bit. Know that I will not do such things inside the ward around the Barrows, lest I break it and allow Aiakós to go free. I will not permit that at any cost. I am forbidden to tell you more."

"Mother, is Marisol with you? I heard her, but . . . is she . . . ?"

"Marisol is alive. If she were not, I would know. I do not, however, know where she is." The Mother drifted closer. "One of the things that most distresses me is that occasionally my children think that I am omnipotent. I see much, but not everything. I can intervene, but not always in the way my people wish. Marisol is hidden from me."

"When I called this evening, she did answer faintly."

"I heard. But I feel she is weakening. You must find her soon."

"I will. One more thing. Can I trust Etienne?"

"I understand your concern. He is a stranger. A powerful stranger. He is occasionally brutal, but left to his own conscience he would harm no innocent. Although I suspect his perception of innocent is a bit flexible. You *must* teach him to trust *you*. That is your considerable challenge. He is a complex man with complex secrets. Twice set upon by witches, once with his knowledge and once without, he has good reason to be wary of all magic. Consider Etienne my gift to you. He would suit you, I think. But the choice is yours."

The Mother laughed and all the birds in the forest sang, in a magnificent melody in perfect harmony. One question spoiled the beauty of the moment. Etienne, damn him, I had to deal with the man no matter what. The Mother hadn't really said I could trust Etienne. While she soothed me with the idea that he would harm no innocent, she waffled on it with the words *flexible* and *innocence*. It both comforted and terrified to know that my powerful patroness, my demigoddess, could be unsure of herself. That she could be less than omnipotent, more human. It terrified me because it meant that she could fail. She could be wrong. I listened to her song for a few minutes, then fell back into true sleep.

I woke when Herschel grabbed my foot and dragged me off the bed. My butt hit first, then my head. Thank the Mother for carpet. I yelped and let out a few choice words, then threatened to send him to the dog pound.

I sat up and looked around. Etienne stood at the foot of the bed, laughing. He'd obviously bathed and found clean clothes. He looked just fine. *"Consider him my gift to you."* The Mother's words.

"Good morning," my so-called gift said.

He grinned. Oh, he did have a nice smile. I had to smile back, all the while telling myself it was a bad idea. The Mother had said I should teach him to trust. I just wasn't sure that would be good. This was not a man a careful woman should find attractive. But then, when was I ever more than moderately careful?

"You said your dog understood if I talked to him.

Madeline had a lizard once that she talked to. It understood. I asked the mutt if he would wake you."

"Yeah, but he could have barked." Damn, I hurt.

My stomach growled loud enough to be heard three rooms away.

Graceful as a giraffe, I forced myself off the floor to sit on the bed. "Where am I?"

"My apartment. My bedroom." He laughed a little more. "My bed."

"You couldn't have put me on the couch?"

"Oh, I'd be a poor host if I did that." He tossed a bundle of clothes on the bed, a pair of black fatigue pants and a blue T-shirt. There were socks and panties there, too. "I thought you might want some clean clothes. I got these from one of the women. They should fit you."

I accepted the garments. "Guess this covers everything except . . ." I picked through the garments. "No bra?"

"No. Hers wouldn't fit you. She's a bit more . . ." He grimaced, apparently unsure of the words he needed. Finally, he found one. "Substantial, I would say."

I looked him up and down and gazed pointedly at his crotch. "Substantial. Yeah. You either got it or you don't. Not that I've ever had complaints. Of course, with me, a good surgeon could work wonders. Others have to accept things as they are."

Etienne gave another good-natured laugh. He was in a good mood this morning. I wondered how long it would last. "The bathroom is there." He pointed to a door. "And in case you're wondering, I had Darrow come and get you out of your wet clothes."

I hadn't noticed. The man seemed to be dominating my thought process. I was wearing a man's T-shirt and a pair of boxer shorts. Etienne had shown me a small consideration in having Darrow come. I'd worked in really close quarters with Darrow and other men and by necessity we'd occasionally had to get naked. As long as I knew them, I got used to it. Embarrassment didn't hold up when we were hiding from people who wanted to kill us. It would have troubled me a bit if Etienne, a stranger, had stripped me.

Etienne frowned as if he'd taken a quick, emotional step back from his pleasant mood of only minutes ago. "Why didn't the fire burn you last night? It didn't even dry your clothes."

"There are different kinds of fire."

He wasn't satisfied. "I felt the heat. I couldn't get close to you."

What did I tell him? I wasn't into soul baring yet. He didn't need to know that fire was a part of me. I could start one as hot as the sun, but no fire would burn me. "It works different with magic, that's all. I used magic to protect myself."

He watched me for a moment, then left. I could tell he wasn't satisfied.

Bathroom, yes, and a shower, too. The garments Etienne brought fit me quite nicely, in spite of the lack of substance in my chest area. Not that I'm super small, but I didn't complain. They'd been described as perky and just the right handful. Big breasts would have been a hazard considering some things I'd had to do. My shoes, dried, sat on the floor by the bed.

I also checked my cell phone. Dead, but the charger was in my backpack, which someone had conveniently brought from the car. I plugged it in. I really needed to call Karen and warn her of the firestorm of official demands that were to descend upon her. When I finished in the bathroom, Etienne was in the living room and Herschel had disappeared. Etienne led me down the stairs. Once outside, I found that Gran's car was missing.

"What did you do with my car?" Irritation made me clench my fists.

"It's parked in a building. We don't permit vehicles outside here. It draws attention. There are plenty of empty buildings."

"Which building?"

Etienne shrugged. "I don't know. I just ordered it moved. I'll check on it for you."

Sure he would. Not that it mattered. Herschel would find it if I asked. If I located the miserable mutt anytime soon.

Etienne led me across a parking lot to another building, a large bright dining room where breakfast was in progress. It was served buffet-style and about fifty men and a few women sat at tables scattered around the room. They were all dressed in crisp black fatigues, as Darrow had been when I met him earlier. Only my blue shirt set me apart. They all stopped talking when I walked in with Etienne, but quickly went back to their conversation, their voices hushed.

Darrow greeted me. "Come on. Get a tray." He led me away to the buffet line, where I was able to fill my plate with what would probably be considered, for a normal person, an enormous amount of food. Bacon, sausage, eggs, and good Southern grits topped with gobs of butter, and I would consume it all. I added a couple of muffins and three sweet rolls. Magic depleted my body and I had to refuel. I grinned at the serving staff behind the buffet as they stared.

"I see you can still eat like a pig and not gain weight," Darrow said.

"You bet. Nice gourmet setup you have here, Darrow." I elbowed him. "Don't you miss boiled goat?"

Darrow chuckled. "No. Occasionally have a yen for fried monkey, though."

Our overseas employers had fed us well, though some of the food was unusual. Between jobs and in certain critical situations we'd eaten some pretty gross stuff. It was a cultural thing, too. We often ingested unknown rations offered in friendship. I'd discovered that food is food and if you put enough ulcer-inducing spice on it and swallowed quickly, it usually stayed down. There'd been hard times when we went hungry.

I glanced around. Etienne was gone, apparently leaving me in Darrow's care. Darrow led me to a table where Rocky and Salvatore, a couple of old companions, waited. They'd been with Darrow long before I joined him. They had to hug me and hold me tight for a minute. They also laughed and poked fun at me for a while, and told me how boring things were after I left.

"You gonna work with us?" Salvatore asked. Salvatore was a good man and a good friend, but age was streaking his hair with gray. He'd led a hard life. It was time for him to retire. Past time, actually. I knew he had money because it was he who taught me about numbered bank accounts in the islands where I had amassed my comfortable retirement fund. The bitter truth was that the troop was his family. As with almost all of them, he had no one else. Men and women with families didn't usually live the lives of guards in the war-torn areas of the world. If he quit, he would wither away. Which was one of a long list of reasons I quit when I did. The life I was living then was one of adrenaline highs and numbing fear . . . followed by more adrenaline. I'm not an oracle, but I could see the future and it went to hell. I'd had one friend too many die a bloody death in my arms.

I reach over and patted his hand. "Me work here? No, at least not now. Although it seems like a pretty cushy job."

"It's a job," Rocky said in a soft voice. Like Darrow he was dark, thin, and wiry. "Pretty much same as always. Nothing to do but train. Waiting for the next time . . . Sometimes . . ." His voice trailed off as if he was unsure what to say. Rambling and vague, not like Rocky at all.

Darrow glanced around.

"Boss man standing over your shoulder?" I asked. "You worried?"

Darrow shrugged. "He's okay. Had worse. Pay is good. I get the feeling something may be coming down soon, though. Maybe I spent too much time with you."

"Maybe." I had a reputation for sometimes being prescient and knowing when something bad was pending. When I thought about it, that feeling had been the norm since I came into the Barrows.

I had to ask. "Is Etienne the same one that lifted our cargo and kicked our asses out of that town in Nigeria?"

"He is. He doesn't know for sure about Nigeria, but he'd heard of us. We had a good rep. You know that. My contacts met his, he was hiring. The three of us came. The others wanted something else." Darrow didn't look at me. "Are you okay with him?"

I knew his concern. "For now. It's cool. Your boss isn't my enemy—yet. And thanks for taking care of me last night."

"You want to tell me what happened?"

"Not today. But we need a good sit-down and talk."

"Will you explain some things to me?"

"Yeah. I will. You have to promise to believe me, though."

"Oh, Nicky, I can assure you that I will believe."

I laughed and concentrated on shoveling my food down. Then I went back for more.

After we finished, Darrow gave me a grand tour of the compound. It was a nice setup compared to some places we'd worked. Spread out in several warehouses in what used to be an industrial park were bedrooms, not barracks, an exercise and training room. There was absolutely nothing on the outside to show that the buildings were inhabited. The one place he did not show me was an armory. Etienne carried a gun, but no one else did.

Like the ruins to the south, Etienne's compound was surrounded by other warehouses, some on the verge of collapse. It allowed a great deal of room to expand, should redevelopment ever reach this deep in the Barrows. I wondered exactly how many men Etienne had here, but doubted I'd get an answer if I asked. And I hadn't seen my car.

I had Darrow show me back to the building where Etienne kept the apartment. I needed my cell phone to call Karen—and I needed my backpack should I choose to leave. He hadn't locked the apartment door at least.

I'll admit he confused me. He hated witches, but stood for me against one in a particularly nasty challenge last night. I had to wonder why. I sort of liked him, but I'd had a tendency to like rough men in the past. Sometimes with disastrous results.

Since I was almost unconscious last night and focused on other things earlier, I took the opportunity to look around. A single living room and a kitchen divided by a bar with stools. Modern furniture, browns and blues, with clean lines, but absolutely no personal touches like photos or a stack of unopened mail. The small kitchen looked like nobody ever cooked there, which wasn't surprising since he provided three good solid meals in another warehouse. The bedroom I'd slept in last night was the same. Spare and masculine, with no hint of the man who lived there. And there was no cell phone service.

I knew a few tricks, though. I could use the magic to find service and plug in. Those calls couldn't be traced. I mentally patted myself on the back again for learning that little trick. Minor magic, in which I excelled—most of the time. I made my call.

"Hello, super secretary, how goes it?"

Karen sighed, loud and long. "The good news, Harold is apparently lost in a sand trap. Haven't seen him in a while. MacLellen is gaining speed—finally—and I threw your plants in the trash. The bad news is that I'm turning away new clients and the accountant is grumbling about a bottom line, whatever that is."

"What about the information I asked for?"

"That's not good, either. Duivel, Missouri, apparently doesn't exist, never existed, or existed and went extinct. However, one of the business databases has an entry for a place called the Archangel in Duivel. I haven't figured that one out yet. It's listed under exercise studios of all things. Nothing on Bastinados except a soccer team in South America. When I type in *Abigail* and *Duivel*, I get all sorts of sites that are wacko on witchcraft. You're not into that, are you?"

Only since the day I was born. "No, Karen, I'm not into witchcraft. What about Etienne? Africa? Asia?"

"I hope you are not into that, either. That is one badass dude. Chat sites say he's stolen just about everything imaginable. He's the essential antihero. Murder, armed assault, you name it. Everyone is looking for him. Not bad-looking guy, though. Saw a picture on the Internet. Lots of rewards out there. If you see him, call the police. Or the FBI. Or the CIA. Call Interpol. Mega rewards. You'll get rich."

Nothing new there. Last night's experience had enlightened me. "Hey, do you think you can find a way to pay my utilities at the condo?"

"Sure. Honestly, honey, when are you coming back? I'm worried about you. Miss you."

"I don't know, but I miss you, too. Listen, this is important. You can expect a visit from the police soon. Maybe FBI. Tell them the truth, don't lie. I'm in Duivel visiting a friend. You don't know her name. They'll have all your computer searches so you can't hide anything."

Karen gasped. "Are you in trouble?"

"No. At least not yet. I can take care of things. I'll call you again as soon as I can. Everything will be okay." I spoke with a confidence I didn't have.

I hung up the phone.

The police would see the searches for Etienne, too. Maybe his hideout down in the Barrows would hold.

I turned at a slight sound to find Etienne standing in the doorway.

chapter 15

Etienne leaned against the doorjamb. His expression was one of extreme curiosity. His dark eyes drew me as they had the first day I'd met him. A gift for me, as the Mother said. As gifts go, I could do worse.

"Tell me, witch, how'd you get that cell to work? There's no service in the Barrows except along River Street and the docks. We had to run landlines ourselves to get it in the compound."

I shrugged and turned the phone in my hands. "Magic."

"You know, if you wanted to know about me, you could ask." He grinned as if he found it amusing I would be that interested.

"And you would tell me?"

"Maybe. Are you looking for something specific?"

"No. You're a stranger I seem to be spending a lot of time with." I looked into his eyes and spoke the truth. "You're a dangerous stranger. That's obvious. But Darrow wouldn't work for you if you were into pure evil."

Etienne came to sit beside me. Not super close, but close enough I was majorly aware of him. I think my body temperature actually rose a few degrees. My girl. Oh, yeah.

"You need to define pure evil." He spoke in a light voice, still amused at me and my questions.

"Define?" How did I do that? I'd seen so much. "I met an old woman in Sudan. She said, *They have the blood of innocents on their hands.* Raiders had come in the night. We helped her bury her grandchildren. That kind of evil. You've walked the same paths in the same places that I have. You know what I mean."

Etienne looked straight into my eyes. "By that definition, slaughtering children, I am not evil. I have killed men. Some because they attacked me and some simply because they opposed me. I've procured some very valuable goods in my time. By almost any definition I am not a *good* man."

No, he was not a good man. And yet, last night, he had stood between me and what seemed to be a madwoman. By all the tenets of the Mother and her earth witches, I should have been safer with Laudine than him.

Etienne leaned forward, elbows on his knees, and stared straight at me. "I don't like witches. But I'm truly sorry I caused you trouble. You need to go to the police and say I kidnapped you, forced you to come with me. They'll search River Street and the docks, but they won't likely come here. Then you should leave town."

I shook my head. "I'm not leaving without Marisol. Last night was partly my fault. The only reason they noticed you was because you took me to Abigail. As for witches, I guess you have your reasons. Some of us are evil. I won't deny that."

I liked the feeling of him sitting next to me, talking about the Barrows, but I had a mission. I needed to be on my way. "What are the odds of me talking to this demon of yours?"

"Not good. Why would you want that?"

"Laudine says he killed Marisol."

Etienne froze. "And if he did?"

"I'll do my best to destroy him."

"You have no concept of what you're proposing."

"I'll build a hellfire under him so hot there won't even be ash left." I didn't elaborate on a relatively empty threat. I knew Marisol was alive. Maybe weak, but alive. My tenacious, bulldog nature would force me to tear at all possibilities.

Etienne stood. "Let's go see a few people I know. We'll ask about your sister. The faster you find her, the faster you'll leave. We'll take my car."

"What, you don't like my grandmother's tank? Just because it doesn't have air-conditioning and can't pass a gas station . . ." I punched him in the arm. Ouch. A really hard arm. As long as he was willing to take me where I wanted to go, I'd play the game.

When we walked outside, I could see the day had moved from early to late morning. The sky, a bright blue cap over the world, had no hint of clouds. Last night's rain, having fulfilled its irrigation duties, had moved on. I loved SF, but the gray days wore on me at times. I could become accustomed to this place—except for the crazy witches and so-called demons.

Herschel was waiting at the foot of the stairs.

"Did you get anything to eat, Hersch?" I'd have to hit a fast-food restaurant if he hadn't. Unfortunately, I'd have to borrow money to do it. The cops still had my wallet.

"He's eaten." Etienne spoke in a terse, irritated voice. He glared at Herschel. "He went into the kitchen, stared at the cook for a few minutes, and they immediately fed him. He apparently ate enough for ten men. Is he a witch, too? Is that possible?"

I glanced at Herschel, who was licking his balls with loud slurps. "To tell the truth, I'm not exactly sure what he is."

"I believe that."

Etienne had a new SUV outside. Obviously the SUV fairy had worked overtime to produce another one. Or maybe he had a whole warehouse full that I hadn't seen. Herschel indicated he wanted to accompany us, so I let him into the backseat. Etienne stepped away when a man approached. He spoke quietly with him, then nodded. When we climbed in, he said, "You get to meet the demon after all. Someone obviously told him about you. Or maybe he saw. He walks the Barrows at night." Etienne did not sound happy.

"What if I believe he killed Marisol? What if I try to kill him?"

"I'll be expected to throw myself in front of him."

"Because you're immune to magic."

"Something like that."

"And if I try to shoot—"

He snatched my arm near the wrist and his fingers bit to the bone. "This isn't a joke."

He released me. Dull pain spread from my wrist to my elbow. I would probably bruise. His instantaneous anger stunned me into silence.

Etienne stared out the window. His hands lay in his lap, but they'd clenched into fists. Slowly, a few fingers at a time, he let them relax.

"Nyx, Aiakós is the premier predator in the Barrows. I can guarantee that you have never met one like him. He talks about being vulnerable to earth magic, but no one knows exactly *how* vulnerable. I watched Madeline empty an entire magazine of large-caliber bronze bullets into his gut one night. It barely slowed him. He almost tore her apart. I was wounded, couldn't move. Only Michael saved her."

He slowly reached and grasped my arm again. Gently now, but it still hurt. He slid his fingers down to take my hand. "You need to be afraid of him, Nyx. If you've never been afraid of anyone or anything in your life, fear Aiakós."

He released me and started the engine.

What did I do about this confusing man? Etienne seemed drawn to me, liked me, but I was a witch, to the very depths of my soul. He hated witches. He'd protected me and now jumped to instant violence to make a point. He hurt me, then half-ass apologized.

Though the road was clear, the buildings around it soon went back to what I'd seen previously. Abandoned apartments and storefronts lined the street. Crowded together, gloomy and forsaken, none showed signs of habitation. Not even a heavy winter snow would soften these abandoned boxes.

From what I'd seen so far, the inhabited Barrows appeared to be a patchwork of fiefdoms. Etienne had his military, the docks still belonged to the city, River Street was a strip of blighted commerce, and the Archangel made a stunning example of a well-guarded mansion in a crime-ridden ghetto.

"Where do Dervick and his Bastinados hang out?" I asked.

"To the south. You really should avoid them. We don't know much about them."

"The ones I saw didn't look all that dangerous. They looked . . . frightened."

"And that's what makes them dangerous. Fifty or so armed men. Once there were several hundred. Once they were the scourge of the city. They're afraid. Of what?"

I could see how Dervick, with his ability to manipulate fire, could frighten them, at least initially. I knew the concept of a team with a leader, though. Dervick wasn't—or he didn't seem like—a true leader. He seemed a simple little fire starter, with the attitude of a man who had always had to look up at the other men around him. I doubted he could hold a group of gang members together forever.

Etienne drove into a plaza surrounded by taller buildings, but none higher than four stories. The streets coming into the place met at odd angles and a few cars were parked at the curb. The buildings here did show evidence of patchwork repair and habitation, though nothing seemed shiny and new. Windows had glass and all buildings had doors, a rare thing on the streets we passed earlier.

As soon as Etienne parked, I climbed out. Something boiled in the plaza's exact center. Invisible, but I could feel it, though it remained invisible. The power emanating in colossal waves from the thing caused a chill deep in my guts. The warm summer day fled and left me standing in stunning cold.

"What is it?" I whispered to Etienne, who had come to stand beside me.

"What is what?"

Could he not see? I stood shivering, my shoulders hunched, arms crossed protectively over my chest. Even the aftermath of my spectacular, fiery oops last night paled beside what I felt just then.

Etienne's arm curved around my shoulders. At that moment, I did feel oddly fragile. I thought I would shatter if I should trip and fall.

A pickup truck entered the plaza. It drove straight toward the spiral of energy and right on through it as if it were not there. I'd expected that much power would have swallowed it.

"Is this the Zombie Zone?" I asked. "Abigail said . . ."

"Yes. That's it." He frowned. "You can see something?"

I shook my head. "Mostly I feel it."

"How does it feel?"

"It's cold. Bitter cold. It's an aberration of time and space. It does not belong here in the Earth Mother's world."

I remembered Laudine's words. *"The heart of evil, the Zombie Zone. That's where the demon hides. A door between worlds."*

I'd seen many odd things in my life and travels. A place in the Okefenokee where the ghosts of ancient peoples gathered to dance to the beat of now-silent drums, a pit in Africa where the bones of animals collected and rattled and almost formed words—they awed me, but I would walk through them without fear. Should the Earth Mother grace me with her presence again, I would ask only one question. *Why did she allow such a dangerous thing to exist here?*

chapter 16

I suddenly realized I was standing on the sidewalk in the arms of a stranger who might be a friend or might be an enemy. Whatever power was parked in the center of the plaza frightened me. Nothing that involved magic had ever actually frightened me before. Etienne had seen a moment of weakness I really hadn't wanted him to see. When I pulled away, he instantly released me. He did give me a roguish grin and that managed to draw a smile from me in return.

"Let's go inside," he said. He didn't move. Instead he caught my arm in a firm grip. He put his lips close to my ear. "If something happens, if I tell you to run, will you do it?"

"What do you think? Run? Yes, I'll run. If necessary and if you run with me. Don't ever think I'll leave you to fight alone. To fight for me. As long as I have the strength to stand, I will."

Etienne turned his face away and muttered under his breath. "Darrow said . . ."

"Darrow said what? I've probably heard it. 'Nicky, you are the most stubborn creature on God's earth.'"

Etienne's face relaxed. He almost smiled. "Darrow said you had the courage of a tiger with cubs. That I would find no better warrior to stand at my back—if I could persuade you that I am worthy of your loyalty."

"Damn. Darrow's getting to be a philosopher in his old age." I made light of it, but it pleased me deep in my heart that my old friend thought that of me. "Let's get this over with."

I walked with him across the sidewalk and through glass doors that whispered as they closed behind us. We entered into a marble-floor room with expansive ceilings and hand-carved woodwork. This place had been either recently restored or carefully protected from whatever disaster befell the ruins outside. The most striking thing in the massive room was not the marble under my feet, the high ceiling, or the wide ornate staircase leading to a second floor.

I held my breath as I approached a statue, the human representation of Earth Mother I'd seen in my dream last night. What artist could have created such a rare and perfect image? Certainly one who had been graced with her presence as I had. Human-sized and absolutely perfect, it seemed as if it would come to life if I touched it. Carved from a single, perfect opal, her eyes were closed, not as if she slept, but as if she prayed. That emphasized the perfect symmetry of her hands and arms. The first men and women had bowed to and worshipped her, changeless and eternal, for thousands of years. They had left their crude representations buried in the earth. Those humans lived within her cycle of life, birth, and death. They took careful note of the seasons as they foraged the land, herded animals, and grew their crops. Then as now, witches, healers, and oracles were the keepers of the world's magic. Idolatry had no appeal for me, but seeing this, I could understand why humans would choose to fall to their knees before her.

"She is beautiful, our Innana." The voice, deep and soft, came from my right.

Etienne stood behind me. His hands clamped on my shoulders with a grip that would probably defy any effort on my part to dislodge them. Not that I wanted to move just then.

Beyond a doubt, the melodic voice came from Laudine's demon. He stood at least seven feet tall and was masculine as the statue of the Earth Mother was feminine. Golden skin and deeper golden eyes complemented magnificent crimson hair. Or maybe it was hair. It stood like a crest over his head and fell down to his shoulders. How exquisite, how . . . breathtaking.

Speechless, I simply stared as I had at the statue.

The demon favored me with a personal smile, a sensual smile, and it carried the promise of pleasure beyond imagination. At the same time, the offer came with the arrogance of a noble looking down upon his favored servant.

"Nyx." Etienne spoke in my ear. "This is Aiakós."

"Ah . . . yeah." Could I sound more stupid?

Aiakós stepped closer. His clothing appeared to be modern, upscale, and flattering. It had to be custom-made for his size. It was the eyes, his eyes, that broke the spell. He'd dropped his guard to study me, and those perfect golden eyes turned black as a basement in hell. Only an instant, but my witch instincts shrieked. Etienne's warning held true. Something deadly, something evil, approached.

I backed up tighter against Etienne. His breath remained steady, and his body rigid. My arms still hung at my sides.

"No magic," Etienne hissed in my ear. "He won't attack you."

His words didn't reassure me. Aiakós stopped.

"No. I won't attack your witch, Etienne," Aiakós agreed. "Innana"—he nodded at the Earth Mother's statue—"has made that quite clear. I am only permitted to strike at her witches if I am attacked first. It seems unfair, but I remain her captive." He gave the statue a glance that could only be taken as annoyance.

Desperate to change the subject, I nodded at the statue. "Where did you get that?"

"Oh, some diligent grave robbers found it deep within a cave in the Middle East. It is priceless, I'm told, though certain merchants were persuaded to accept a substantial amount of money and send it here. My son was most perturbed at the cost. That, too, was priceless, to see him so vexed. Apparently he feels there are some limits to wealth. You've met Michael."

It was not a question. He'd been keeping track of me, probably since I first arrived.

My initial stupor at his appearance quickly changed to curiosity. Curiosity and my occasional reckless absence of fear had defined my life—and caused me endless trouble.

Etienne, apparently sensing I had overcome my initial shock and wasn't planning an assault on his employer, slowly released me.

Aiakós studied me for a long moment. "I'm told that you are searching for your sister. Marisol. I have met her. To my utter surprise, she walked in one day and introduced herself. After that, she came to visit me occasionally. I certainly enjoyed her company. She was well versed in areas of earth magic that were of interest to me and had traveled extensively around your world. And quite a lovely young woman."

"That sounds like Marisol." Marisol had a far greater

deficit of good healthy fear than I. I didn't know she had traveled *extensively*. I thought I was the only wanderer in the family. "How long since you've seen her?"

"I don't actually mark time as you do, but it has been the equivalent of five weeks. Now that I know she is missing, I will search for her. I lead a rather barren existence in this place. I value the few people whose company I enjoy."

I nodded. "I take it Etienne isn't much of a conversationalist."

Aiakós laughed. "Oh, Etienne and I have communicated excellently at times." The demon's laugh carried an edge that made me shiver. Etienne still stood behind me, close enough I could feel his body grow stiff and his breath ragged. The man feared witches. He also feared his employer. But he somehow found the courage to face both those fears with only minor hesitation.

I'd relaxed a little since it didn't seem likely that we would fall into an immediate violent confrontation. Maybe Aiakós would answer some questions. "What's that thing outside? In the plaza." I'd been told, but I wanted his understanding of the Zombie and its uses.

Aiakós nodded. "Marisol found it quite intriguing, too. That, my dear, is a most dangerous and difficult passage between worlds. Many who use it do not survive." His voice and expression grew cold and hard. He changed a bit. His eyes narrowed and took on a really scary shine. A demonic shine. And his hands? He had claws. I hadn't noticed them before. He reached out with a clawed hand and stroked the statue's arm. "That wretched door is closed now, but it opens occasionally. With spectacular results. It is the portal that your—our— precious Earth Mother used to drag me here and make me a prisoner."

I'd heard about the prisoner part. "Dragged you from where?"

"From a place where I was quite powerful. A place I enjoyed very much. I had the best of that world and the Barrows. Now I have . . . nothing."

I broke from my awe and raised an eyebrow at his assertion. "You have a lot more than nothing."

Aiakós suddenly relaxed. He went from demon to magnificent charming alien in a single instant. "Yes. I have money and servants to create a luxurious cage. It is not an alternative to freedom. But of course, my prison is not your fault. Will you join me for some wine? I'm curious about you." He gave me a beneficent smile.

"No, thanks. Maybe later." I'd like to talk to him, but my mind had to process things first. "I really need to be searching for Marisol. I know something is wrong, and I feel like time is running out."

"Another time, then. Please. You will be safe here. I can promise you that." He nodded politely.

Voices came from the side of the room as several men and one woman entered. All were dressed in expensive tailored business suits. It seemed innocuous at first, until I heard a voice I knew. Alcides Spaneas.

To call Alcides Spaneas Greek was an insult to the people of that land, but he claimed it as his home. The nicest thing he'd been called was a gunrunner. The worst, a mass murderer. If Etienne's picture was in the post office, this man's face was everywhere. Wanted. Wanted by more countries than I could count. I had personally walked through some of the blood he'd spread across the world.

Aiakós laughed, soft and deadly as if he'd heard some secret joke. His attention was no longer on us. I had heard rumors of Etienne as a mercenary, but in conjunction with Spaneas? My horror must have shown on my face.

I turned to Etienne.

"Do you . . . have you . . . ?" What could I ask? *Have you killed for Alcides Spaneas?* I turned away.

Aiakós went to the group and herded them in another direction, thankfully away from us and the Earth Mother's image. He towered over them and laughed with them. He allowed them to enter another room ahead of him. Before he went in, he looked straight at me and smiled. Alcides Spaneas wasn't a demon here. Spaneas was human, only a small evil man. Aiakós would lead them. What evil did he have planned for the Earth Mother's world? Would he use men like Spaneas as a tool to spread death and destruction?

Anger, a sense of horror . . . rage. I could do nothing about atrocities I'd seen. That was the past. This was about the future. The fire rose in me. I could follow them into that room and everything, everyone, demon and man, would burn.

Etienne lowered his mouth to my ear. His voice was cold and steady as steel. "Those are Aiakós's . . . slaves. They think of themselves as comrades. They will receive what they truly deserve eventually." He shuddered. "As I have received."

He held me as if I was his anchor, this time. The flame in me descended to a flicker. I swallowed and drew a deep breath. Etienne released me.

"Let's go. We'll talk somewhere else."

I started to turn when I realized Herschel was sitting on my feet. I guess he'd felt the fire rise in me. Did he plan to help or hinder me if I built an inferno? How did he get out of the SUV? What was this animal? What powers did he have—and what did he do with my lovable childhood companion?

"Herschel?"

A blob of slobber dropped from his mouth. He farted loudly and Etienne and I quickly backed away. Things dropped to something that approached normal for a witch and a mercenary soldier.

"Does he always do that?" Etienne asked.

"If you mean drool and pass gas, yes, he does. Standing between me and what he thinks dangerous, not often."

"He felt you were in danger?"

"Possibly. Or maybe he was warning me not to do something . . . reckless."

Aiakós was most certainly dangerous on his own, regardless of his *comrades*. I would not ignore the possibilities. The demon might not have harmed Marisol, but who's to say he wasn't holding her prisoner somewhere? Powerful Marisol was not immune to the witch's curse of arrogance. Perhaps she had misjudged him, and he saw a way to use her. He might have made her a prisoner.

As for Etienne, Great Mother, what should I do with him? I could only find some consolation in the fact that the Earth Mother offered him to me and move on from there.

I had now met—or at least I hoped I had met—most of the major "players" in the Barrows. Etienne, the demon, Michael and Madeline, and Dervick had all put in an appearance. I'd even talked to Abigail, the High Witch. I'd spent very little time with Dervick before Etienne chased him off. Of course, any or every one of those

I'd met could have lied actually or by omission. The two Sisters of Justice were a bit of a mystery. Like most witches, I was not likely to invite them out to play if I didn't have to.

We walked outside and I stared again at the Zombie. A portal to other worlds, obviously closed since another vehicle drove by and passed right through it without harm. I managed to find a bit of courage and stepped toward it. Herschel grabbed my leg in his mouth. I staggered and started to fall, but Etienne caught me. Herschel held on. His teeth poked into me to the point of pain.

"What's he doing?" Etienne asked.

"Urging me to resist my wildly curious nature. All right, Herschel, I'll stay away."

Herschel released me.

"Where to, witch?" Etienne asked as we climbed into the SUV.

"Back to your place, where I'll clean your backseat and get my car."

"No point in that." He grinned and spoke with obvious pleasure. "I'll take you where you want to go. I have people who can clean the car, or get me a new one."

"Suppose I want to go somewhere without you?"

"That's too bad." His voice tightened with determination. "Unless you want to go to the police, straighten out your life, and go home."

"Why are you so determined to play bodyguard?"

"I don't want to get blamed if something happens to you." His voice sounded flat. What didn't he want to tell me?

"Etienne, who would care if something *happened* to me?"

"Abigail, Darrow. Maybe Madeline . . ."

I could read the truth behind his words. Damn, I did not need this. Why had this man suddenly decided there was some umbilical cord between us?

"What do you want from me? I am absolutely nothing to you. Besides, if I hadn't helped you last night at the road block . . ."

"I remember helping you, too."

"You dragged an unconscious woman home and dumped her in your bed. You could have left me lying on the ground. Herschel would have protected me from Laudine."

"You're sure about that?"

No, I wasn't. And yes, I was beginning to like the man a little, but I wasn't going to give him any say-so in my life. Immune to magic, my ass. I'd see about that. I gathered a minuscule bit of magic. I ever so gently brushed him with it.

It slammed me back so hard I cried out and jerked in my seat. Blast furnace light blinded me. My head smacked against the window. My legs went numb.

Herschel lunged forward. His massive mouth closed on Etienne's neck. Etienne clawed for his gun.

"Herschel," I screamed. "Stop!"

I used what little strength I had to throw myself over and grabbed Etienne's wrist so he couldn't draw. He froze.

"Let him go, Herschel." I gasped out the words.

Herschel held for a second, then released him. My familiar growled in warning. He had let go physically, but kept alert.

My body still trembled as I collapsed across Etienne. At that point he could probably have drawn his gun, but he didn't. He placed his hands on my shoulders and sat me back straight in my seat.

I drew deep gasping breaths, unable to pull oxygen in fast enough. My stomach churned and my heart raced. What a disaster. Etienne had red marks on his neck where Herschel's teeth had come deathly close to removing his head. I'd seen my unusual familiar bite the head of an alligator. A man didn't stand a chance.

I wasn't the only one breathing deeply. Etienne had both hands on the steering wheel as if he would lose control of them if he released it. When he spoke, his voice was rough, but edged with deadly calm. "If that animal ever tries that again, I will kill him."

I could feel the rage rolling off him.

His anger was justified—but not at Herschel. I'd always taken pride that my use of magic had been for an absolutely necessary reason. This time, I'd gone a little beyond a line I shouldn't cross. I had no cause to touch him with magic and I'd paid the price. It didn't dampen my curiosity about his immunity, but I would have to find another way to learn more.

"I understand. I'm so sorry. It was my fault." My words sounded inadequate. My humiliation ran deep to the core of my life. "He thought you attacked me."

The Mother had said I should teach him to trust me and I'd created a mess.

"If you're sorry, you'll tell me what happened." Etienne had relaxed a bit. His voice was still tight as a steel coil spring.

"I wanted to know about this immunity-to-magic thing Laudine talked about. I touched you with magic. Only a tiny bit, a single finger tap, and it backfired. Herschel thought you had hurt me."

Etienne's jaw clenched and he clutched the steering

wheel tighter. He'd break it soon. "And what did you try to make me do?"

"Make you do?" His question stunned me. "No. No. I can't . . . I never . . ." I sat back and closed my eyes. He'd made a harsh judgment of me. I told myself he had reason, but it hurt nonetheless. I tried to relax, let myself settle into the moment. When I could speak calmly, I tried to explain.

"Etienne, I was born into a family of witches. I've had certain lessons drilled into me from the time I understood I had the power to do things." I rubbed my hands over my face and tried to work a little saliva into a parched mouth. "A witch can sell or give you a potion for you to use. Laudine sells arthritis and hot flash meds to old women. A witch can defend herself when threatened. Like I did with the rain and blowing out the street and car lights.

"The Mother's First Law binds witches, though. It's carved into our souls. It is absolutely forbidden to use earth magic to force a person to take any action against their will. I can't tell you how many times I've recited the mantra of the First Law since I was six years old." I blew out a breath.

He had relaxed a bit. His hands had dropped to his knees, but he tensed again when I shifted in my seat. "What happens if a witch is . . . bad?"

"I was born with my power. It's in my body and comes from the earth itself. The only way to stop a witch is destroy her. When the Earth Mother finds out a witch has been using spells in a *truly evil manner* she sends the Sisters of Justice to send the offender back to the cauldron of death and rebirth. Minor transgressions might be overlooked. Witches are human after all. But willful intent to harm? The Mother knows. It may take a while to get the details, but then . . . There's no trial. No mercy. It's not negotiable. When the Sisters arrive, it's usually for an execution."

He nodded as if he understood that part. "What did you just do to me?"

I sighed. I hated to admit I was wrong. "I acted with bad manners and bad judgment. I did something very rude. I was curious. Laudine said you were immune to magic. I couldn't see a spell around you that gave you that immunity, so I very gently touched you with magic. Just a tap."

I held up one finger. "The equivalent of a single drop of water in a twenty-acre lake. That tiny tap bounced back like a lightning strike. You are immune to magic. I don't understand why. Do you know?"

Etienne gave a brief shake of his head, which was not a convincing denial. I didn't blame him for not wanting to spew his secrets and leave himself vulnerable to me.

"So," I said, as perky as I could manage. "Are you my chauffeur? Or are you going to kick me out on the street? I don't mind. The street, that is. I completely understand. I'll walk back and get my car."

"No, I'm still with you."

"Well, damn." I didn't know whether to be pleased or irritated. I leaned back and flexed my shoulders. Every muscle in me ached. "If I'm stuck with you, I need to go find Dervick. He and I need to continue the conversation you and Darrow so rudely interrupted yesterday. But first I need to talk to Laudine."

Etienne shook his head, but he headed toward River Street. "I hope you know what you're doing. You're a walking disaster."

"Oh, how sweet. I love it when I'm surrounded by supportive people."

"Of course I'm supportive. I haven't tried to kill you yet. Magic isn't your only weapon."

Not my only weapon? Now what did that mean? It made me smile. I think maybe he liked me, or wanted to like me, but we probably had too many obstacles between us and a truly satisfying relationship.

"Tell me about the men at Aiakós's place," I said. "Alcides Spaneas I recognized. Am I to assume the others are in the same class?"

"Definitely. I can tell you what's going to happen. It happened with some others about six months ago. They're wanted all over the world."

"Like you."

"Like me. Aiakós is going to offer them sanctuary, use them, then steal all their money. If they happen to have any other skill he can use, he'll let them live. In the meantime, the Barrows is their haven."

"Yes. This meeting is one of the first stages of his plan."

I rubbed the back of my neck. I hadn't realized how tense I was. "And you know this *plan*? How?"

"He told me. He regularly reminds me that I'm as much a prisoner of the Barrows as he is. I betrayed him once. He'll keep me as long as I keep his army sharp. As long as I'm useful."

"You betrayed him?"

"Yes."

"And he didn't kill you?" That sounded a little out there.

"No." His voice was smooth and dark without a trace of fear. "I screamed a lot for a few weeks. Did I mention he's fond of torture? I survived."

"Great Mother." That came out as a prayer.

"I told you, Nyx. I've earned most of what I have received. One way or the other."

Of all the thoughts and conjectures running through my mind, one thing stood out. Etienne feared Aiakós for good reason. That was healthy, given what he'd told me. But damn it to hell, he feared witches more.

chapter 17

Two cars were parked in front of Laudine's. Apparently the lull in harassment by Etienne's men continued. I didn't know if he called them off, Darrow intervened, or they were now afraid to approach. Two elderly women came out as we entered. Laudine stood alone behind the counter. She stared at me with her typical stony expression when we entered. As usual, she didn't look at Etienne.

"I see you've joined the demon," she said. She glared and contempt filled her voice.

"I haven't joined anyone, Laudine. Stop making assumptions about me. I only have bits and pieces of a puzzle to work with here. My options are still open. Right now I'm simply taking advantage of a free ride." And without my credit cards or money I couldn't go anywhere. Etienne would probably give me money, though, if I'd leave.

I approached her, but Etienne hung back, maybe giving me some space.

"Talk to me about Dervick, Laudine. He's really pissed at you. What did you do to him?"

"The toad. That weasel. He came here and ..." She sneered.

Toad? Weasel? Now, there was an odd image to get stuck in a mind. "What did he want you to do?"

"That's not your business." Laudine's hands shook. She noticed them and clasped them together tight to still them.

"Okay. The toad-weasel. The one you won't talk about. Where can I find him?"

"I have no idea. Now take your lackey and leave. You're a disgrace to witches and your sister's memory." She flipped a dismissive hand at me.

"You're sure she's a memory?" I felt myself grow colder. "Why is that?"

Laudine hissed between her teeth. "Get out!"

I left. Etienne followed me.

"Damn." I smacked my fist in my hand. "I should have grabbed my clothes." We climbed in the SUV. "I guess I can do it later. Since you're my friendly neighborhood lackey, do you know where I can find Dervick?"

"I might. Unless you call me a lackey again."

"You would prefer minion or subordinate. How about—"

"How about you shut up."

I laughed. "Okay, does that mean we're best friends again?"

"No. It means if you stop talking, I won't try to maim you in the next ten minutes."

His mouth twitched in a smile. Had he forgiven me for my little magical transgression? I'm not sure why I even cared. Except that it felt good sitting in the car next to him. I still hadn't had time to process his words about guilt. He didn't seem to feel sorry for himself, so I doubted he would want sympathy from me, even if he were able to find it. I watched him as he maneuvered a massive vehicle through the ruined streets of what had once been a vibrant part of a city. He was barely able to skirt around some buildings that had crumbled. It seemed as if we might come to something impassable, but we didn't.

I saw them ahead, the so-called Bastinados. About thirty of them lounged on abandoned cars, boxes, and broken benches in what had once been a midblock park. A few scraggly trees still reached desperate branches to the sky. Copious piles of garbage littered the ground and many of them held enough beer cans to build a small aluminum house. Etienne parked the car in front of a three-story building not far from the congregation of badasses. The Bastinados all leaned forward toward what might be a threat. Several drew weapons.

When Etienne stepped out, those sitting stood and stepped up, ready to rumble. When I did the same, they sat back down.

How incredibly odd.

Etienne stared at me with suspicious and curious eyes. "They're afraid of you." His words said he wasn't happy about that.

"Of me? Surely not. You're mistaking something else for fear, Etienne."

"Like what?"

"Indigenous cultural hospitality? Indigestion?"

Some of the Bastinados had probably been watching when I'd taken their boss's fire and thrown it back at him. All men were wise to beware of fire, but these were also armed with guns. Herschel was lying asleep on the backseat with all four legs in the air.

"That's disgusting," Etienne said, nodding at the dog.

"It's okay. He'll guard our ride." Herschel did look disgusting, but I'd never admit it out loud.

The building we entered was mostly open on the first

floor, except for some massive steel columns. Carpet had covered it at one time; I could see the remnants around the edges of the room. Now we walked across bare concrete.

"Hey," I said to Etienne. "If Dervick starts shooting fire, I'm going to stand behind you. You being immune to magic and all."

"Shooting fire?" He drew his gun. I noticed that the ready firearm had become a semipermanent accessory when I was around.

I snickered. "Damn. You forgot the extinguisher, didn't you? What were you thinking? Don't worry. I can handle a little fire." I walked on into the building. "Dervick? You here?"

"What do you want?" Dervick stepped from behind one of the massive columns. He sounded absolutely sulky. His baggy suit looked like he'd been run over by a truck. I paid no attention to his sullen attitude. "We need to finish our conversation from yesterday. I think we ended it at the part where you said something about your men dying after Laudine refused to work for you."

Dervick came closer. He didn't seem frightened. More like unsure of how to deal with me. "After I spoke to Laudine, the men began to die. They're still dying. You saw them out there." His voice sounded as pretty as his face.

"I'll admit they weren't very energetic. There aren't many of them, either." He had a point. The Mother might be upset with Laudine poisoning his men without immediate threat. "Why are you here? This *derelict chic* show seems like a pretty unlikely lifestyle for you."

Dervick grimaced. "My mother wanted me to come. I was supposed to take control."

"Control of what?" I really tried not to laugh at the

farce. Under the circumstances humor was difficult to restrain.

He shrugged one shoulder. "Control of . . . everything. The Barrows, I guess. I made them afraid of me, those men. I do own the ones you saw, but a lot of them left town. And there is that creature." I presumed he meant Aiakós. He rubbed his hands together as if washing them. "I thought if I could persuade Laudine to join me . . ." He rubbed a hand through his hair, then vigorously scratched at one point. This boy had a problem.

"Your mother is a witch and you don't know how incredibly arrogant they are? You should have known better, Dervick."

"You don't know that Mother is a witch."

He was right. I'd made an assumption that because he had power, he had to be related to the keepers of magic. He spun quite a tale. Most of it probably lies. Could a witch's kid be that naive?

"Dervick, you're the first person I've ever met, except for myself, who plays with fire like we did."

"Huh! What world have you been living in?" He cocked his head and smiled. His voice softened with his words and hinted at something else, something far stronger than his demeanor implied. He continued. "I'll tell you something, even if you don't believe me. The world of witches is new, only a few thousand years old. There was a time before then when the Earth Mother had other servants. Servants far more fantastic and powerful than men or witches."

"Really? Where are they now?"

"She hides them, keeps them away from us."

"And you know this because . . . ? And it's important to me because . . . ?"

He gave me what I would call a smug, shit-eating

smile. "I just know. And you'll find out how important soon, I think."

He was right about some things. It had been a long time since I lived in the world of witches and when I had, it was in the most backwater isolated town in America. I had purposefully rejected any deep, informational lessons on the cultural diversity of the Earth Mother's children. My knowledge of the differences came from the people I'd met in my life. I had no clue why he'd given me a lecture on ancient history. I dealt with the now.

"You sent those men to attack Laudine the other night?"

"Yes. I just wanted them to harass her. They failed, thanks to you."

"Harass?" The little shit pissed me off. "They were shooting real bullets."

"You burned—"

"They burned. They threw a firebomb and I tossed it back at them."

This was bordering on unbelievable. The word ludicrous came to mind, too.

I plunged on. "So, you have these men, these Bastinados. What do you plan to do with them?"

"I have no idea." He was hiding something, of course.

"Maybe you should call your mom and ask her for advice."

He didn't answer me.

I had to go. "I'll see you later, Dervick. Try to stay out of trouble."

As I turned, he called me back. "Nyx?"

"Yes?"

"Are you . . ." He made one step forward. His pretty face wrinkled in a frown. He glanced at Etienne. "Could we talk? Sometime? We can find an impartial place."

"Yeah. We can talk. Not right now, but as soon as I can." I did need to talk to him after I found Marisol. There was still something familiar about him, and he was the only person I'd ever met who could play with fire.

When Etienne and I walked back outside, the Bastinados remained where they were. Well, I walked out. Etienne staggered because he was laughing so hard. Oh, I understood the humor. Dervick, the insecure and slightly pathetic fire mage, leading a bloody gang. Doing stupid, childlike things in the worst possible places.

I threw my hands up. "This place is paradise. We have a demon who acts too kind and sophisticated to squash a bug and a militia leader on the whole world's most wanted list." I poked his ribs with my finger to see him flinch. "There's a pretty boy gang leader who probably calls Mom every night, and a malicious earth witch who . . . well, the Mother only knows what she wants. It's imminent Armageddon."

And I was no closer to finding Marisol.

chapter 18

Herschel didn't wake when we climbed back in the SUV. The assembled Bastinados had relaxed and gone back to their tedious pursuit of absolutely nothing. Once we were rolling again, I opened my phone. I called the office in San Francisco. On River Street I had service, but I spiked it with a little magic to upset anyone trying to track me.

"Single-Eye Investigations," Karen answered all bright and perky. "You lose 'em, we find 'em."

I laughed. "You sound happy. Your *boyfriend of the week* pick you up for a nooner? Not in my office, I hope." Karen changed boyfriends like I changed socks.

Karen sighed loudly. "In the absence of all managerial authority I have adopted a new attitude. It's called, *I don't give a shit*. I have also decided to give myself a raise. One of my bosses is camping out on the golf course and the other is wanted by the police. They did come by—the police, that is. FBI, actually. I did what you said. Told them you were in Duivel, but I didn't know exactly where." Her voice softened. "Are you okay? I didn't really give myself a raise BTW."

"I'm okay. Need something else. Run a deep search on Anton Dervick. Not totally sure of the spelling. I'll

take care of the raise when I get back. You've earned it."
I loved that girl.

I hung up and turned to Etienne. "You know what I want. I want to find my sister. What do you want? You insist on following me around. You won't tell me why." I tried to ask with some honesty. He'd attached himself to me for no apparent reason other than possibly a feeling of mild attraction.

He didn't speak for a moment. Then he said, "I value Darrow. He, however, seems to value *you* a bit too much. As long as I keep you around and safe, he won't leave me. Or turn on me."

Now, that was an interesting bit of logic. It was also absurd. This man walked in red-hot danger zones and had most of his life. If you had doubts about one of your men's loyalty, for your own safety, you fired and replaced him. Darrow didn't mean that much to him. Oh, had I actually thought his interest in me was personal? Had I wanted it to be? I wasn't sure about that yet.

Darrow greeted us when we parked back at the compound. He moved in close when Etienne opened his door. "You got a cop waiting for you in the office. Told him I never heard of you, but he didn't buy it."

Etienne glanced at me. "Why don't you go upstairs and—"

"What? No way. You stick like chewing gum on my boot when you're messing in my business. Payback is hell, buddy."

He jumped out of the SUV and slammed the door. I was right behind him. Darrow chuckled. "Damn, girl. I'd forgotten how stubborn you can be."

I gave him a one-finger salute and stayed on Etienne's heels.

Etienne's office was on the ground floor under his

apartment. The man waiting there introduced himself as Captain Flynn of the Duivel Police Department. He produced a badge and ID. The next thing he said was, "Abby sent me."

Etienne raised an eyebrow at that, but said nothing. He went to sit behind a desk and Captain Flynn sat in front of him. Flynn had a firm voice, a nice pleasant face, and a strong body. The tone in that voice said he'd seen more than he wished to see of the Earth Mother's world. I sat in a chair at the side of the room so I could see both of them.

Flynn started the conversation. "Abby called and asked that I check into something that happened the other night. Someone supposedly spotted a fugitive at a license check. It's not my case, but I told her I'd find out. She said the Mother . . ." He stopped, bit his lip, then continued in a steady voice. "The idea that an internationally known felon, Etienne Durand, is in Duivel is interesting. The only proof they have is a fake driver's license with the picture of someone who looks a bit like Durand. Unfortunately, the officer who swears he saw Durand is a crime-buff rookie who has memorized a lot of wanted posters." Flynn glanced at me. "Are you Nyx Ianira?"

I nodded.

He frowned. "You shouldn't have run. There's nothing on you."

I stretched my legs out and tried to relax. "It seemed like the right thing to do at the time. People were yelling and pointing guns."

Flynn stared for a moment, then went on. "I have a friend at the FBI. He said Interpol is looking for Durand. I don't think they'll send someone to Duivel on the say-so of a rookie cop." A roguish smile twitched his lips. It made him look much younger. "I've heard a lot of rumors. Exactly how much gold did you—did Durand—steal?"

I sat up straight. Gold. Oh, this was getting interesting.

Etienne kept a straight face and a level gaze on Flynn. "What gold?"

"Of course," Flynn said. "But it was suggested, privately, by certain authorities that if the gold was returned, other things might be overlooked." Flynn stood. He pulled out a card and laid it on Etienne's desk. "Call me if you need to make arrangements for a safe delivery of . . . anything. Abby said you should do the right thing." He paused. His mouth twisted in a mocking grin. "Of course, Abby's idea of the right thing might not be what you or I would like."

He walked out. As soon as he was gone, I moved closer to Etienne's desk. Consumed with curiosity, I asked, "How much gold is he talking about?"

Etienne gazed at me with cold eyes. "A ten-wheel truckload. Millions, maybe a billion."

My mouth dropped open. I don't think anything I'd learned here surprised me more. "And where is it?"

He shrugged. "I don't know. The witch I stole it for hid it exceptionally well somewhere in the Barrows. The Barrows is a big place with lots of hiding places."

"The witch . . . ?"

"Is dead. Madeline took her down and one of the Sisters finished the job. It's been over two years."

"Would you give it back? The gold. If I can find it after I find Marisol?"

"What do you think?" He gave a quick, almost boyish smile.

"I think I need to be out of here. I'll go up and get my things. You send for my car. You really don't want me to start looking for it by myself."

"No! You—"

I jumped up, shoved the door open, and went out and up the stairs. He followed me and walked in before the door closed behind me. I whirled to face him.

Before I could speak, he laid his hands on my shoulders. I didn't pull away, mostly because his grip wasn't tight—and the hungry look on his face interested me.

"I appreciate what you've done," I said. "You took a hell of a risk going out of the Barrows. You guarded me, but I can't sit around here, hoping for the best."

I knew it was going to happen. Maybe it was destined from that first moment we met. Maybe it was the way so many things about us fit. His hands slid down and caught my waist. His mouth came down on mine. He drew something from me I hadn't savored in a long time. I'd had lovers, some skilled and quite adept at making sex an incredible experience. None made me feel like he did. Delicious anticipation and slow burning desire filled me, and the taste of him made me cling to him and hunger for more.

I broke the kiss and realized I was shaking.

"I don't have time for this." I tried to release him, draw away. He grinned at me.

His smile was that of a man who knew what he wanted—a man who knew what I wanted, too. He drew me closer and I gave in to the warm demand of his mouth.

I had a few minutes for this, didn't I? A half hour wouldn't make . . . oops, my pants were around my knees. Then I was sitting on the couch with him kneeling in front of me. He'd managed to strip off my shoes and pants and his hands slid under my shirt and over my breasts. I tried to touch him, get that leather vest off, but my hand caught on his gun holster.

"Get that off before one of us gets shot." Oh, this seemed priceless.

He laughed again and stripped the vest, T-shirt, and gun. I ran my hand over the bronze skin of his lean, hard chest. Not perfect. There were scars. He was a fighter, after all. I'd seen the masculine arrogance on his face. Given his reputation and my knowledge of the paths he'd walked, he'd earned it. The fact that he was still alive should earn him some kind of medal. Survival of the fittest. This man was the most cunning of his kind, the one who would use all his guile to take what he wanted by right or by force. He kissed me again.

Passion makes normally sane people act like rutting monkeys. I'm not immune. I didn't even think when I laid my palm on the amulet hanging from a chain around his neck. If I'd looked at it instead of gazing stupidly into his eyes, I'd have seen the markings and known not to touch.

Searing pain tore through my wrist. It blazed up my elbow before my mind could register it and jerk my hand away. I shrieked, fought blindly. He instantly moved, so I doubled over, trying to breathe. The carpeted floor loomed as I collapsed. The world around me blurred, blinding me.

I could vaguely hear Etienne calling my name over the roaring in my ears. Unable to get enough air to scream, all I could do was ride a giant wave of agony and pray for release. It rolled on, like a giant wave that would never crest and fall.

It did come, just as I thought I could bear no more and would lose consciousness. Each beat of my heart sent agony racing along my nerves. Pain has a tendency to slow the perception of time. After what seemed like an hour, sounds became more distinct and my vision went from fuzziness to moderately clear.

Etienne had picked me up, taken me to the bedroom, and laid me on the bed. I drew deep breaths. At least he didn't hover over me, didn't press me. Neither had he called for help.

My heart rate slowed, but a few muscles still twitched. My nose was running and I fought nausea. Great Mother, nothing in my life prepared me for that. I'd endured broken bones, being sliced by shrapnel, but this went beyond even that agony. I sucked in deep breaths, desperate for oxygen.

"What happened?" Etienne asked. He sounded concerned, but his face betrayed no emotion.

My body still jerked with the occasional spasm, but my vision had cleared and my mind started working again. It didn't take long to figure things out. I don't know why I hadn't thought of it before. Etienne's little amulet was a Solaire and the source of his immunity to magic. Gran had told me about them. The Solaires—there are rumored to be three of them—were created by the Earth Mother and given to the Sisters of Justice to protect themselves, make them immune to magic, when they had to execute a witch. I'd never seen one, but it could be nothing else. As I'd grown up, we young witches had chattered and speculated, but the adults wouldn't speak of any witch that might have been condemned. The Solaire and the Morié, the bronze execution blade, were a complete shield. The outlawed witch could not use magic to defend herself when the Sisters finally ran her down. I'd bet that knife on Etienne's belt was also the Morié. We witches were absolutely forbidden to touch either Solaire or Morié. I now knew why.

Etienne brought me a glass of water. I was able to sit up, but I cringed away from him. He set the glass on the nightstand beside the bed and stepped back. A guarded look, eyes narrow with speculation, remained on his face as he waited for me to explain. I needed answers first.

"Where did you get that amulet?" I managed to ask after a couple of tries. My voice wasn't working right.

He brushed it with his hand. "It was a gift."

"From who?"

"Not your business." His guarded expression told me nothing.

"Not my business!" I shouted, and pain spread from my hand again. I held it close and waited for it to ease. "You almost killed me, Etienne."

"I didn't want to kill you. I wanted to fuck you."

"Well, you're not going to as long as you wear that thing around your neck."

The room grew still. The only sound came from outside where men and vehicles moved briefly. They always moved fast because of the rule that all things remained inside. Finally, he said, "I'll tell you where I got it if you'll tell me what it is."

I gritted my teeth and tried to straighten from my hunched-over position. My fingers still curled tight in an instinctive need to protect the injured palm. The pain had eased, but I was not in a gentle state of mind. Certainly not gentle enough to talk. I wasn't going to give in to him and blab about the thing. I was the injured party here.

"Abigail," he suddenly spoke. "There was a fight. A battle, actually. I was dying and she healed me. After she did, she had me remove the amulet and knife from one of the Sisters of Justice who was knocked unconscious. She said . . ." He paused, then continued. "She said that as long as I wore them, I didn't have to fear magical traps again."

"Again? Some witch trapped you." Well, that made sense of things.

Etienne shrugged. It looked casual but was filled with determination. "Your turn."

I gave him a brief explanation of the Morié and Solaire—and I warned him. "Those objects of power, artifacts infused with earth magic, are powerful things. I'm told the Mother created them herself, thousands of years ago. The Earth Mother's High Priestess may have given them to you, but she doesn't control the Sisters. If a Sister of Justice catches you with them, she won't need magic to get them back. You better hope Abigail is around to protect you. The Sister will carve you to pieces."

I realized that he had not intended to hurt me. He'd wanted sex as much as I did. I also realized that he was not prepared to trust me, a witch, enough to remove them. I'd have to work to earn that. Did I want to? His kisses had been sweet—a disaster—but sweet. The question would be, could I spare time from my search for Marisol to deal with a complicated love affair?

chapter 19

I had to get up and move on. Etienne ignored me and I ignored him as I struggled to stand. I staggered to the bathroom. I held my hand under the stream of cool water. I'd expected a burn or some other mark on my palm, but there was none. The chill of the water helped and I could move my fingers again. I splashed my ravaged face, too, trying to forget the pain.

I'm not a deep philosophical thinker. I rarely have stunning mental revelations. Most enlightenment comes when someone or something slaps me up the side of the head. So, as I stared in the mirror at my red-eyed face, it came in utter shock that I realized I knew a place where Marisol might have left me some clues. I had only to find it. Had I stayed at Laudine's, I might have thought of it sooner.

I went back into the bedroom. Etienne was there, waiting, as if to see what I was going to do. At that moment, he seemed a complicated mix of a proud warrior and a wounded conscript. I couldn't change that. But he hadn't left. I didn't know why. For now, I was going to pretend nothing had happened between us.

"I need to find Marisol's Grimoire," I said.

"Grimoire?" He stepped back as if I'd suddenly pushed him off-balance.

"It's like a diary. Some witches keep them, some don't. Marisol always did. She put in spells she used, told about things that happened. She may have left me a clue to what she was doing here."

"If it wasn't with her when she went missing, Laudine probably has it. Will she give it to you?"

"Laudine won't give me shit, but I bet Marisol hid it. If I find the location, Laudine won't stop me from getting it. Marisol's spells are like size twelve boots and Laudine a cockroach to be stepped on. No way could Laudine find or open it if she did."

"So, you can't find it, either. Or open it." He had his T-shirt in his hand. The amulet, the destructor of what would have been a pleasant few hours, still hung around his neck.

I had my tank and panties on, but would need to find my pants. Oh, yeah, he pulled them off in the living room. I forced myself to my feet and swayed a bit. A sudden memory of pain made my fingers curl into a fist.

"Marisol may have left some key, some mark on it, for me," I said. Or for Gran, who wasn't here. At least I could try. Witches who kept Grimoires guarded them well. A Grimoire could be used to injure or kill its creator if it fell in the hands of an enemy. I could only hope my sister trusted me enough to leave a marker that would allow me to find it.

I had to rest for a while, and eat again to regain strength. Etienne made a call and ordered sandwiches brought up when I mentioned food. He remained with me. He didn't talk. He didn't leave. He merely watched me, seemingly interested but at the same time not giving a shit. For some ungodly reason he was still committed to following me around.

Eventually we were in Etienne's SUV and headed for the cul-de-sac in front of Laudine's. Neither of us spoke of the aborted sexual encounter.

I went to Laudine's because the Grimoire was most likely in that vicinity. I didn't need to do a physical search.

Herschel, not surprisingly, wasn't around. My familiar, who stood between me and Aiakós and threatened to take Etienne's head off when I had my blowback of magic, had disappeared again. He hadn't even shown up when I'd been mad with pain. If I thought it would do any good, I'd sit down and have a long talk with him. We weren't communicating very well at the moment.

The sun stood just above the western horizon when we arrived, sliding orange light across the silent water of Sullen Bog. Another day had passed and darkness would fall within minutes.

If Marisol's Grimoire was hidden inside of Laudine's building, I might have to mount an all-out assault. I'd thought all the way there about how to do it. Go in and ask Laudine or start spinning a spell, calling for the book to tell me where it was. I chose the spell. I stood facing the Bog, leaning against the flimsy protective railing. The section I'd burned off had not been replaced.

Each witch's Grimoire was different. Each had its own personality, a bit like a summer dress. Dresses came in different colors, styles, and Marisol's book had its own look, its own feel. At least I'd seen that in the days before I'd left home and swamp. I'd never read it, but I knew what it looked like.

I called my favorite magic. Fire. Not literal fire, but I let the image burn low in my mind. Then I pictured her

Grimoire as I'd last seen it. Details: a leather cover, the size of a magazine, hand bound with thread. Then came the hard part. A flower, a perfect swamp lily, had been cut into the leather by Marisol's own artistic hand. I had to come up with a clear image to project through the magic. While I worked, I also touched it with memories, not just of her, but of us together.

Unlike my previous powerful sending, I carefully spread it out over the larger area including Laudine's store, calling it, searching for it. Theoretically, if I touched the Grimoire, I would know where it was.

As with all things magic and me, disaster struck.

I heard Etienne speak. When I glanced his way, he had moved into position, gun drawn, facing Laudine, who had come out of her storefront. She appeared to have no weapons. But again, he stood between us, again protecting. Then one of the massive events that filled my life commanded my attention.

A water dragon lifted its immense body from Sullen Bog. Its thick black head rose twenty feet in the air over me. Muddy water dripped from it and it swayed like a cobra ready to strike. Sleek, with midnight scales, it was far larger than Penrod.

I stared up, mouth open, in total awe. I'd taken Penrod, my friend in the swamp, for granted. This dangerous stranger had to be faced. I swallowed hard. I stared up at it, into its reptilian eyes. As I had with Penrod, I sent a message with magic.

I am Nyx. I pictured Penrod. *This is my friend.*

The dragon swayed. *Nyx,* the dragon answered. *I am Chalice.*

I probably should have seen it coming, but facing a sixty-foot serpentlike creature with a mouth full of big sharp teeth tends to require a serious quantity of mental capacity. The dragon dropped something from its mouth. I had the impression of a rectangular shape. Impression only because it hit me smack on the head. A flash of white light blasted before my eyes—and I crashed to the ground.

chapter 20

I woke lying on a stretcher, surrounded by men dressed in black fatigues. Someone was applying pressure to my head and speaking firmly. "She needs a doctor. A hospital. I'm just a medic."

"Get her there." That was Etienne. Why did he sound so distressed?

I wanted to shout no. It came out as a wheeze. My head throbbed.

Etienne leaned over me. "You'll be okay."

"Grimoire? Thing. Dropped. Where?" I could only manage single words.

"Your dog has it."

"Herschel?" My mind could not comprehend his words. Why would . . . ?

I heard the siren, wailing, coming closer. Etienne had disappeared. The next minutes dissolved into shouts about a head injury. Yes, my head was injured. When they asked what happened, I didn't answer. The Mother knows what I might have said. Nothing they would have believed. Then I fell asleep.

I woke in a hospital bed hooked up to various machines. I choked on a paper-dry mouth. After a moment of pure panic, I relaxed. At least I didn't hurt anymore.

Not until next time. Damn this place. What had happened? Memory, often a casualty in head injuries, seemed intact. Water dragon, something rectangular and solid, crashing down on my equally solid head. That just about covered it.

A nurse with some experience came to stand by me. I knew she was experienced because she immediately stuck a straw in my mouth and I sucked down some precious liquid. She knew what I needed. I sighed in relief.

"Where am I?" The words sounded odd.

"Duivel General." The nurse had a soothing voice. All nurses should have soothing voices. They should give them lessons in school.

"What happened?" Okay, that was better. I could manage more words.

"I don't know. They brought you in with a head laceration, severe concussion, and hairline skull fracture."

"Okay."

"You've had visitors. They don't seem to know anything, either."

"Oh."

"Your grandmother Abby—and the police."

"Oh." Nyx, the mistress of one-word answers. I needed to do better than that. I struggled. "I want to leave."

"Sorry. The police, a Captain Flynn, said no, not until he talked to you." She straightened my covers. "I doubt you could escape anyway, at least for a few days." She eyed me, drew a breath to speak, then shook her head.

"What is it?"

She bit her lip and glanced over her shoulder. "The docs in the emergency room said you would die—or at least be a vegetable. But you're not. They call it a miracle.

What happened? My sister, in a car accident, not hurt as bad as you, died."

"I don't know what happened. I'm sorry." There was nothing I could tell her. My "grandmother" Abby was a healer and had probably helped me a little. She would not have completely healed me as long as she felt I'd be okay in the doctor's hands. That would be too obvious. Etienne may have called her.

The nurse left me and several hours later my next visitor was Captain Flynn of the Duivel Police Department. He, too, wanted to know what happened. I told him I couldn't remember, which often happened with head trauma victims.

"I suppose you can't remember anything about Etienne Durand, either." He smiled when he asked.

"No."

He laid my wallet on the stand by the bed. "The incident at the traffic stop has pretty much been forgotten at the station. I only knew about you being here because Abby called." He gave me a wry smile. "That forgetfulness happens rather often in Duivel. Especially when it involves incidents or people connected to the Barrows. I brought you your wallet. No one will miss it."

"Thank you."

"And there is a hysterical young woman in San Francisco you should call as soon as possible. I tried to reassure her you're okay, but she needs to hear that from you." He sat on a chair that had been placed close to the bed.

I had to ask him. "How come you know about ... things? Abigail, the Barrows."

He grinned. "I'm one of the blessed, it appears. Once upon a time my wife was called the Earth Mother's Huntress. She was that when I met her. She introduced me to the Barrows. She calls us chess pieces. Abby is the queen—"

"And the rest of us are pawns."

He raised an eyebrow. "I like to think of myself as a knight."

"I agree with that. Who's the king?"

"I'm not sure. I thought it might be . . ." He stopped. I figured he meant Aiakós.

"I've met him," I said. "He might want to be king, but I don't think he's there yet." And he was so evil, decent people should not acknowledge him as such.

"So, the power struggle continues." Flynn nodded. He laid a business card beside the wallet he had returned. "Call me if you need anything. I'll see what I can do."

"Thanks." He seemed so personable, not like many cops I'd known. "Tell me, Flynn, is your wife a witch?"

He glanced at the empty doorway again. "No, but we have twin daughters with red hair who do some pretty strange things at times."

"Oh, boy. The Mother help you on that one."

"I'm counting more on Abby."

I had no other visitors. Etienne, of course, did not come. He couldn't take the chance again. They released me the next morning, but I'd lost three days of search time. I'd given them my Single-Eye insurance card from my returned wallet and they reminded me I'd be responsible for what the insurance didn't pay. Since I had my wallet with money and cards, I figured I'd get a taxi. My former guard buddy Rocky, dressed in civilian clothes, met me as I was discharged. He helped me climb in a nondescript gray sedan and, of course, headed straight for the Barrows.

chapter 21

The first thing I wanted when I returned to the compound was to find the case that Chalice the water dragon had so imprudently used to break my skull. I'm sure Chalice didn't mean to damage me any more than Etienne meant to hurt my hand, but I'd endured a lot of pain and shock in that single day, hand and head. When I thought back to my first night here, I'd bet that Chalice had also been the massive body hovering over me, protecting me from the assault. I'd have to thank her for that.

Etienne greeted me in front of his office. Feet planted, arms crossed, he stared at me. He shook his head. "You really fucked up that time." But his eyes were filled with sympathy.

"Thank you." He looked very desirable just then. Dark eyes, sensual mouth, I forced myself not to flinch when he laid a gentle hand on the side of my face. You'd think he was actually worried about me.

Rocky cleared his throat. He looked curious, as if Etienne's action, his seemingly concerned touch, surprised him. Then he frowned.

I'd known Rocky as long as I'd known Darrow and he'd been witness to a few disastrous love affairs. That really handsome warlord in Asia was quite entertaining until he wanted to make me his third wife. But the team stuck together and they spirited me out of the man's clutches before I had to create a problem using magic.

Was Rocky trying to warn me? Of what? I nodded to acknowledge his concern. We'd been close working companions, friends. We stuck together and it worked. It was definitely not the same here. This place had an undercurrent of magic that existed nowhere else in the world. My sudden brain activity hurt and I laid a hand over my bandage.

Etienne moved in close, holding me steady. "I'm told you had thirty-five stitches in your head," he hissed through his teeth.

"And a cracked skull." I kept said head very still. "They took the stitches out, though. I'm taped together now." I reached out and grabbed Rocky by the arm. "I know you haven't seen much action here, Rock, but I think you know this place isn't normal. Not like Africa or Asia."

Rocky grinned and his solemn expression vanished. "Normal? What's normal? Remember that time that monstrous herd of cows surrounded the bastards chasing us. That wasn't normal."

"Okay. I'll admit I had a talk with them. The cows, not the bastards."

Rocky nodded genially and walked away. Ah, I understood. Rocky was warning Etienne, not me. Warning him that I was not exactly a kitten he could play with. I'd bet Etienne already knew that.

Etienne remained close as I climbed the stairs. He didn't touch me.

"So," I said as I carefully lowered myself on the couch in his living room, "what happened? Out by the Bug, I mean. What did you see?"

He removed his shoulder holster and gun, and placed it on the counter that divided the kitchen from the living room. "I have no idea what I saw. That damned giant snake . . ." He blew out a breath. "I've seen some strange things since I came here. That was the strangest. It must have come out of the Zombie."

"It didn't come from the Zombie. That giant snake was a water dragon. Her name is Chalice. I have one of them living by my house in the Georgia swamp. His name is Penrod. I'd thought he was the only one of his kind. They belong to the Earth Mother. To this world. I'll admit Chalice's delivery method sucked. She didn't mean any harm. Not having hands limited her. What was it by the way? The thing she dropped on me. It felt like a truck."

"It looked like one of those waterproof aluminum camera cases. I didn't have time to inspect it. The minute it—and you—dropped, Laudine closed in. I backed her up with the gun, but you were bleeding all over the place. It needed to stop. I had to put a compress on you."

Etienne's face carried an uneasy expression. Chalice certainly shocked him with her sudden appearance. I didn't think she frightened him. Despite her size, she lacked the impressively dangerous look and feel of Aiakós.

He went to the kitchen, pulled a whiskey bottle out of the cabinet, and poured a good amount in brown into a glass. He chugged it and poured another, then brought it into the living room. He sat on the couch beside me, a good arm's length away, before he spoke again. I wondered if this was something ordinary or if I had literally driven him to drink.

"I figured you wanted that case, so I grabbed it, got it close so I could draw if she came at me. I used my shirt to make a compress for your head. Then the damned case was sliding across the asphalt toward Laudine, all by itself. I didn't want to let go the compress." He tossed down the rest of his drink. "Laudine almost had it in her hands when here comes that mutt of yours. Running like a fucking greyhound. He snatched the case before she got it and ran away." Bitterness filled his voice. "I should have shot her. Tossed her body into the Bog."

I wanted to ask why he didn't, but I figured I knew. While he might drive a witch out of the Barrows, he simply wouldn't shoot one who posed no real threat. He had no idea what was in that case, no idea whether he'd be killing for treasure or trash.

"I'm glad you didn't. We're playing the Earth Mother's game. Laudine might have another critical part to play."

"Witches' games."

"Yeah. That's my life. I consider it a priceless learning experience." I wanted to move away from his personal bias.

He continued. "I called for an ambulance, then my men if the ambulance didn't show. That happens sometimes in the Barrows. They forget about it before they get on the road. This one came quick, so was probably close by."

"That's shitty. People live here, too, not just us criminals. They need that kind of service. Where's Herschel—and the case?"

"I have no idea."

At that point, Herschel ambled out of the bedroom. He carried the case in his mouth and dropped it on my foot.

"Ow . . . Herschel!"

Etienne stood and walked to the bedroom door. He stared inside.

Oh, boy. Another Herschel disaster. "I'll change the sheets, Etienne. I'll buy new sheets," I tried to console him.

While Etienne spit out some innovative curse words in several languages, I cautiously rose and let Herschel out. I caught him by the scruff of the neck before he exited. "I know you are not always a great communicator, but we really need to talk. I'll ask questions. You can bark once for yes and twice for no." I released him and he unceremoniously lumbered down the stairs.

"How does he get in and out when no one is here to open the door?" Etienne asked when he came back into the living room. He carried an armload of bedding, which he quickly tossed in a corner. "He wasn't here when I left earlier."

"I don't know. I've always taken him for granted. He always stayed outside at Gran's house. She didn't like the drooling and gas thing." Herschel always preferred to be out anyway. He'd probably come in and tossed and slobbered Etienne's bed for spite. Or maybe he was bored.

Etienne brought me paper towels from the kitchen to wipe the slime off the case. He sat beside me on the couch, much closer this time. Maybe he'd decided that, *Yes, she's a witch, but she's so incompetent she's no danger to me.* He leaned back and his body relaxed. "If that bastard mutt can actually open and close locked doors on his own, why can't he stop this shit?" He pointed at the pile of wet paper towels.

"You got me." I smiled. I had a strong suspicion that Herschel might have gone through the door. He wasn't the average familiar. "Strange things have happened in my life. Even for a witch. Gran called it bizarre. Herschel showed up the day I was born and I'm told he was already grown when he arrived."

"Right, and that would make him . . ."

"At least twenty-eight. He's aged well, I think."

Etienne sighed.

"What? You're surprised by Herschel? You have play-dates with a demon."

I put the case on the coffee table and examined it. It looked standard, but I'm sure Marisol would have placed more protection on it. I ran my fingers over the lock and whispered my name in magic. The lock snapped open. The world around me stopped moving. She had spelled the lock and I was caught. But the spell recognized me, and I heard Marisol's voice in my mind. *"Well, big sister, something momentous must be happening or you wouldn't be opening this. I hope it isn't too tragic. Isn't Chalice lovely? I wanted her to go meet Penrod, but she said it wasn't time. If you have difficulty reading my little book, remember the Summer of the Frogs."*

I gasped as the spell released me. "The frogs?"

"What frogs?" Etienne frowned.

I clapped my hands. It was joyous to remember a wonderful time of innocence. "Oh, one year there was a massive hatching of frogs in the swamp. The Okefeno-kee. We grew up there. Some fluke of nature, I suppose. The sound was so horrendous we couldn't sleep at night. Marisol and I found that with a little magic and her toy xylophone, we could manipulate the croaks to imitate some simple songs. She was six and I was nine."

"I take it you didn't have television?"

"Not until I was eleven. We finally harassed Gran un-til she broke down and got one."

I opened the case and there was Marisol's Grimoire. I wondered if I would need a spell to open it, but the delicately etched leather cover moved easily when I lifted it out. I scanned the first page. It was a recipe for strawberry shortcake.

I flipped through the other pages. Nothing but more recipes, some for food, some for potions, appeared. Of course, I knew there had to be more. Summer of the Frogs.

I let my mind travel over that memory. Marisol on the porch with the xylophone, banging the colorful metal strips with her little knobbed sticks, me singing at the top of my lungs in a voice that made Herschel head for the woods, and . . . of course. The xylophone.

"I have a problem," I said.

"I'm not surprised." Etienne lifted his glass as if contemplating another drink.

"I need a xylophone."

"Xylophone?"

"Yeah, a small one. Like a kid's toy."

"Maybe you should go lie down for a while."

"It's okay. I have my driver's license back. I'll run get one. A discount store should have one." I stood—too fast. The apartment lurched to the left and right and the floor dropped a few inches.

Etienne caught me by the arms and held me steady. I wished he'd drawn me closer. But he couldn't. The amulet might be under his shirt but it was still there. "You're crazy. Be still. I'll send someone for a damned xylophone." He carefully lowered me back to the couch.

chapter 22

Etienne left me there on the couch with a pillow and a blanket. It was only early afternoon, but I hadn't slept much in the hospital. I carefully placed Marisol's Grimoire under the couch cushion and immediately fell asleep. I did dream. Odd scenes of an undisciplined childhood came, then drifted away into the foggy swamp. I rode on Penrod's head as he glided among the cypress trees and across the wider lakes, where we would hide when the occasional boat came by.

When I first learned about the fire within me, I discovered I could throw tiny sparks from my fingers like the Fourth of July sparklers. To Marisol's delight, I would dance around waving my arms — until some stray embers had drifted in a window and set Gran's curtains ablaze.

Gran tried to find a witch to teach me about fire, but none had my ability. I had some difficulty accepting that I was the only witch in the world who was a pyromaniac.

I woke when Etienne came back to the apartment.

He stalked in, clearly furious. He slammed the door behind him. I jerked into a sitting position, but couldn't otherwise move. He froze me with his rage, though it wasn't directed at me. He stood rigid, arms straight, fists clenched, dark eyes shining, one of the most powerful men I'd ever met. The dark tattoos on his copper-skinned forearms stood out sharply and . . . Great Mother, did I see them move? There was a caustic wildness about him, one of the Earth Mother's children whose every move, every gesture, could be a weapon.

If Darrow was to be believed—and I saw no reason to think otherwise—Etienne and I had been unidentified opponents in the past. That was business. This fury was personal.

I remained quiet and sat very still. No way did I want to draw his attention. His breathing slowed. After one final deep breath, he won his battle with rage. Those dark eyes focused in my direction.

"There was a problem." He sounded calm, but an edge of violence remained in his voice.

I nodded my head, afraid to speak.

"I went to Laudine's and asked for your things." His face flushed. He hadn't relaxed much.

"She objected?"

"No. She didn't object. I took two men with me. They loaded everything of yours in plastic bags and carried it to the car. When they finished, she said there was more." His fury returned. He drew deep breaths. "The men went in and carried out another bag . . . and it . . . just outside the door it exploded in fire. They're dead. Two men. I used a fire extinguisher, but the fire still burned." He stared straight at me. "She kept screaming that she didn't do it. Fire was *your* thing. That you put a spell on your possessions to stop thieves."

Thousands of things passed through my mind in that instance. The need to defend myself, to proclaim my innocence, came first. It would probably sound pretty hollow. "What do you think, Etienne?"

He spoke with a low, brutal voice. "I think that the world would be better without this plague of witches."

No way would I argue with him. "Yeah, we are a bit of a plague. We're too powerful to run loose like wild animals. But we have rules, and no witch, not me, not Laudine, is above them. There will be justice. I promise you." I held out the palm of the hand that had so brutally been burned with the Solaire. "I will swear that on my life."

He seemed calm now, but I tightened when he came and knelt beside me. He stared straight into my eyes. "Nyx, one of the men was Salvatore. He burned alive and there was absolutely nothing I could do."

The world closed around me. Etienne's fury was a kitten's mewling next to my roar. The double-damned witch had killed my friend. With a power I didn't know I could muster, I screamed my rage, not with my voice, but with my heart and soul. I shrieked it across the spectrum of magic. Every witch in the vicinity, every being with the power to do so, would hear my cry. I focused on finding one . . . and find her I did. Laudine. I felt her heart jump and pound in fear.

Murderer! I accused. *Run. Hide. I will destroy you.*

Laudine didn't reply. She simply shut herself off from the magic like a blown-out lightbulb. Not that it would do any good. I would find her. I would file a charge with the High Witch and they might or might not send the Sisters of Justice to execute her. I'd get her first.

I came back to myself. Cold. I was so cold. I huddled there on Etienne's couch and . . . Etienne? He no longer knelt by me. He stood in the doorway, rigid, holding the frame tight with both hands. What had he seen?

"Do you . . ." I choked on the words. I shivered and wrapped my arms around myself. "Cold."

"Cold?" He made a single step toward me. "You were on fire. I saw you . . . but you didn't burn. Nothing around you burned. Your eyes . . . changed."

I didn't care about my eyes. I curled up in a ball and sobbed. I wanted to sink into oblivion, but I couldn't. So I simply cried until I lost my voice. The hurt wouldn't go away. Salvatore had taught me how to survive. I was strong when I joined Darrow's troop, but a bit naive. Salvatore had appointed himself my guardian. He protected me, guarded me when I was hurt. We had risked our lives together, laughed together, and cried when we lost a comrade. Now I cried for him. I didn't know Etienne's other man, the one who died with Salvatore, but he would be avenged, too.

I don't know how long I cried. Etienne didn't come close. I don't blame him. The fire was something I did lose control of at times. I forced myself to stop.

I made it into the bathroom to wash my ravaged face in cold water. My right cheek was swelled to twice its usual size and my black eyes had faded to nasty yellow. The bandage on my head had come loose, so I carefully removed it. I think Abigail had done a little healing on the wound. I could see it was drying nicely and I resisted the urge to scratch the itch that was beginning to make its way across my nerve endings. Unfortunately, I had a two-inch-wide bald strip where they'd cut my hair.

The door opened and Darrow stepped in. Then I had to cry all over again. He held me close in his arms.

"Me and Rocky went down there," Darrow said. Unshed tears pooled in his eyes. "Etienne said not to. But we did. We burned her place. I hope she was inside."

"She probably wasn't." I hated to give him that news. I'd warned her I'd come for her, so she probably ran the instant she heard them. "But don't worry, Darrow. I'm going to take care of it."

He brushed away the hair that had fallen in my face. His fingers briefly touched the long red line on my scalp.

"Nyx, I want to be there. When it happens. You can do it, but I want to watch."

"I'll do my best to arrange it."

Darrow nodded. We both knew what came next. We'd lived with loss before. We would submerge our need for retribution under a layer of ordinary—or in this case extraordinary—life. But every time we thought of her, of Salvatore, we would think of and plan vengeance.

He left me. My body ached and my mind still rolled. When I opened the door, I could hear low murmured voices from the living room. Darrow and Etienne. Darrow's voice was muted, but when he raised it slightly, I understood his words. "Damn it, Etienne. Five years. I had that girl for five years in the most dangerous parts of the world. I never let her get hurt like that!"

I couldn't hear Etienne's reply. He'd kept his voice very low.

That wasn't quite fair. Etienne had done a good job watching over me given my own actions. He'd used the weapons he had, his gun and the immunity, to stand in front of me. Darrow didn't understand. He still saw the Nyx who worked with him in a different context. He'd dealt with a young woman, trained but untested in a true battle. He, Salvatore, and Rocky had protected me until I could stand on my own. That time in my life only occasionally brushed up against magic, low-key magic at that. Nyx the guard and Nyx the witch lived in two different worlds. None of these men could protect me from the world of magic in the Barrows.

After Darrow left, I went back to sit on the couch. Etienne sat beside me. He'd placed a small brown case on the coffee table.

I swallowed. "Darrow said they burned Laudine's place down."

He nodded. "They did. Big fire. Engines actually came from uptown. Surprising."

"Any sign of the witch herself?"

"No." He picked up the brown case and handed it to me, carefully keeping an arm's length distance from me. I didn't blame him. What do you do with a woman who keeps bursting into flames? He'd remained, though, stuck with me.

"This was in the things we brought from Laudine's." He offered me the case.

I opened it and there was Marisol's toy xylophone.

chapter 23

When Salvatore and Etienne's other man had gone to Laudine's, they'd entered the room that had been Marisol's and, very briefly, mine. Apparently, they'd gathered up everything there, including her possessions. They would not have noted the difference between the belongings of two women. Then they had gone back for the single bag, the deadly trap, Laudine had prepared for them—probably prepared for all of them. It must have been prematurely triggered. Laudine's incompetence maybe. If that bag had gone into their vehicle, all would have burned, with the possible exception of Etienne. Possible because I didn't actually know the extent of the protection of the Morié and Solaire.

Unfortunately, I had to push my sorrow aside and deal with the present. I needed to think critically at this point. I would have time to mourn Salvatore when I stood over Laudine's burned bones and ashes.

That Marisol actually kept the child-sized xylophone as she matured had to mean something. I lifted it out of the case. It was about a foot long with multicolored strips of metal attached to two rails. The two sticks with knobs on the ends used to make the sound were included. I tapped the red strip and it gave me a low note. I'm not musically inclined and this would be a challenge.

There was a knock at the door and Etienne went to answer it. My stomach growled at the fragrance when one of his men brought in a box apparently filled with edible things. I put my toy aside and joined him at the bar that separated the two rooms. He'd set out quite a feast.

"You have a good cook," I said. I forked another slice of roast beef on my plate.

"He is. Complains a lot. Now he wants another assistant. To cook for your dog. What is it with that beast? He walks in, wants something—and gets it."

"Herschel just is. I grew up in a swamp with odd creatures. A water dragon, like the one you saw the other day, and Gran had some birds that talked. Actually talked, not just mimic words they heard. Only I'm not exactly sure they were birds." I didn't want to talk about Herschel and his bizarre nature. "What about you? Where did you grow up? How long have you known about witches? About earth magic?" I set my plate aside. "You know a lot more about me than I know about you."

Etienne watched me for a few moments, face closed to expression. When he spoke, his voice kept a level matter-of-fact tone. "I grew up in Virginia. Family of French descent, lots of money. Happy childhood. One of my uncles was a mercenary. After college, he got me into a training camp, then a job. I learned about magic . . . somewhere else." His smile was gone.

I wanted to know more. "You met a witch?"

A shadow passed over his face. His jaw tightened; he grew very still. "I met a witch. A witch that made Laudine look like a first-grade schoolteacher."

And that witch had burned him, scarred him as deeply as any fire I could create. After he spoke, he relaxed.

Maybe he hoped I wouldn't ask more about her. I had questions, but I'd save them.

"What about Aiakós?"

"Aiakós just is. Don't talk about him. He might hear." He handed me a container with a massive slice of cake.

The man looked so benign, so rugged and sexy, sitting there offering me dessert. He was just trying to console me about Salvatore, I'm sure. I couldn't figure him. He wanted me—and yes, I wanted him—but he wouldn't trust me enough to remove his protection from earth magic. The witch who'd hurt him had done a jam-up job. She hadn't broken him, though. He'd helped me, saved my life twice; I still had no clue to what he really wanted. He hadn't let me get that close.

We went back to the living room and I placed the Grimoire and the xylophone on the coffee table. *The Summer of the Frogs,* Marisol's message said. She had a beautiful singing voice and I croaked worse than an alligator looking for a mate. The frogs, however, had far fewer notes in their musical repertoire. We kept the songs simple. Mary and her lamb, "Twinkle, Twinkle," and so on. Today, all I could do was pong on the xylophone and try to figure out which notes to use. After fifteen minutes of ponging, Etienne apparently reached his limit. He reached out and snatched the instrument away from me.

"What?" I had to protest. "I can't help if I'm tone-deaf."

"And I had piano lessons for ten years. What are you trying to play?" He played "Mary" correctly the first time. Nothing happened.

"Try changing the notes." I offered my somewhat logical but less than expert advice.

"Nyx, if I change them, it won't be the same song. It's

not like we have a vast range of notes available." He tried it again. Still nothing.

I leaned back and sighed, searching memory. Then I laughed and bounced a little, which tugged painfully at the healing wound in my head. "I know. I remember. It went, *Mary had a little lamb, little lamb, its fleece was white as snow,* and then there was a pause."

Etienne raised an eyebrow. "Pause?"

"Oh, yeah. When the pause came, all the frogs would go silent." I frowned at the memory. "Actually, the whole swamp went silent. Marisol and I were young, untrained witches stumbling through earth magic. Earth magic is strong in the Okefenokee and it seemed to concentrate around us. It was really creepy when everything stopped. We kept making that pause longer and longer. That silence ... I don't know if I can explain it ... it had a weight. A power. I guess that's why Gran made us stop doing it."

He shrugged and played again, this time with a brief pause.

Again, nothing.

"Make the pause a little longer," I said.

He complied. Seconds after he played the final note, the pages of the Grimoire fluttered. I watched. I didn't touch. I had few formal lessons in magic, but I knew better than to mess with a spell in progress.

Excited, I grabbed Etienne's arm and leaned against him. I jerked away. My hand ached with the memory of pain. He hadn't moved—but he hadn't shoved me away, fearing fire and magic. We had a powerful wall between us. He could remove the Solaire and Morié. I could not remove the earth magic in my body and soul.

The first page, the one with the strawberry shortcake

recipe, shivered. It spit along the edges and suddenly became multiple pages as if it had been glued together. I waited until I was sure it was finished before I opened the new section to review its contents. Two separate pieces of paper loosely stuck in the fold.

The first page was a confusing drawing with numerous lines and symbols. In the center was a pentagram with an X in the middle. There were other markings, too, but I couldn't instantly decipher them. The second page I could see was written in Aradian script. Aradian was the secret language used by witches, a common denominator in all their spells. I studied and failed it in school, just as I had excelled in English and history. No one found it surprising that I wound up more people oriented than witch oriented. I was never a good student and I hadn't even tried to read Aradian script in over ten years. I took the page with lines and symbols and laid it on the table.

"This is a map of the Barrows," Etienne said. He pointed to the center. "I'd say the X is the Zombie Zone."

"Point out where some other locations might be."

He studied it. "That's the Archangel."

Easy, the spot did contain the symbol for an angel. I found Laudine's place marked with a general symbol for a witch. Across the street from her was one I didn't recognize. It looked a bit like a gargoyle.

"What's that?" I had seen the abandoned building. Laudine said it was a nightclub.

"The Goblin Den. It's closed now. Going to be torn down."

I was able to pick out a few other things, but as near as I could see, the whole page was simply a map with symbols marked and numbered. The Goblin Den was number one.

"This looks like Marisol was searching for something," I said. "Some marker, maybe a trail. As she found each place she needed, she marked it on the main map."

I picked up the second sheet of paper. The list written in Aradian. I could probably read it, but it would take time to translate. I held it out for Etienne to see. He stared at it, then turned as pale as a man with dark skin could. Whatever it said, he understood. I doubted he spoke Aradian, unless the witch who hurt him had taught him.

He surged to his feet, snatched up his still holstered gun, and left me alone. Etienne was not a man to run from battle. He would face bombs and bullets with a cool head and grim determination to survive. Whatever the witch had done to him had a profound impact on his soul. It had scared him as if she'd laid a red-hot knife on his skin.

Stunned and a bit alarmed, I watched the closed door as if it would burst open and he would charge back in. It had been a long time since I had dealt with a man on a personal or semipersonal level. I wasn't sure I could classify Etienne with either of those terms. We'd sort of accidently fallen together and for some reason, he stuck with me. And I was really too tired to deal with it. Too tired and, remembering Salvatore, too hurt. I glanced at the clock. Ten and really dark outside.

Since I wasn't going to leave the Grimoire alone, I packed it back in the case, leaving my hard-earned papers separate. I did find clean sheets in a closet, made the bed, and crawled in. Herschel ambled into the room. He'd done his thing with getting inside a closed door again. I gave some thought about getting him to teach me how. But then, I'd never actually seen him do it.

He lay on the floor beside me. I finally fell asleep and,

thank the Mother, didn't dream. The smell of coffee woke me in what seemed like five minutes. The sun peeking around the curtains told me it had been longer. Herschel, as he was wont to do, had disappeared. Another day in the Barrows had begun. I really hoped no one would throw any skull-busting objects at me today, or die and leave me with a hole in my heart.

chapter 24

The plastic bags of mine and Marisol's things had been conveniently piled in the corner of the bedroom. One bag produced jeans, a shirt, underwear, and socks. I dug through Marisol's clothing and found a blue silk scarf. I'd given it to her as a solstice gift the year before I left Twitch Crossing. It made her cry, which upset me, but she said the tears were because it was so beautiful.

I stared in the bathroom mirror. The bruising under my eyes had turned puke yellow. Most of the swelling had receded as the inflammation causing it faded away. Tiny sprigs of hair stuck out like soldiers at attention across the shaved strip on my scalp. They itched like hell, too. The scarf covered it, but the itching continued. I sucked up my willpower and ignored it, only digging at it with a fingernail occasionally. Ready to face the day — hopefully without injury — I followed the scent of coffee into the living room and to the tiny kitchen.

The room was empty, so the blessed and anonymous maker of coffee had done his thing and departed. How thoughtful of him. I'd seen so few women I doubted it was a her. One cup later, I decided to get to work. I retrieved Marisol's papers from the case.

I was sitting at the coffee table with my second cup of

its namesake in my hand when Etienne walked in. His expression carried no evidence of what had caused him to bolt the previous evening. He made his own coffee and casually strolled over to sit beside me.

I realized that he'd changed clothes and shaved. He had basically moved out and left the apartment to me. He gave me a half smile that said *I'm being polite*. It did not say *I'm glad to see you*. "So, witch, what's on the agenda today?"

Witch, he'd called me, as if to remind me, or maybe himself, again that witches were evil—or at the very least a hideous amount of trouble. I was not exactly a friend. And while I liked him most of the time, I had to remind myself that he had an agenda, one that would probably be radically different from mine. Oh, yeah. He wanted to fuck me, too. I would not permit that until he removed that nasty amulet from his neck.

"Isn't it boring training an army when you don't have an enemy?" I asked him.

Etienne's mouth pursed as if he was trying not to smile. "There's always an enemy in the Barrows. A battle will come. Another dark moon will rise. Not every dark moon brings a battle, but I think we're overdue. I'm prepared."

Okay, we needed to move on from that. "I'm going to take Marisol's map, visit the places she marked, in the order she marked them, and see what I can find. Am I to assume you're stuck to my ass in my endeavors?"

"Assume away."

"Will you tell me why?"

"I'm bored. You're entertainment. Watching you burst into flames or almost get killed every day is better than a special effects thriller movie." He grinned.

I remembered that mouth had been incredibly soft

and sweet in that one kiss we had shared before it turned to disaster. Damn him, he would save my life, protect me, but not trust me. Not to mention the shit was laughing at me.

I picked up the page that had so disturbed him last night, leaned back trying to make sense of it. As with the map, some of the symbols and words I recognized. Others looked familiar.

"Can you read that?" Etienne asked.

"Some. Can you read it? It seemed to . . . disturb you."

"Only some?" He ignored my question about why it disturbed him.

"I can't do everything. It's a weakness, but I'll admit it. I was born a witch, Etienne. I have certain innate powers that I can use. You saw some of them."

"The fire."

"The fire. Moving objects. There are a few others. I don't like or use certain aspects of witchcraft. Casting spells, making potions, requires years of study. I'm too lazy, too . . . wild. When I was young, I didn't want to devote my life to the required, all-consuming rote and ritual that makes a powerful witch. I still don't."

"Why?"

"That is the question every witch in Twitch Crossing wants answered. And if I ever come across that answer, I'll let everyone know. I've always been . . . me. Restless, undisciplined."

I wanted to change the subject, so I turned to the paper in my hand. "I totally failed the class in Aradian. Maybe I can decipher some of this. It appears to be a list of objects. Objects used in magic. There are cups, cauldrons, statues, and . . ." I studied it closer. The temperature in the room seemed to plummet. Could I be reading this correctly?

Etienne remained quiet beside me.

I drew a deep breath. "This is a list of some of the most powerful objects in the world of witchcraft. The Cauldron of Aradia, Isis's bracelet, and more. Powerful relics. Most have been lost, or hidden and forgotten. They're in the history books." I eyed him suspiciously. "You know who wrote this, don't you?"

"I've seen the handwriting. Oonagh. I told you. She's dead." His voice sounded flat and hard as the asphalt parking lot outside. Is that what caused him to run last night? Had this been such a powerful reminder of its author that it caused such panic in a man who obviously wasn't given to such?

"Did she actually have these things before she died?" I really needed to know the story of Etienne and Oonagh. As dangerous as this situation had become, knowledge was imperative.

He didn't answer.

"Etienne, I need to know if this is an *actual* list, not just a glorified wish list."

"I retrieved certain objects for the witch." His hands clenched into fists. "She considered herself a collector. I can't tell you which ones they were."

"And where are they now? Those objects." I suspected I already knew.

"She hid them in Barrows in the truck that contains all that gold."

I leaned back and closed my eyes.

"I take it that's a problem." He spoke with a light uncaring voice, but I heard the concern.

I tossed the list on the table. "It's a problem. Not the gold. Most witches usually don't want or need gold, other than a small amount to work a spell. The objects, however, make a witch very powerful."

"What about you? Do you need gold?"

"I don't remember ever craving vast wealth. I don't want to be, and have never been, dirt-poor. But I prefer ... sensation to riches. Life, people, doing things."

"If witches don't usually need gold, why did Oonagh want so much of it?"

"It depends on what she was afraid of. Wealth can buy a security. Rich people have a tendency to be more afraid than everyone else. Mostly that fear involves losing the riches. Money buys high walls and gates. Enough of it can hire people like me and Darrow to protect you."

"She feared death. She was dying." He spoke with certainty.

"There isn't enough gold in the world to protect her from death. She had to know that."

"She did. Madeline said she feared it so much she was willing to take a chance on destroying the world to gain immortality. She failed, thanks to Madeline."

"Why? I don't understand. I love life, but returning to the Earth Mother is not to be feared. Death is only another beginning. An earth witch would know that."

Etienne leaned forward, elbows on his knees. "Madeline told me Oonagh was hiding in the Barrows. Hiding from the Earth Mother. And the Sisters of Justice. She'd committed some crime ... crimes. Those crimes were unforgivable. "

I'd seen a lot of unforgivable crimes. There were other issues here, too.

I had to explain. "The objects Oonagh collected are usually in the possession of individual witches. The Earth Mother forbids a witch from having more than one or two." Which brought up another problem. "Did you steal any of them? From other witches. Did she help you steal?"

Words might cause discomfort, but stealing objects of power from a witch could get him killed if the witch discovered his part in the theft. And witches have long memories.

He shrugged. "Oonagh had most of them before I came along. I lifted a few, but focused on the gold. Guards disappeared, cameras and alarms shut off. Me and my men . . . we walked in and took what we wanted. What she wanted." He rose and went to the kitchen. He watched me from across the bar. "Before she died, Oonagh had an object from another world in her possession. Madeline called it the Portal. That object is gone now, but if Aiakós could have laid hands on it, he might have been able to escape from the Barrows." Those dark eyes of his focused on me. His next words carried gravity and warning. He pointed at the paper. "Would any of those objects let him do that? If he finds them?"

I glanced down at the parchment in my hand. "These are some of the most powerful magical objects in the world. Odds are good that one or more might help him. But can he make them work? Do you know about his power? The source of his power?"

"No."

I'd bet Marisol had been looking for the missing treasure truck. I'm sure she was interested in the artifacts and returning them to the Earth Mother for distribution to the witches where they would be safe. I was equally certain that she was not interested in the gold. Given the map and list, I now suspected that if I found the gold and artifacts, I would find Marisol.

chapter 25

Etienne left the apartment. He told me he'd be back in an hour and not to go out until then. I nodded politely, then ignored him. I was hungry and needed to see if it was possible to have a bit of the communication I'd threatened to have with my familiar. Food first.

When I walked into the dining room, breakfast was still available, but most of the troops had gone on to other things. Good enough. If I saw Darrow or Rocky, I'd remember Salvatore and start crying again.

I had a chance to talk to the workers there, the food servers, compliment them on their work, even if they were suspicious of me. One thing I'd learned in my years abroad was to pay attention to the people considered *less important* in the grand scheme of things. It saved all our lives once, when a grandmother I'd befriended at a market came to warn us of an impending attack.

Then on to find Herschel. The buildings around me, large and small, had nothing outside to let anyone know they were inhabited. I called Herschel's name once and he walked from around the corner of one building. He fell in step beside me and I went back to the apartment. Etienne's SUV wasn't there, so I assumed he hadn't returned.

Once upstairs, I fixed another cup of coffee and Herschel immediately went to the bedroom. He returned with the thick arm bracelet Gran had called my heritage. The Dragon's Tears.

"What? Are you dressing me now? My backpack was closed. How did . . . ?"

Herschel dropped the bracelet at my feet. Ew. Ick. I picked it up with two fingers and carried it to the sink to wash. When I returned to the couch, he sat patiently waiting. He had an air of expectancy, this dog who could not be a dog. Herschel, my childhood friend, my magical familiar. Gran told me familiars for witches were rare and he certainly surprised her. I guess she wondered why the Mother would give him to a half-assed witch like me.

"Okay. I take it you want me to wear this thing. I can do that." I laid my hand on his head and gazed deep in his eyes—and saw fire. Distant but compelling, drawing me in, deeper, deeper. Fire surrounded me. I could feel its searing heat, but it did not burn me. Something moved toward me. Something, massive, ponderous . . . and it roared. The sound shook the earth, filled me, was me . . . until I snapped back into the world of the Barrows.

I gasped for breath. Like I'd run up a set of stairs or been someplace where the oxygen was low. Herschel sauntered away. He dropped to the carpet with a weighty sigh, stretched out, and closed his eyes.

I turned the bracelet in my fingers. I'd worn a tank top, leaving my arms bare. With care, I slid the bracelet on, up over my elbow to just below my shoulder. I thought it might fall off, but it remained. It was as if it tightened to fit me. Again, I felt the flame. Not around me, but in the distance.

Etienne opened the door and walked in. He froze. He stared for a long time, then asked, "What happened?"

"Nothing happened that I'm aware of." I stood and faced him. He came closer until he stood within . . . kissing distance.

"You're different." His fingers brushed my cheek and for a brief second, his eyes narrowed. Suspicious, always suspicious. He shook his head as if to deny the change he thought he saw. "Get your map and let's go."

chapter 26

"Where to, witch?" Etienne asked as we climbed in the SUV.

"The Goblin Den." My plan was to go to each place Marisol had marked on the map in the numbered order she marked them. I believed that it was possible she found something at each location that led her to the next. I might find that, too, if she left me a sign.

Etienne slid the key in the ignition without hesitation. "The Goblin Den has been empty for a year. Michael used to run it, but when they built the new Archangel, he closed it."

Herschel had followed me. He twisted and circled on the backseat, trying to find a spot he could sprawl without falling on the floor. He found it and flopped down with a sigh that blew bubbles of slobber from his jowls. I winced and whined as I had so many times before. *Why couldn't the Mother have sent me a cat or a canary or even a cockroach?*

Etienne started the vehicle. He drove toward River Street to go south to the building.

"Who pays for your operation here, Etienne? Someone with deep pockets, I know, but who writes the checks for the everyday payroll?"

He didn't speak for a moment; then he said, "Michael. I'm told there is a grand plan for the Barrows." He chuckled. "I once heard a very angry Madeline ask him how low he would go to keep Aiakós amused."

When we arrived at the Goblin Den, he pried a boarded door open and we went inside. He carried a high-power flashlight, which he needed to see. It totally interfered with my night vision. The empty building, pitch-black to him, came into focus in shades of gray.

"Do you want a flashlight? I have another." His voice created an echo in the darkness. He stood close behind me, so close I could feel his breath when he spoke.

"No, I can see."

"You're weird." He sounded annoyed. "Normal people need light."

I took the dig in stride. "Normal? Is that the best we've got? I'm a witch who works pretty good magic—sometimes—and you're a man wanted by every police authority on the planet. Screw normal. Let us bask in infamy, buddy."

He sighed.

The building had been hollowed out and that abated the sense of deterioration somewhat. It didn't seem on the verge of collapse, either.

"What did they do here?" I asked.

"When Michael had a restaurant here, it did a good business. Or at least it did when Michael came down and played Prince Charming every night. When they built the new Archangel, he closed it. He was going to reopen it as a higher-end restaurant, but then he said he was too busy for two places. Madeline said she didn't like the place. He almost got killed here one night. That's a long story. You should get her to tell you sometime." He flashed the light around the cavernous room. "Before that, it was a really wild nightclub call the Goblin Den."

"Nightclub? Here?"

"The only place it could be. They wouldn't allow it uptown. Loud heavy metal bands, lots of drugs." He laughed softly. "I heard stories."

The building held an eerie silence. If the walls once rattled with heavy metal, it was long forgotten now. For some reason, Etienne had relaxed. He stood closer to me now, even touching me occasionally.

I let myself fall into witch sight and scanned the rooms for something magical, something that stood out. It came as a vibration, barely a whisper from another room. A symbol, the one Marisol used for the Goblin Den, was drawn on the floor in the main restaurant area. To my eyes it glowed. It had my name on it. It spun out and touched me and the room shifted a tiny bit.

"Wow!" I spoke softly because the situation—dark, spooky, empty building—seemed to require it. Marisol had created this perfect drawing, and she'd spelled it with a marker that only I could see. For some reason, she'd wanted the spell to touch me, to give me something. I had no idea why, or how she would have known I'd be here. As I watched, it faded slightly to reveal another symbol. It was not the number two spot on her list. She'd written the order of symbols on paper, but created another order just for me. Why?

"What is it?" Etienne asked.

"A message from my sister. You can't see it. We need to go to the place marked as number four, next."

"Four? Not two?"

"Her instructions. I'll trust that."

Etienne grumbled, but he went along. Good thing, too, because back in the SUV we had to take block-long detours around obstacles and holes in the road. I could have walked, but it would have taken days.

Number four turned out to be an apartment house — a three-story apartment house. And with it came a major problem. I did a quick search and found nothing on the first floor except that the stairs to the second floor had collapsed into a pile of sticks and boards on the floor. Collapsed or maybe been torn down. Somehow, I had to get up there.

Etienne came to stand beside me as I stared at the crumbled stairs. "I don't suppose you plan to leave this alone, do you?" Resignation filled his voice.

"Absolutely not. The fire escape, maybe?"

The outside metal fire escape lay in ruins. The rusted metal had long since pulled away from the building walls. Etienne solved my problem by driving the SUV across the sidewalk and dangerously close to a front wall that might disintegrate at any moment. We climbed on the hood and he boosted me into a second-floor window. He'd given me a rope so I could anchor it to something inside and lower myself back down. Good old Etienne, always ready to solve a problem or rescue a witch in distress. He climbed the rope, hand over hand, to get in. Impressed the hell out of me. Not too many men were strong enough to do that.

The apartment house symbol, drawn in one of the second-floor apartments, pointed me next to number three. When I touched it with my sight, it told me to go not there but to number two. Near that number two symbol was a warning I knew. Danger. This spell also touched me, as if it was adding to the previous spell. It was a cumulative spell. Once I had all the pieces, it would give me an answer. The problem was, I didn't know the question.

Etienne caught me and steadied me as he tied the

rope around me to lower me down from the window. I froze in his arms. I couldn't help it. They were strong and comforting, but I knew that damned amulet was hanging on his neck. He didn't speak as we climbed back in the SUV.

"You have your gun?" I asked.

"Of course."

"You may need it. There's something dangerous in this next one. Marisol left me a warning."

"What kind of danger?"

"I don't know. She didn't indicate whether it was magical or something else. Magical, I can deal with."

"Bullshit." His jaw tightened and his hands squeezed the steering wheel in a white-knuckled death grip. "You witches talk in circles. Your magic is way overrated."

Irritation skimmed through me, but I fought to remain calm. Now he was mad again. Here was a man, a powerful, competent man, a man that wanted me, a man I wanted—and he was clinging to his dangerous lucky charms and prejudice against witches like a kid.

"*I don't know* is an honest answer, Etienne. There are a lot of things I don't know. You've got a big *unknown* circling around you, too. Those trinkets Abigail gave you make you immune to magic. But is it only magic that is specifically aimed at you? Or any magic you touch? What if we go into a dangerous situation and you accidently touch me when I'm using earth magic?"

"You might consider that I can protect you. That you don't need magic. I have a track record there." He stared out the window at the ruins. Distracted, he suddenly jerked the wheel to avoid a pothole. His jaw was set and he projected anger . . . or maybe frustration.

Having someone protect me was not in my nature. "The Earth Mother said I should teach you to trust me, and . . ." Oops. I'd said too much. "Never mind. Let's finish this. Be careful what you shoot. And try not to get too close."

He said nothing as he drove on. The day had warmed, making me grateful for the tank top I wore. It was still early summer here in the Barrows, but I could feel sweat in my hair and across my upper lip. We parked and climbed out of the vehicle. This time Herschel came with us. He growled as we stood facing the building and I laid my hand on his head.

This one was a single story and high ceilinged. Maybe a grocery store once, I imagined. The floor that we could see was cluttered with junk, what might have been metal shelving. The rest stretched into darkness. Worse, it had a fetid animal smell of wet fur and ripe shit.

"Something lives here." I spoke softly. Etienne had already drawn his gun.

Herschel growled again.

"Etienne? You have any ideas?"

He shrugged as if I'd asked him the meaning of the universe or some other useless unanswerable question. "Let's get this over with, witch."

I started into the building. I picked a path between piles of debris, then took note of the fact that there actually was a path. A path used by whatever lived here.

A slow rumbling growl came from the back of the building. It filled the air with warning. Etienne pointed his flashlight in the direction of the sound.

Something moved under the circle beam of Etienne's light. It rose to stand on four legs. As near as I could see, it looked like a giant black bear—until it raised a face that could only be described as a monkey's. Traveling as I had through some more exotic parts of the world, I'd seen a lot of strange animals. They were all a *part* of the world. This thing felt far different. It had an air of something alien, something that didn't belong.

Herschel barked. Once, a single sharp sound that echoed in a virtually empty building. How incredibly uncomfortable. Should we kill this animal? Did it really offer us harm? I wouldn't kill any man or creature simply because it appeared fearsome.

"Should I shoot it?" Etienne asked. He seemed to be taking it in stride. I appreciated the fact that he wasn't so quick to pull the trigger. I also appreciated the fact that his gun, while massive by human standards, probably would not stop something the size of a small elephant. As I stood contemplating the situation, the creature opened a large mouth full of sharp teeth and charged.

chapter 27

The air exploded in massive sound as Etienne pulled the trigger. The rapid blasts came like a single long explosion as they hammered my eardrums. Ten feet from us, the thing stopped and staggered. It swayed. That gave Etienne time to reload. Not necessary. It moaned, then toppled over, stiff legged like a statue.

Etienne and I stood there and waited for it to rise, but it did not. Black fluid drained from its mouth. The air hummed, still vibrating from the shots. Hearing returned slowly, but Etienne's voice sounded tinny as he spoke. "What was that?" He gestured at the creature with his gun.

"I don't know." I toned it down a bit when I realized I was shouting. "I never saw one before."

"The thing from the Bog." Etienne raised his voice, too. "You knew what it was."

"Yes. A water dragon, yes. But dragons of all kinds have been depicted through history. They're part of this world. They belong to the Mother. This thing doesn't. It feels . . . wrong."

"It came through the Zombie, then." He holstered his gun.

I grabbed his arm. "What the hell? You mean things from other worlds just wander in?"

"Indeed." The deep soft voice spoke from behind us.

We whirled and Aiakós stood there, smiling. Sunlight illuminated his form from behind, giving his magnificent crimson hair a glow. He walked toward us.

"The Zombie is a trap, actually." His voice was rich and compelling. "A one-way door. Most of the time. Any intelligent being on another world would recognize and avoid it. Any intelligent being on this world should avoid it, too. Simple creatures like this one occasionally wander in and can't get home. There is no place for them here. I usually put them out of their misery. Or I have Etienne and his most excellent troops take care of it."

I glanced at Etienne. He said nothing. His face, as usual, betrayed no emotion.

Aiakós came closer. "I've watched you all day. You are looking for your sister in some unusual places. And you have a map of sorts. May I see it?"

Now what did I do? I didn't want to show him the map. I would not show him the map. "I can't show it to you. It has a heavy spell on it. It's a spell directed solely to me. Marisol drew it. She is one megapowerful witch. Unintended consequences, but it might bite you."

Aiakós cocked his head and smiled, but those gold eyes went narrow and cold. Obviously he wasn't used to being denied anything he requested. "Well, thank you for your consideration of my well-being, Nyx. Please, continue your search." He inclined his head, regal as a king. But his voice had carried a menacing note. He turned and walked away, back into the sunlight.

"He'll just follow us," Etienne said. "Maybe he was all along. He's curious now. That's not good."

"Yeah." I walked farther into the building, carefully skirting the creature lying dead on the floor. I studied it a moment. "How did you kill it? I know about firepower. You got a big gun, but not that big."

"Bronze bullets. Everything that comes through the Zombie seems to be abnormally susceptible to bronze. Except maybe him." The *him* had to be Aiakós. "Bronze hurts him, even if it doesn't kill him."

"And they, these things, come here? All the time?"

"Not all the time. Usually just on certain moon cycles. They come in, they're starving. There's nothing here for them to eat. And nothing to keep the carnivores among them from snacking on the general population of the Barrows. Some just come through and die. We find them lying on the plaza. I don't think they can breathe the air."

"It's a one-way door. They can't leave."

"Not without help." His voice had been neutral, but now it thickened with anger.

I figured he meant the artifacts, those objects imbued with earth magic. They would work—if a being knew how to use them.

"And you kill them?"

"Yes, Nyx, we kill them. A hole to the greater universe has been poked in your Earth Mother's world. Somehow, I got appointed to defend this little corner of hell."

"Rocky said he hasn't seen much action yet."

"No, but there's a major dark moon coming in a few months. Let's find your next clue, Sherlock."

The symbols left on the floor in the back of the building sent me on to the place marked three. It also added to the cumulative spell I was gathering for my sister. Next was an abandoned school.

The place of the fifth symbol was a six-story building. Another building had crumbled into the street and we had to park a block away. The sun fell behind a cloud bank in the west as we climbed the thankfully solid steel and concrete stairs and searched the rooms. There was nothing there.

"What about the roof?" I asked as we finished searching the fifth floor.

"Dangerous." He hadn't talked much since Aiakós had left us. He merely followed me as I followed my path.

"I have to get up there." I was adamant about that. I wouldn't leave until I found it.

All of the windows were gone and a strong wind blowing through the openings cut a fierce path at times. It whistled and moaned as it pushed against us, battled us as if it wanted to keep us away.

I started searching for a way and found a locked door with a plate on it.

"See." I pointed at it. "Roof."

"I suppose you want me to shoot the locks off."

I laid my hand on it and the locks popped loose. Not quietly, since they had long since rusted shut. "No. I got it." I gave him a smug smile. "I'm good with locks."

"So was Oonagh."

So, he wanted to compare me to ... her. I glared at him. I hadn't expected an instant metamorphosis, but it would be nice to see a gradual change in his attitude. Instead I got erratic attitude bouncing between *all witches are evil* and *you're okay even if you are a witch*.

The roof was a scary place. The wind glided unhindered by walls and threatened to push us off. At least it was clean and not like the stink that sometimes came off the Bog. The roof dipped in places as if the foundation had deteriorated from underneath. The symbol left there was nothing but a small spiked wheel. When I touched it, the last of the cumulative spells locked into place. All it did was make me blink a couple of times. That was it? There were no further directions.

We carefully eased our way down the stairs and outside. A fruitful day was apparently not going to happen. The need to find Marisol sat like a knot in my stomach. It coincided with the knowledge that I might not ever find her. My shoulders slumped in defeat.

"We're doing the best we can, Nyx."

I'm sure Etienne meant to comfort me. He'd suddenly morphed back to his *you're okay for a witch* attitude. At the same time he was scouring the area around us. The SUV sat a little more than a block away.

"Let's go," he said. Sudden tension filled his voice. So much tension that I wasn't inclined to dawdle.

He set a pace. A really fast walk. He had his handgun drawn.

"Ah, we could run," I offered. I stumbled in a hole, but I caught myself in time.

"No. Not yet."

"Are we power walking toward something or away from something?"

"Both."

A scrabbling noise came from behind us.

"Don't turn around." He picked up the pace.

"Okay." I quickly drew a little magic, making sure I kept it away from him.

Ahead, the SUV seemed farther than ever. The scrabbling came closer.

"Shit," Etienne cursed. He whirled and started shooting.

I turned, too.

Chasing us were . . . crabs? Spiders? My first thought was that the aliens had landed in force. More than I could count, the size of a large dog, the sick gray creatures scrabbled toward us. They made the sound of rustling leaves as multiple legs propelled them easily over the rubble in the streets. Antennae bristled above each head, a head that sat directly on a flat oval body.

Etienne picked them off. Each bullet brought another one down. More came like an invasion of killer crabs. Creatures from another world via the Zombie. No spaceship required.

Okay, I could fight. And here I would be limited by only my strength. Given the number, though, it would be best to escape. I threw a line of fire between us and them. The first twenty feet of them flashed and burned. Oh, goody. They were flammable.

"What the . . ." Etienne stopped shooting.

I just grinned. Unfortunately, it didn't last. Others came scrambling out of the ruins around us. Thousands of them—or at least hundreds. I exaggerate when filled with utter terror. I could surround us with a ring of fire, but we'd be trapped.

Fire is an excellent weapon. Unfortunately, it's capricious, horrifying, and often goes in unintended directions. At least here, almost everything that could burn had long since rotted. And were my sister and others not here, I would be ecstatic to burn these empty ruins. I hated to kill anything. But in defense, to avoid becoming lunch, I would.

They had moved closer. I threw a sheet of flames directly at a group of the creatures. The fire covered them—and burned. They screamed—I think. The sound was more like a high-pitched whistle, like a lobster dropped in a boiling pot of water. Mother help me, I was going to be sick—and I'd probably never eat lobster or crab again.

Another group was almost on us. Another sheet of fire and the street filled with shrill cries of agony tearing at my eardrums. The bracelet on my arm, the Dragon's

Tears, suddenly turned white-hot but did not burn me. It gave me strength.

Etienne grabbed my arm and dragged me toward the SUV. My stomach twisted in terror—my mind roared with fire. In it I could see a circle with markings like the Dragon's Tears. Through it was a deep, wide searing canyon of fire. With every inch of my being I understood. Those massive flames would come racing toward me at my call—and I wanted to call. May the Earth Mother help and forgive me, but at that moment I felt as if I could joyfully set her wonderful world ablaze.

Next thing I knew, Etienne threw me—literally threw me—into the SUV's backseat. My poor abused head hit the far door and the other door slammed behind me. Just once, couldn't I land on my ass? I heard the engine start. Light faded. The hideous creatures scrabbled up and over the SUV. They blocked the light. Their crustacean faces pressed against the window like a mad jigsaw puzzle. Multiple eyes gazed at me, eyes filled with hunger, stupid mindless hunger, and purest pain.

The fire came again.

Oh, Great Mother, how was this happening? I couldn't control it. I'd played with fire, used fire, but nothing like this. It seared, scoured, and burned everything around us. I'd lost control and I would burn us alive along with our assailants.

Fire surrounded me. It shifted, warm and caressing. I shaped it. Balls of fire, streaks of fire, red, gold, white, and blue, it swirled into insane tornadoes that roared and shrieked of destruction. I controlled it. I was made of flame, glorious flame. I wanted it, grabbed at it desperately as it suddenly began to fade away.

"Nyx!"

Someone called me.

"Nyx!"

I didn't want to go, but the voice refused to leave me alone.

I came to in semidarkness, cradled in Etienne's arms. He'd crawled from the front seat.

My throat, my mouth, rasped, parchment dry. Finally, I worked up a bit of saliva. "What happened?" I coughed out the words.

He helped me sit up. "I don't know. You burned them."

Was that actual wonder I heard in his voice? Of course it was. I had stunned myself with something incomprehensible—how could he not be shocked?

I realized then that the windows were covered with oily soot, hence the darkness. The SUV's engine was still running, so apparently I hadn't damaged that part. Maybe some sense of survival and control had kicked in and I'd unconsciously protected us. Good to know I actually could look out for myself when I totally lost control of magic. I didn't know if I could make a repeat performance of what just happened, though. I didn't want to try—at least not in the next hundred years.

Etienne left me and crawled back into the front of the vehicle. I didn't move, trying to regain my strength. He used the wipers to clean a patch of windshield and started slowly forward.

"Herschel?" I screamed. "What about Herschel?"

I opened the door of the moving vehicle and started to jump out—just as Herschel jumped in. We collided, him on top. The door closed behind him and we were moving again. His toenails punched through my clothes like spikes and his face was smack in mine. Not drooling this time. His arid mouth smelled of smoke and ashes. I wasn't ready for a repeat performance of my great burning, but maybe I could figure out a way to stop his excess saliva.

After a rough struggle, I managed to get from under him. Exhaustion overwhelmed me, and my head throbbed. During a few days I'd seriously abused the fine body the Mother had given me. I laid my head on Herschel's back as Etienne slowly made our way through the rubble-filled streets.

I couldn't see much at first. Some of the soot had peeled off as he drove, making twists and turns through the ruins. The Barrows became visible in small places. I saw it then, the spiked wheel. The last symbol Marisol had left me at the top of the building. It glowed on a high wall, between two buildings, a faint glimpse and it was gone.

"Etienne, stop!"

"What? No. Are you crazy? Never mind. I know the answer to that." His usually deep, voice resonated with emotion. Anger and fear twined in the few words he spoke. My magical display had a profound effect on him, just as it had me. How could it not?

"Please. I saw it. The spiked wheel. On a building."

"Later. Not now."

I fumbled with the door handle to jump out again. This time they locked. I realized that I was too weak to tug at the locks or even conjure a spell to release them. It would have to wait.

chapter 28

True darkness had descended when we arrived back at the compound. Darrow greeted us. He studied the soot-covered SUV with a flashlight. It didn't get away completely unscathed. Paint bubbled in great scaly patches and the tires had peculiar bulges in places. It carried a distinct odor of burnt carrion.

Darrow simply said, "Another one."

"It was fun, Darrow." I linked my arm in his. He grabbed me when I collapsed and steadied me while I regained my footing. I felt drunk, as if I'd consumed a couple of bottles of hard liquor. I giggled. Now, this was new. A true magical high.

Darrow glared at Etienne. "You still aren't taking good care of her. I told you . . ." Anger rumbled in his voice. He tightened his hold on me. Oh, my. Had Darrow threatened Etienne? Charged him with my safety?

"No." I patted Darrow on the chest. I knew he wanted to protect me. He'd always done that. And I'd fought the same battle for independence. "No one has to take care of me. I built a big, massive, gigantic, humongous fire. You should have been there, buddy. It was magnificent." I waved my arm wildly, narrowly missing his face. "It was sooo bright, brilliant, shining, dazzling . . . and bright. Oh, the colors I made."

"I wasn't invited." Darrow's gaze remained on Etienne.

"You are now," Etienne said. "Get a couple of teams together—with flamethrowers. We have work. If there are any left."

Any left as in *Nyx slaughtered all.*

I giggled. What in the Mother's name . . . ? I'm a soldier witch. I don't giggle.

Darrow grinned. The warrior was happy to fight. "You coming with us, Nyx?"

"No." Etienne spoke before I could draw a breath. "She'd done enough. She doesn't look too stable right now."

He was right. But I'd seen the marking on that building and I needed to find my way back. Being able to see in the dark was an asset, but no way could I take on the creatures that attacked us alone. Not without food and rest. And I really needed food and rest—and to come off this fire-induced high.

Darrow led me and got started on the stairs, but I could feel his impatience. He wanted to go fight. I pushed him away, assuring him I'd be okay. I trudged up the stairs to the apartment and clung tightly to the handrail the whole way. Once there, I knew I needed food, which thankfully came from a gallon of milk, a package of cookies, and a loaf of bread. It was all I could find. I ate and drank everything. Taste wasn't the objective. I needed calories.

Pure fire, and it was pure, was so new to me. I'd never thought it existed, never called upon it in the manner and to the degree I had hours ago. I'd never had it give me a drunken high. I didn't know I could do more than small fires that got out of hand and grew to be monster blazes. Gran had worried when she couldn't find a witch to teach me about fire. Apparently her worry was justified. The lack of control I displayed earlier may have saved our lives, but it could just as easily have made Etienne a barbecue crisp. No fire had ever burned me.

Hunger abated, I stripped off my soiled and soot-crusted things and threw them in the trash. When I tried to remove the Dragon's Tears from my arm, it stuck. Nothing I did budged it. Soap, a bottle of Marisol's bath oil, nothing moved it. Too tired to continue the struggle, I surrendered. I'd try again tomorrow.

The shower revived me some. While I wasn't as tired as I was before, I was too tired to hunt up clothing. I crawled naked into Etienne's bed. If he followed his usual pattern, he wouldn't show up until morning. I could dress then.

I slept and woke when Etienne entered the apartment. A surprise—or was it? He crossed the darkened room and headed straight for the shower. He came out wrapped in a towel, carrying his gun and knife. The only light spread softly from the bathroom. The door was partially closed and left the bedroom in shadows. With great care he laid the weapons on the nightstand. He waited for a moment, then lifted the amulet from his neck and laid it beside the gun and knife.

I lost interest in all his weapons except one when he dropped the towel. This was a magnificent man. He radiated power, purpose, and intensity. He had the hard body of a warrior—a body that seemed to shout with sexual possibilities.

I'd admired him physically from the beginning. He caught the covers and dragged them off and stared at me. He smiled, so I guess he was pleased. He lay beside me, within reach but not quite touching.

"Have you decided to trust me?" I had to ask.

He smiled. "I have decided that your power, no matter what you say, is beyond any protection those trinkets can give me. You've been tearing down my defenses since the day I met you."

"Etienne, that's not true. It is possible that *those trinkets* were what protected you today. When I tried to touch you with magic—"

He reached out and touched his fingers to my lips to silence me. It did.

My finger traced a scar that ran across his chest. And another that cut across it. The pinched round circle at his waist, a bullet wound, told of a shot that should have killed him. Scars, straight, even, lay across the tops of his thighs. Burns. At his side, curling around to his back, were the rough lines I'd seen before. Whip marks. When you've lived the life I have lived, been the places I have been, you knew the signs of torture.

"Who hurt you?" My finger traced one of the whip marks.

"It doesn't matter."

"It does." I found his scars both compelling and exciting. Here was a man who had lived and traveled the same paths, lived some of the same life I had for years. He, however, had lived on the aggressive side and I on the defensive. Each carried its dangers as each carried a reward. He'd paid a far higher price than I had and had achieved more. More wealth, more pain, more abuse, everything that comes to those who live on the edge. I wondered if he had secret death wish, a wish hidden from himself. I laid my hand on the bullet wound. "If I had been with you, I would have fought for you. No one would hurt you."

"No. It's all past now. Let it go, witch, let it go."

Witch, witch. Again he reminded me of what I was to him. The protection of the Solaire and Morié was gone, but not far. They were only physical weapons and shields that I had temporarily overcome. He had other defenses, far deeper and stronger, inside.

My body gave its typical reaction to a man so long, hard, and muscular. A primal desire rose in me. He drew a quick breath as my fingers slid lower. He closed the distance between us in an instant.

There was a fierce desperate urgency in him and I matched it with ease. This was going to be a delicious but quick experience. It had been some time since I'd allowed myself this kind of pleasure, a long time since I'd met a man I wanted to be with in such an intimate way. This physical craving was so often denied by the more critical things in life. His hand slid between my legs and I realized I was moist and more than ready. My need, his need, filled us to capacity. Later, we could move slowly through the process of exploring how our bodies could feel. We could tease and torment and draw out the hours given to us for being a man and a woman.

When he moved on top of me, I spread my legs, welcoming him. I gave in to the warm demands of his mouth. As with the events that had plagued me since I arrived in this bizarre place they called the Barrows, the fire started to rise. The ascent of desire created it. It flared and surrounded us. I contained it, held it tight.

"You have fire in your eyes," he whispered. His own eyes remained dark and mysterious. "I see you. You burn."

And I did. I was no virgin. I had cared for and loved

men before—but I had never burned for one. I burned now, knowing that this man, above all others who had briefly passed through my life, was beyond hope, beyond expectation, created for me. My gift. The Earth Mother had chosen him and I should accept him. I would not be the first woman who had accepted a man she could not trust, praying all the while for a miracle.

Earth magic. Nothing was more fundamental in the realm of natural things than the binding between a man and a woman when they made love. In those minutes we bathed in the splendor of living emotions and exquisite physical touch of a man and a woman. His skin against mine, they rhythm of bodies, it didn't last long. In a sudden rolling release, my mind went blank with pleasure. Again, the fire came. This time, I couldn't control it. It was a priceless experience as white-hot flames surrounded us, but did not burn. He shuddered and groaned. He whispered words I couldn't hear. The fire faded to the darkness of a simple room, a simple bed.

We lay there, holding on tight, allowing the warmth, the satisfaction of release, flood through our bodies.

"Witch," he murmured against my throat. For the first time, he said that single word without making it a curse. "Earth, water, wind, and fire. Elemental. You are fire."

"Witch I am, Etienne. Witch I will always be. And the fire lives in me. You'll have to accept me or let me go."

He rolled over and lay at my side. I didn't speak again. Disappointment filled me. What had I wanted? What had I expected? A declaration of true love? Not that, but I wished he'd say he trusted me now. Trusted me not to control him, not to hurt him. He might not call me *my love*, but I wished he would at least call me *my witch*.

By the Earth Mother's grace, I was there with him.

But he didn't know that. She left it up to me to enlighten him. She charged me with creating a relationship. That seemed so unfair. She could see into his heart, his mind, but she left me blind and struggling. Whimper, whine, and complain was all I could do.

His forearm was so close I could see the solid ebony tattoos clearly.

The fireworks faded, but in that final glow, I made an astounding discovery. The tattoos on his arms writhed and their purpose became unmistakable.

Earth magic had Etienne firmly in its grip. Like me, he'd been born with it in every molecule of his body. I had seen the tattoos, but never thought of their meaning. I'd not felt a hint of magic in him. But why should I? The tattoos, the symbols on his arms, were like padlocks. They were a potent and effective ward like the Earth Mother's ward around the Barrows. Gran told me that the few men who can use earth magic are vastly different from us. She only knew of one, and she did not often speak of him, her own brother. Would the Solaire have burned Etienne as it had burned me if he hadn't had those tattoo guards? Or were they created only for women, the vast majority of witches? The vision faded. Another Barrows mystery rose to the top of the pile.

Etienne groaned softly. It trailed off to a sigh. I didn't groan, but I did suck in a deep breath of oxygen. I laughed breathlessly. "You sound like Herschel when he's eaten something he shouldn't."

"Do not compare me to that dog."

I rolled over and rose up on my elbows. "Oh, I think you're pretty much incomparable."

He chuckled. "Flattery will get you a reward." He raised his head for a moment, then dropped it back down. "In a little bit. Your reward needs a little power nap."

"I think a nap is justified." From me, though, Etienne needed more than to be told he was a great lover.

I pitched my voice to speak true words. "I swear, in the Earth Mother's name, no matter what happens, I will never use magic to harm you." I kissed him lightly on the mouth. "Please, will you tell me why you hate witches?"

He didn't speak for a moment. Then he said, "Oonagh. She . . . I was in South Africa. We'd tried to rob a diamond convoy and it went wrong. I took one here." He laid his own hand over the bullet scar. "We were hiding out. No doctors. Pain was pretty bad and the guys kept me full of alcohol. I was dying and I knew it. They knew it, too. They were standing a death watch. It was night . . . everything quiet, she just walked in. She got past my men on guard and walked in. Apparently she'd seen me days before. I don't know where. Or how. She asked if I wanted to live. I did, but deep inside I knew something was wrong."

"You were in pain and full of booze. That doesn't make for rational decisions."

"No. Is that in the rules? For witches? To ask if someone wants to be healed."

"It is." Surprising, that she asked, but maybe a tiny bit of conscience remained in her. I knew nothing of her life. Oonagh, as we all did, had served the Mother at one time.

"I would probably have made the same decision, even if I knew the consequences. I wanted to live. I don't remember much after that," Etienne said. "I woke up the next morning, feeling tired but okay." He reached out and brushed a hand over my hair. "A lot of my men deserted me that day. They were a superstitious bunch and seeing a dying man heal overnight spooked them. When they came in expecting to take me out and bury me, she was sitting by my bed. They marked her for the evil creature she was.

"My life seemed easier after that, the stealing, whatever she wanted I got for her. Money in the bank. There were few obstacles. Then I got nervous—and bored because it was so undemanding. I wanted to get away."

I understood. "You couldn't. She'd bound you to her service when she healed you."

"I fought." He stopped speaking for a moment. His fingers trailed along my arm to my hand. "I fought for a long time. Do you know what it's like to want to leave, but be frozen, unable to move? I became a trapped animal. She won, of course. She trained me well."

I did understand his despair at being caged. That had happened to me a couple of times, physically, not magically. Physically was bad enough. "Etienne, that spell she used on you is called a Soul Binding. It's powerful. Like everything else, it's okay for us to use it as defense, but not to make people slaves. It broke when she died. I'm surprised you didn't die when she did. That's one of the violations that get the Sisters of Justice called in. I told you, a witch who binds and controls another without cause receives an automatic death sentence."

"Could you do it? Make someone a slave? She had control over even my mind. Could you?"

"No. I really am an incompetent witch. I can toss you across the room, burn the room around you. Bind your soul? No way. Things like that take years of training, the thing I've always rejected. Much to my dismay, I can't heal, either. Abigail can. And Oonagh might not have had as much power as you or others believed. The artifacts on that list could possibly help even a poor witch become a strong witch. If she had them . . ."

"I learned the futility of fighting. I wanted to kill myself and couldn't." Etienne sighed and kissed me on the ear. "It got worse. After she got that thing she wore around her neck, the thing Madeline called the Portal, she changed. She was okay at first. She seemed . . . healthy. Then she started to . . . decay. Her body . . . I can't explain it." His voice went low and strained. "We came here and she sent me to serve and spy on Aiakós— and betray him. It all ended when Madeline defeated her and one of the Sisters of Justice killed her. If Madeline hadn't come, looking for the Portal . . ." He shuddered.

"I thought Aiakós would kill me then. I had built his army, much as it is now—and used it against him. I got men who trusted me killed. He . . ." He stopped and drew a breath. "He was unhappy, but you understand how he has limited options. So he agreed I could live. After he hurt me to show that he could hurt me. He owns me now, too. Just not in the same way she did. I have more autonomy. I could run if I wanted to. But where would I go? That's often the fate of a successful criminal. Eventually, everyone knows you. My world, thanks to Oonagh, is much smaller. But Aiakós lets Michael run things. Michael is reasonable."

Etienne had one long arm stretched across me. I snuggled close to him and relaxed. This man had strength and power. He had the strength to mold soldiers, to guide an army. Though he didn't know it, he had power to manipulate earth magic, the magic he had every reason to hate. I didn't understand it, but I had to try. Now I could actually feel the magic under the tattoos binding it. What would happen if those bindings broke and he suddenly became filled with something he could neither understand nor control?

"Where did you get these?" I touched the stark midnight tattoo on his arm.

"Don't know," he murmured, seeming contented. "Always had them."

"Always?"

"Adoption people told my mother I came in that way. I never looked for my biological parents. I figured they dumped me for a reason. I had a good mother and father." He shifted and held me closer still. His breathing slowed and I knew he'd fallen asleep.

I slept a little then, but near dawn I had to rise. Etienne continued to rest. He'd been out last night long after I'd gone to bed. My usually depleted witch strength seemed to be full force now. Maybe sex did that. I quietly dug out panties and a T-shirt, dressed, and went into the kitchen.

My sister needed to be found and I was close. My gut told me I was close. Or maybe it was desperation, the knowledge that she might be dying every minute I delayed.

chapter 29

I'd just put the coffee on when a tap came at the door. I only opened it a crack, then opened it wider to let Darrow in.

"You dig out many creepy-crawlies last night?" I asked.

"A few. Etienne said you probably frightened the survivors enough they went out and drowned themselves in the Bog. He didn't give details, but he was pretty surprised. I saw where you burned. That's a little bigger fire than you usually toss around, girl."

"Yeah. I'll admit to being nervous. Got a little wild. I was scared. But don't tell anyone."

Darrow chuckled. "A little wild? So, if you get totally terrified, I should look for you to blow up half the Barrows."

"Probably. Is that really a bad idea? Blowing up the Barrows?"

"No. I thought about it a time or two myself." Darrow went to sit on one of the barstools. He was actually one of the few people to have seen me throw fire. I tried to be discreet. Discreet with the throwing thing. Fire itself is rarely discreet.

I'd left the bedroom door open and he could see Etienne sprawled on the bed, facedown and minus clothing.

I doubt Darrow was impressed, but it was a fine sight to me. If Darrow hadn't come, I'd probably have sucked down a cup of coffee and gone back to bed myself.

"You sure about that?" Darrow spoke softly and nodded at Etienne.

"Sure of what? True love? No. Or a one-night stand? Definitely. He's . . . talented."

"I'd advise sticking to the one night. That's because I know both of you. An oil-water thing." He mouthed the next words. "Nyx, be careful. He's . . . different."

I nodded, accepting his words. I wanted to say he was right. Odds were good he was right, since he was a very wise man. But he didn't understand the forces involved. Etienne and I were the Earth Mother's children. We belonged to the same club. In her wisdom, she'd pushed us together. I had to keep reminding myself that she said I should get him to trust me, not necessarily that I could trust him. It might end in tragedy, regardless of my patroness's platitudes.

"Nicky, honey, I thought when you left Africa . . ." The worry lines between his brows deepened.

"What? You thought I'd go home, find a man, have a two-car garage, couple of kids, live in a subdivision?" I stared at the slow, thin stream of coffee gliding into the pot. "I did try to be normal. Not the husband-kid type normal. That isn't me. I had a life in SF, a job, not typical, but no danger I couldn't handle. I'm different. You've heard the saying, 'out of step, out of time.'"

"That's exactly how I'd describe the Barrows. Out of step, out of time. It called you, didn't it? This place."

I shook my head. "No. It called my sister." I'd heard of Duivel, of course, in association with the High Witch Abigail. I hadn't known about the Barrows. "How did you end up here, buddy?"

"My network jobber, Karawoski, you remember him? Etienne worked for him some, too. Etienne sent out a call for men. You hire locally, you get political issues and family connections—and lots of questions. Those of us out of the country a long time have fewer complications. And there isn't much that surprises us. The Barrows is a good sanctuary for criminals. If you can keep your head down and survive. Money is good, too."

I remembered Karawoski. I met the highly successful war contractor once. He sat in a fine office in Paris and directed the hiring of mercenary soldiers and guards around North and Central Africa. He also managed certain loathsome business and directed billions of dollars in blood money between Swiss and Caribbean island banks.

The coffee finally finished its drip and I poured us each a cup. We carried them into the living room. "Did you get a chance to see those spider-crab thingies close-up?" I asked. "Or did the troops just blast everything in front of them?"

"I saw what was left of those you blasted. Never had that many crawlers come through, before. Last ones died the minute they hit the street. We did clean-up duty." Darrow was his usual steady self. All the years I've known him, I've only seen him break down once. He cried when I said good-bye. At the same time, he kept urging me to go, to have a different life. Now, sitting over coffee, he seemed as companionable as ever. Or maybe I had dropped back into the Nicky he knew from the past. Had leaving that life changed me? I like to think it had, but now I doubted.

I blew on my coffee to cool it. "How does something like that happen? Things just wander through that Zombie thing from . . . wherever? Don't you keep watchers posted?"

"Aiakós won't let us watch. He says he'll call us if he needs us."

"Does that mean he actually approves of some things coming in? Things he can control? Things he can use?"

Darrow smiled, but it was in irony, not humor. "Mostly I think he likes to kill things himself. He doesn't want us to see his bloody hands. Oh, I expect he's up to something he doesn't want everyone to know about. That's what he is. Dangerous."

Oh, he was. Spaneas and those other criminals proved that.

I really needed to talk to Abigail. Why did the Mother allow such a thing as the Zombie to exist? A hole, a fucking hole in the universe. Did she care no more for us and her world?

"How well do you know the Barrows?" I asked Darrow. "I'm looking for a building."

He chuckled. "Well, Nicky, there's thousands of them."

I described the wheel on the building. "I only saw the corner, but the building is at least five stories high."

"Don't remember seeing it. 'Course, when I go down there, I rarely look up. That's a bad idea."

I sighed. Of course it wouldn't be easy.

After Darrow left, I went in, woke Etienne, and, instead of making love again, demanded that he dress and take me back into the Barrows—or I would go by myself. I did make a half-assed effort to explain the growing urgency that time was running out. I needed to eat again, but after that I had to move. He grumbled, bitched, and finally fell silent as the SUV crossed streets and drove around rubble, searching for a symbol I couldn't find. I even lay on the backseat and ordered him to drive the exact route from where I burned the spider things to the compound. Nothing.

"Nyx." Etienne laid a hand on my shoulder. It would be dark soon, and the search would end. "Why are you so sure she's here?"

"She left me signs, markers. Personal markers. I should be able to find her." We stood by the SUV, his shoulder close to mine.

"Maybe they're wrong." He hesitated. "Maybe you're wrong. Maybe she's not here at all."

I closed my eyes. I wanted to cry. This was something I couldn't work out, something I had no way of moving on.

"She's probably okay for now." He spoke in a soft casual voice that sounded too condescending. But then, he had nothing to lose here.

"What?" Something hit me then. An odd feeling, something I shouldn't ignore. His words. *Okay for now?* How did he know that?

Etienne drew me into his arms. He gave me a sweet, gentle kiss, probably to comfort me . . . only it didn't. It certainly felt good with my head lying against his chest. Carefully lying against his chest and carefully avoiding the proximity of the Solaire he still wore under his shirt.

"Let's go back to the compound," he said. "We can look again tomorrow. I'll get a team together. Set up a search pattern."

I didn't say anything, but he didn't understand. If Marisol was hidden by magic, his men would never find her. If an abandoned building crumbled on them, or some hidden beast attacked and they were injured, it would amount to men being hurt solely in my personal interest.

Darrow waited for us when we arrived back at the compound. He drew me aside. With his arm around my shoulders, he turned me away from Etienne. "Me, Rocky, and some of the guys are going to Larry's tonight. You need to go, too. You need to get away from . . . him. Have a few drinks. You can't search at night, so it won't make a difference."

There was no animosity in Darrow's voice, just a tiny bit of concern, of warning. *Get away from him. Away from Etienne.*

"You know something I don't?" Something strange was happening here. I had no tangible evidence that Etienne meant me harm, other than the fact he seemed to be glued to my ass 24-7.

"I know a lot of things you don't know, Nyx. I know you. Something's not right. You're not thinking right. This isn't my Nicky."

I punched him in the ribs. Not hard, but he winced. Then I hugged him.

"Okay. I'll go. I won't run into those two clowns I met on my first day here, will I?"

"Nope. They're business security. Locals who live in Duivel. They work out of an office on River Street. Oh, Etienne's not invited. We made that clear a long time ago." Darrow stared at Etienne. His face was stern but without malice. "It's our place, a place to get away from and bitch about him and some of his rules." I understood. When I worked for Darrow, we troops had our own place to escape the boss, too.

Last night, Etienne had trusted me with his story of captivity by a witch. And he'd inadvertently let me in on a dark, powerful secret that he didn't know himself. I needed to talk to Abigail, but didn't have time. Perhaps I should go there instead of a bar to have fun. But wouldn't Etienne insist on going with me? Would that cause a disturbance that might force Darrow to choose sides? Etienne's magic had been bound a long time and he didn't know it existed. It could wait. "Okay, give me an hour. I need to eat and—"

"You always need to eat."

"Yeah, but I need to shower and change, too." I hesitated. "Darrow, you think Etienne will try to stop me from going with you? I know we're on better terms now, but it's still shaky."

"No. He won't." He grinned. "I haven't pushed him on it, because I haven't noticed you fighting to get away from him. If you really wanted to leave, you'd have done it on that first day."

"He offered me something I needed. Hell, he saved my life a couple of times. Why leave?"

Darrow laughed. "Okay, Nicky, see you in an hour."

I didn't tell Etienne about going anywhere. I simply headed for the food hall and fueled up. Then I went looking for Herschel. I found him in the kitchen, in the head chef's office. The chef was quietly discussing the next day's menu with him. At least the chef was discussing. Herschel looked like he was paying attention, even if he didn't talk. It was, without a doubt, the weirdest thing I'd seen since I'd entered the Barrows. I quietly backed out and left them there. The chef and the witch's familiar had something in common. The chef produced food and Herschel consumed it. If I chose to leave here, Herschel would have to make a hard decision.

My clothes were limited, but I did have a pair of nice black jeans and a couple of tank tops. Since I still didn't have a bra, I put on both tanks. The Dragon's Tears, the band on my arm, looked a little barbaric, but not bad. I brushed my hair and dug through Marisol's things for a tube of lipstick.

Etienne drew a startled breath when I walked out of

the bathroom. He'd been sitting on the couch, drink in hand. I didn't wait to let him ask. "I'm going out with Darrow and Rocky a while. Maybe get drunk. They'll take care of me."

"I'm sure they will." He rose and came to me. He caught my chin in his fingers and kissed me, long and sweet. Tempting, persuasive, but after a gut-wrenching battle, I managed to ignore it.

"Do not distract me." I stepped away.

"You shouldn't go. It's not safe out there at night. You know that."

"And yet, many people come and go with a certain degree of safety."

He shrugged. That lean, tanned face of his seemed calm, but his eyes narrowed. "I'll go with—"

"No. Let's get something straight. Am I your prisoner?"

"Nyx. You—"

"It's a yes or no question."

"I simply want to protect you."

"Liar. Or maybe half a lie. You don't do anything *simply*. You're painting a damned confusing picture." I stepped back and crossed my arms.

He did the same, his face hard and hands clenched into fists. He stood between me and the door. I heard a vehicle pull up out front. I didn't want Darrow to have to come in and get me. If a fight started here, it would be me and Etienne.

"Get out of my way, Etienne."

We both held steady amid the stillness that often preceded stupid violence. The joyous elemental forces that had united us last night, desire and loneliness, now stood against his inexplicable need to control me and my understandable need to act out my desperation and fear.

I jumped at the knock on the door. Darrow. I pushed toward it and ran into Etienne. He caught my arms below the shoulders and held me tight. Then he released me. I shoved by without looking at him.

When I opened the door, I twisted by Darrow and hurried down the stairs. When I reached the bottom and stepped outside, I had to stop and breathe. My guts felt like a four-car pileup with multiple injuries. Stupid. I should never have made love to him. That act had always created a binding, even if it was temporary. Now everything I did, every word I spoke, was in that personal context.

I waited there until Darrow came down to me. I didn't know how long it had been. I didn't know if Darrow had words with Etienne. I didn't ask.

chapter 30

"Come on, Nicky." Darrow wrapped an arm around me and pulled me to the car. Rocky was there, but obviously he'd recognized my need for a few minutes alone.

Larry's Place wasn't bad. I inspected it with a critical eye as I did all new places. Critical as in *How can I escape if I need to?* as opposed to *My, what an interesting decor.*

It had the typical beer odor of a bar. No matter what they served, all but the highest-class cocktail lounges smelled of beer. I liked it because beer remained my perfect beverage. The U-shaped bar was long, but narrow enough you could yell across it if you needed to. Wood floors, wood furniture, low lighting, the decorations consisted of neon beer signs. Entertainment? A jukebox in the corner spilled out country-western, but a band was setting up on a small stage in front of a dance floor. Perfect. A plain Jane establishment, with no nonsense. The people who came there were interested in the basics. Having a good time by getting drunk and/or getting laid.

Most of the men in the bar I recognized as Darrow's troops, though there were a few I'd never seen before. Most of those were women. Darrow, his arm still around my shoulder, dragged me to the bar, where a bartender promptly handed me a bottle of my favorite Belgian beer. It was also his favorite, so I knew he'd had the relatively obscure brew specially imported. I downed my first swallow and suddenly felt very happy.

Darrow led me around, personally introducing me to all the men and women, all the time flattering me with adjectives directed at proving what a great fighter I was. About the third time I'd had enough.

"Darrow, are you wanting someone to pick a fight with me? See how tough I am?"

"No. I want them to know that you are not some ordinary piece of pussy our esteemed employer picked up."

"Oh." I raised an eyebrow at that. "Is he in the habit of picking up *ordinary* pussy?"

"No. He doesn't. That's got them a bit confused. I don't like confusion or speculation in my troops. When we worked, you and I, we all knew our places. That's important. This bunch doesn't have that ... cohesiveness ... yet."

"Am I a problem?" I reached up and smoothed the frown line between his brows.

He grinned. "No more than usual."

The band started playing a slow dance. Darrow drew me into his arms and onto the dance floor. He spoke softly. "I worried, when I hired you, years ago. I thought, she's trouble. So young. Then I thought, what will happen to her if I don't hire her? Then you stood your ground at Kimbica. Never once did I think you'd desert us, run away, or betray. That's what scares me. Etienne is a good boss. He'll fight, he won't run. But I can't trust him. He won't let me in, refuses to tell me things his second-in-command should know."

I sighed and relaxed against him. "It's hard, Darrow. Sometimes, when I had to use a little magic, you asked me questions, questions I couldn't answer because ... I couldn't. I haven't taken any official witch's vows. I don't want to. But some things have been ground into me from the time I could understand the language. *There are things you don't talk about with people who aren't like you.* This is just a guess, but I'd say some of the things Etienne isn't telling you are too dangerous for you to know." I kissed him on the cheek. "And some of it is pure bullshit. Not many choices there. You can leave. Or you can stay and keep a close eye on your own ass. You were always good at covering your own."

That got me a good laugh. Darrow had become sensitive to the magic in me. That isn't uncommon among witches who live in the general populace. Eventually, those close to you sense the difference. In some subtle way, Darrow could feel Etienne's magic. That made him uneasy, the contrast between two people, one he cared for, me, and another he barely knew. It would not be instantly resolved.

As had often happened, Darrow's men and women, his gang, had taken over the bar. Others, feeling left out, departed. Only those who had already connected with a partner for the night remained.

Darrow and I were sitting at a table when Rocky sidled up close to me. "Come on, Nicky, do the glass thing for me. These guys haven't seen it yet."

I laughed. Easy laughing since I was on my fourth beer. "You aren't going to win a dime, Rocky. This bunch has seen too much here in the Barrows. You won't fool them. And this is a nice place. Don't start a fight."

He'd had a few beers, too. Damned if he didn't pout like a kid. "Please."

I glanced at Darrow. He shrugged, but kept smiling.

It didn't take long for Rocky to set up. All I needed

was ten regular drink glasses, real glass, and a flat table. The trick, not exactly a trick since I used magic, was to stack the glasses in an absolutely impossible manner. The first glass went down and the second balanced with its bottom edge perched precariously on the rim of the first glass. The next one was stacked, bottom to rim, until I had a sawtooth pattern of glasses, held by a tiny bit of magic. I refused to allow gravity to rule the stack.

Rocky got to pout again, because no one would take his bets about when they would fall. Like I told him, these people had seen too much. Unlike the idiots around the world in general, they believed, they knew, that there were things that couldn't be seen. I'd bet they had also seen some things they'd rather forget. Some of them had been there the day I levitated the rock and tossed it through the wall of a building.

I made my way around the room talking, enjoying myself. Sometimes, the conversation turned, sadly, to Salvatore. I was pleased to learn that they respected him, and shocked to learn that he'd spoken occasionally of me. Spoken of me as a daughter he'd cared for.

I passed Rocky and he dragged me onto his lap. "You gotta help me tell this story."

"Oh, no." I shook a finger at the men gathered around the table. "He lies."

"Then you can keep it straight." Rocky pulled me closer. "See, we were guarding this convoy, when along comes some really bad guys."

I pushed off his lap and into a chair. I had to tell the truth. "By really bad guys, Rocky means they kicked our asses and took the merchandise we were guarding." Someone set another beer in front of me.

Rocky nodded. "They did indeed. Big ass-kick. Hurts me to think about it." He laid his hand over his heart, not his ass. "But we followed them, looking for a way to get the stuff back. We found it, but it looked like there was no way, no way in hell, we were going to recover. So, the witch, here—" He grabbed my hand and kissed my fingers. "She decides, all by herself, that if we can't have it, no one could."

"What happened, honey, you make it disappear by magic?" one of the drunker of our companions offered.

I was laughing by then. Things like that are always funny when you look back—when you actually survive your own idiotic ideas. "Magic? Shit, no. I snuck in the place with a significant amount of C-4, set a timer, and ran like hell." I lifted my bottle in a toast. "Here's to my stupidity and high explosives. That's why God made good old C-4."

"Yeah," Rocky said. "But me and the guys had already made our way in and were taking back our cargo, when Nicky comes racing toward us, yelling at us to run."

I held up my hand. "It was not my fault. The good old boys' club conveniently left me out of their recapture-of-merchandise plans. Serves them right. At least I warned them."

The laughter at the telling of that story improved my mood considerably.

When I did sit again, it was with three of the women in the troop. Two of them were friendly, but the third, Helen, was not. Helen, a thick woman, mostly muscle, had a face with wrinkles that had worn into a deep permanent scowl.

"So." Helen spit the word out. "You're one of those witches."

"Those witches? Don't know about that. I'm a witch. Not sure which subspecies I actually belong to."

That got a giggle from the others, but not Helen.

"Blasphemy." Helen muttered the word and the others shifted in their seats, obviously discomfited. She lifted a large, uncomfortable-looking cross from under her shirt. Uh-oh. Zealot with a capital Z. So not what I needed.

I'd met zealots before. They unfortunately come in both sexes and all shapes, sizes, and persuasions. Some are religious and others simply obsessive-compulsive individuals. Basically, they're not live-and-let-live individuals, but they can be ignored. Unless they have enough money to force people to do things their way—or enough faithful followers to force people to do things their way. I doubted that Helen had money or followers, but I wanted no arguments. I did wonder how she managed to reconcile her beliefs with her profession. She enlightened me.

"I fight those beasts from hell that come into this place." Helen rubbed her cross. She held it like she planned to thrust it in my face. "I don't work with them."

"Helen, stop," one of the women said. "You're going to get in trouble."

I stood. I really didn't want to fight with her. "Okay. I'll leave. Actually, I think that the sole purpose of my life as a witch is simply a warning for other witches not to live like I do. I mean you no harm."

I did something incredibly stupid then. Something I would never have done any place else in the world. I turned my back on her. Oh, I heard the scrape of the chair when she stood. I didn't anticipate how fast she was. I whirled to meet her challenge. Too late. She was already on me. My arms went up and a knife sliced straight through one, right above the wrist. Her forward motion slammed me to the floor. She landed on top. Her weight forced the air out of my lungs in a single whoosh.

The woman's weight kept me from instinctively drawing me more in. If I jerked my arm, the knife would slice it apart.

I'd been wounded before. It hurts. Bright, immediate, white-hot. I know the movies make light of it—the hero jumps up and keeps on fighting—but damn. Instinctive self-preservation flared and the magic in me exploded. It blasted her up. She hit the ceiling hard and fast, then crashed onto the dance floor, barely missing the dancers. This time, there was not a hint of fire. An improvement— I think.

She'd held on to the knife when she'd rocketed away. I managed to sit, but not get to my feet. Blood boiled from my arm and quickly dripped from my elbow. Not the gush of an artery, but serious enough. I, in the meantime, offered her a prayer. "Great Mother, please don't let her die. Don't let her die." Rocky lifted me and helped me to a chair. I noticed the obviously unpopular Helen still lying alone and unconscious on the floor. "Darrow?" I screamed. "See about her."

Rocky tied a bandage around my arm, tight. He insisted we go to the emergency room. I didn't argue. In fact, I rode in the ambulance they called for Helen. She had broken both legs and maybe had a concussion. She also cut herself on her own knife when she landed, but that wasn't as bad.

The Mother alone knew what she would say when she woke, or what the hospital people were told. The Mother alone knew why she didn't wake before I was seen to and escaped the white walls and stink of antiseptic. I saw Darrow talking to the doctors. I hadn't seen any police. Maybe he had some official *She's a security guard* excuse.

Rocky drove us back toward the compound.

"What if she starts talking about witches and magic?" I asked.

"She won't. It's in our contracts. No talking outside the Barrows. If she talks while she's drugged, they'll ignore it. When she comes to her senses, she'll remember how much she gets paid and keep her mouth shut. She's been here long enough to know the penalties. She's been on the edge. Darrow thinks . . . well, we've all seen things. He'll take care of it."

While it hurt, her knife had not cut my artery or major veins. I made Rocky stop at a twenty-four-hour discount store and buy me clean jeans and a shirt. Etienne would know what happened—Darrow would have called him—but no way would I return with blood on my clothes. I also had Rocky stop at a fast-food place. I had to fuel up again.

Rocky wanted to go up with me, but I wouldn't let him. I hated myself at that moment. Good old guilt. I'd chosen to go out and have a good time and could have been injured or killed. That's something that probably wouldn't have happened if I'd stayed with Etienne. Flawed logic, but I created a lot of that.

Etienne was on the phone, but he closed it when I entered.

"It wasn't Darrow's fault," I said.

"No. Darrow is too levelheaded to get into a fight."

I wouldn't explain anything to him. The fight wasn't my fault, only the result. "Darrow is also too smart to be running a third world mercenary gang in the middle of the States, too. Maybe you should use some of Aiakós's money to build your own hospital. I'll bet that statue of the Mother is worth enough to start his own country."

He nodded. "That's a good idea."

He was far too calm to suit me.

I plopped down on the couch. "I am not getting in bed with you. I'm not fucking you. I'm not having any more fun until I find Marisol." I crossed my arms over my chest and felt the stupid pout form on my face.

Etienne walked into the bedroom. He returned with a pillow. He tossed the pillow on the couch. "Okay. I'll see you in the morning." He leaned in and kissed me on the forehead, then headed into the bedroom. He closed the door behind him.

I rubbed my hands over my face, closed my eyes, and instantly fell asleep—and instantly fell into a nightmare, a nightmare that really happened. I lost Marisol in the swamp one day. She was seven and we played hide-and-seek. We were supposed to hide in certain parameters around Gran's house where we knew it was safe. I broke the rules and hid in my canoe. I let it drift off in the water, out of bounds.

Marisol rarely broke the rules. She wasn't allowed to use magic to locate me, and she didn't. She wandered away, too far, looking for me. At seven, she already had the confidence and courage to take one of those rare walks on the wild side. When I realized she couldn't find me, I went back . . . and couldn't find her.

The terror I lived through then was just as fresh in my nightmare. I ran, called, screamed, cried for her, searching. When I returned to Gran's house, still hysterical, she was sitting on the front steps. But that wasn't happening in my current nightmare. I ran through the swamp and cried and heard her calling me, her voice growing more distant with each step. My eyes popped open. In spite of my beers, I had no hangover. My arm, though not healed, didn't hurt. Personal disease, birth control, and the ability to avoid the price of overindulgence in alcohol were among the perks of being born a witch.

I still sat on Etienne's couch. I held my breath, hoping to hear her call me one more time. Only silence filled the room. The glowing clock said five a.m. I had to find Marisol. I had to find her today! I knew that as surely as I knew the sun would come up. Time, that capricious bastard, was going to run out.

I wasn't going to be put off any longer. I had to find Marisol and he was hindering me. She was going to die soon. Etienne seemed to want to help, but in fact he distracted me. I'd allowed him to do it. Would he try to stop me? He'd be too late. I quietly walked out the apartment door, down the stairs, and raced for the ruins.

chapter 31

I shivered in the predawn air. My discount store T-shirt from the night before didn't provide much warmth. Summer seemed reluctant to break spring's grip this morning.

It was a good bet that someone watched the buildings and would alert Etienne. I maintained a steady jog. Once I was out of the maze of warehouses and open parking lots and into the more crowded ruins, they'd never find me. As soon as I reached the first building I could slip in and hide, I relieved my overfull bladder. Drip-dry, but I'd done that before.

It seemed that the only way to find the building I needed was to retrace the route Etienne used to get us out, but I'd already done that. It wasn't exactly daylight yet. Herschel fell in beside me, keeping pace. I didn't see where he came from.

"I wish I could figure you out, buddy," I said to him, "but I guess you are what you are." Herschel farted, thereby contaminating the clear morning air. The opening rattle of massive rolling warehouse doors came behind me, then the sound of an engine. Not that it mattered. I was already moving into more crowded buildings and blocked streets. One step, two steps, I could hide in seconds.

I tried not to think about Etienne, but couldn't help it.

He was a sweet lover and I think I satisfied him. The tattoos on his arms, the binding he didn't know had been laid upon him as a child, was another thing entirely. That I had to question. I'd bet they were the very thing that drew that malicious witch Oonagh to him in the first place. Someone in his life must have feared him, feared what power an infant boy might grow into, what menace he might become. Could I remove that binding? Maybe? Did I want to? Not until I knew the nature of that power. What if it was something he couldn't control? A person treated as he had been by a rogue witch would probably never be comfortable using magic. I suspected he would hate knowing it dwelled in him, even if he didn't use it. That situation reeked of disaster. Incompetent witch that I was, I had learned one thing. Some earth magic was best left alone. Witches should never meddle in some aspects of the Mother's world.

I walked on as the sun rose on my left. Warmer, promising a better day, though the sun could not penetrate or illuminate some places in these ruins. I could see why the Mother used them. The ruins were just another wall to protect the Zombie like the barrier she placed around the Barrows to contain Aiakós. The one-way door between worlds obviously touched places filled with nasty, hostile . . . things. I pitied them, those so-called monsters, but I wouldn't let them eat me.

River Street couldn't be that far away. Still, no sound penetrated this place. Only an occasional piece of falling debris broke the silence. Twice I thought I caught a glimpse of something moving in the shadows of a building, but it didn't approach. A vehicle passed a block over. I remained out of sight. I needed to use earth magic. I might draw all sorts of attention, but the need to find my sister grew more urgent by every hour.

I did have something, though. The spell, the clues, the pieces I had gathered as I went to each location on Marisol's map. Those might guide me. Had they remained with me? Some things about me had changed, mostly fire, but . . . I closed my eyes and searched my mind. I found the symbols, the ones Marisol had drawn at each site we visited. I pulled them from memory, one by one.

My teachers had tried to teach me the art of creating magical runes, the supercharged symbols and words that some witches used. I'd made them, but was never able to charge them with magic. They remained dead things, floating in the air, sparkling and buzzing like Fourth of July sparklers, yet totally impotent of any power and meaning. This time, I used Marisol's symbols to create my runes. Then, rather than using regular earth magic, I called upon the fire. They burst into flame.

"Show me," I said.

I opened my eyes. The runes slowly floated around me in a circle. I cast the gentle locator spell, not the power of my previous sending, and sent it out with her name—and every memory I could pull from my heart. As I did, I locked on to the spiral wheel, the last symbol. The circle of runes turned until the wheel moved to the south. I walked toward it. As I did, it moved on. I had to detour a couple of times, but the fiery wheel remained to guide me.

I was lost, without a doubt, but I had a guide. Nothing challenged me, though I did duck into a building once when a vehicle came close. I wondered if anyone but me could see the wheel—or the other flaming symbols that remained in a circle around me.

Marisol remained farther to the south, but closer now. I started to run, then remembered my strength issues and slowed to a fast walk. I had to conserve energy. I had no idea what I would face when I found my sister.

I had my beacon, though, my guide, my source. At last I saw it, directly in front of me, the building with the spiked wheel. A parking garage. I had been by it a couple of times yesterday. The spiked wheel I'd been looking for wasn't visible without magic. The wheel glowed with it. When I'd seen it before, I'd still carried the residual magic of the great burning I'd summoned to defend against the monster crabs. Of course, no one else saw it, either, so no one could guide me. I released the magic leading me. It flared, then faded to nothing.

I counted five stories on the garage. Each level had the open sides required for ventilation. It stood fairly solid given the buildings around it. I didn't hesitate. The wide entrance had been blocked by dense concrete barriers, long straight things that might have divided a highway. I assumed that they had been placed to keep vehicles from entering an unsafe structure.

I glanced down at Herschel, but he had disappeared. I realized I hadn't seen him since I started my spell. Oh, well. Nothing new. I climbed over the barriers. The first level was slightly underground and no light penetrated. I walked slowly on through the cool damp darkness. It hadn't rained since I'd been to the Barrows. If the old drains were clogged, water would stand. I jumped a couple of puddles.

My footsteps, light as they were, made a slight sound. I stopped every twenty feet to listen. Silence. As I went deeper into the solid cavern, I could hear the faint drip of water, nothing more. The concrete path turned up.

On the second level, shaded light returned. There were openings in the walls to allow auto exhaust fumes to escape. Second level, then the third. I turned the corner to the fourth level—and there it was. The truck with the gold and magical artifacts. And it was surrounded with a spell, a formidable spell that felt like no magic I had ever felt before. Magic drawn by the witch Oonagh to protect something she valued. According to Etienne, she'd had possession of an artifact that was no longer on this world and she'd used it here.

I stepped closer. Marisol floated behind the odd, magic shield around the truck, sleeping in a protective bubble of her own spell. Her pretty pink dress fluttered around her as if the spell contained a soft breeze. That spell she'd created had sustained her life for weeks until I could find her. And I couldn't get to her. The vast alien spell surrounding her and the truck stopped me. As powerful as she was, she'd managed to get inside, but couldn't get out. That task would fall to me.

"Interesting, isn't it?"

The voice came from behind me. Etienne.

I turned to him slowly, deliberately forcing all emotion down. I had no weapons on me that would harm him, and yet this might end in violence. "You knew where she was all along, didn't you?"

"No."

He came closer to me and I shifted into a fighting position.

He stopped. "I suspected, Nyx, that's all. I haven't set foot in this building since I parked the truck three years ago. I watched Oonagh use her magic to protect it. It almost killed her. I had to carry her out." His voice carried a neutral tone, low, deep, and matter-of-fact. I'd suddenly become a stranger to him. Maybe I was. He certainly seemed a stranger to me. This man who had held me carefully in his arms, made love to me. The cautious man who had dropped his protection against magic to have me. Or at least to have my body.

I wanted to remain calm, but rising rage threatened to

overwhelm. "And you would have let Marisol die before you told me."

"She seems to have protected herself." Etienne stood beside me now. "I didn't want you to try. See, there by the wall. Another got in and could not escape."

A skeleton lay in the direction he pointed. Rags covered the bare bones. "Can *you* get in?" My voice bristled and I barely controlled the urge to shriek at him, to strike him with my fists. "You're immune to magic. You should be able to pass through."

"Possibly. And I might be trapped like they were. Oonagh caged me once. Should I risk it again? I don't want or need anything that's there. I need no gold and as far as I'm concerned, the things in that truck are protected from the witches and other beasts roaming the Barrows." He shrugged. "They can sit there until this building crumbles around them."

The flame in me stirred, threatened an explosion. "The spell around that truck is powerful. It might hold fifty years, a hundred years. But no spell can hold forever, especially if the spell caster is dead. Marisol doesn't have that much time. She's put everything she had into a spell to suspend her life. When her spell ends, and that will be soon, she'll die."

"I'm sorry, Nyx." His voice carried some sympathy. "I've made mistakes. Mistakes I can't fix. I told you that."

He seemed genuine, but damn it all . . . Great Mother, how confusing. How could he not have told me? How could he save my life and not tell me? He knew. He knew how much she meant to me. He had placed himself in danger going to Abigail's and leading me around the Barrows. But he'd refused to bring me here, to search here. Why? He didn't trust me. He'd never trust a witch.

I pushed that aside. Etienne didn't matter. I had to get

Marisol out. I gently touched the spell around the truck with magic. I felt it shift to protect itself. It was a strange, powerful spell. Only the Earth Mother might have the strength to break it, and I already knew she would not enter the Barrows to do that. Nausea churned in my guts. If I had to watch Marisol die, it would drive me insane. How could I tell Gran?

"I can try to burn it away," I said. I had a problem to resolve here. My emotions would be dealt with later. "That would work with some spells."

Etienne shifted, no longer neutral but distinctly uncomfortable. "No. You don't know enough about it. About what might happen. You said your sister was powerful. She couldn't get out."

"Perhaps we could work together." A voice spoke from behind me.

Laudine. She came walking down the incline leading to the next floor. Her dark hair had turned to silver and wrinkles twisted her face, wrinkles that hadn't existed before I met her. Age that hadn't seemed to touch her before had descended in a day.

"Indeed." That was Aiakós. He came from the other side. He spoke in a voice that sounded so casual, so relaxed. "After all, there is enough there for all of us."

"I agree." The new voice came from behind Laudine. "But then, I don't need gold. I already have too much of it. I can smell it, though. It's delicious." It was Dervick, but not the Dervick I knew. A taller and much stronger version of Dervick came closer. He still had that pretty boyish face, but he now exposed broad shoulders that had been covered in a baggy suit. The suit he wore now fit him perfectly. Confidence moved through him with every step. He had formed an illusion when I first met him, an illusion that fooled even me.

Etienne grabbed my arm, jerked me behind him. He drew his gun.

What? Now he was going to protect me again?

I stepped away. I didn't need or want his protection. He'd deceived me and I wasn't about to forgive. He'd probably turn on me when he realized I'd free Marisol at almost any cost, even giving Aiakós access to a few earth magic trinkets. I'd deal with that problem later.

"Well, hell." I planted my hands on my hips. I faced the deplorable prospect of actually working with them. But work with whom? Not Laudine.

"We're all here. Why don't we have a party and celebrate?" I glared at them, but it was Dervick who interested me most.

Dervick came closer and I stepped back. Etienne sighted his gun.

Dervick chuckled and I heard the crackle of fire in his voice. "Hello, sister. It is good to meet you as myself, not as I pretended to be. I'd send our father's regards, but I doubt if he actually cares." He gave a friendly nod and a smile.

"Sister? Father?" Damn! Why couldn't something like this happen under less critical circumstances?

"You didn't recognize me?" Dervick held out his hand.

Yes, I'd sensed a familiarity with Dervick, but sister . . . ? Curiosity almost overwhelmed me, but I had to remember the task before me. "I don't have time for you now, Dervick. I need to save my sister."

"I'm patient. And by the way, your man's bullets will harm me no more than they will kill the . . . demon. They might take out the witch." He nodded at Laudine, his face thoughtful. "That would clean things up a little."

Aiakós came closer and the air of tension, already

choking, grew heavier. "Now, here is the strange thing," he said. He cocked that beautiful head and the crimson hair shifted like fine silk. His eyes glowed. "Etienne is immune to magic, you say? And he never told me. I'm hurt. That was something he forgot to mention when I questioned him." His smooth voice had the featherlightness of a massive granite boulder.

I didn't speak my thoughts. Aiakós punished him, tortured him, and yet Etienne had managed to keep the secret of his immunity. Etienne had feared witches far more than his demon employer.

"But no matter," Aiakós continued. "We can still come to an agreement." I saw his smile and heard his voice go into the mesmerizing realm of hypnotic control. No one there, especially me, seemed to buy the enchantment. So much for demon powers of persuasion.

I glanced at Laudine. She was smiling.

I'd take time for one thing. One very important thing. "Laudine, I care nothing about gold. Some things are above any wealth or artifact. As soon as I free Marisol, you will pay for killing my friend. I don't care if the Sisters of Justice send three Triads after me. I will demand retribution."

Laudine stopped smiling.

Aiakós snarled. "So, what shall we do? I doubt any of us will walk away. I suggest that since Etienne is immune to magic, he try to get through. It might break the spell."

"I don't think that's a good idea," I said. "We don't know enough about it. If Etienne does go through, that spell could break and destroy us all. Or it could trap him, too."

"And yet, pretty little Marisol and another made it in," Aiakós reminded us. He stepped even closer. His clawed hands clenched into fists. He smiled at Etienne, feral as any creature could be. "I could bodily throw our warrior at it. His bullets won't hurt me. Would that do it?"

Etienne did not react to Aiakós's words.

"No," I said. "No throwing. No one else needs to get hurt." I could use earth magic to toss all of them off the roof, but not simultaneously. And one of them was a witch. She'd know and be able to counter. While I was blocking her, the others would be on me.

Aiakós cocked his head. "Well, Etienne, it seems this little witch has charmed you. She's worried about hurting you. At least she's better-looking than the hag who owned you before."

Etienne's solemn face softened as he smiled, but it was not really a happy smile. Mostly it was sad. Here was a face I had not seen. "Oh, yes, she's charmed me. I'm hoping she'll someday forgive me."

I turned to him. Much had passed between us. I didn't understand it, but some of it had been good. Much as I loved Marisol, much as his betrayal hurt me, I would not ask him to risk his life for her or me. I'd try myself first. "There has to be another way."

"There is none!" Laudine screamed. "You think I haven't tried." She pointed at the truck. "Those bones are my daughter's. I watched her die. She starved. If your grandmother had come when I asked, there might have been a chance. Instead she sent an incompetent little bitch . . ." She broke off in a sob.

By the condition of her body, Laudine's daughter was dead long before she sent that letter to Gran. And Laudine apparently knew where Marisol was all along. Had she sent her into that spell as she sent her daughter? I hadn't even suspected that. I should have. The ideal was that all witches were a family in tune with the Earth Mother's wishes. I'd seen the politics too many times.

Most spells are not visible to the eye without witch sight. I saw the one around the truck as a kind of smooth transparent bubble. I walked closer. I'd made the determination to try to break it.

Etienne approached. He'd holstered his gun and relaxed like a man who had made a decision. This was the man who had held me, made love to me. His eyes carried the gentleness I'd so cherished. He laid his hands on my shoulders and gave me a soft kiss. My lips tingled under his and in spite of the location and danger, I responded. He released me. "So, little witch, can you protect me from the vultures while I try to get in?" He nodded at Aiakós and the others.

"You don't have to risk it." I meant that. "I can try other things first."

My warrior. My totally confusing man. *"Men are supposed to be confusing,"* Gran had once told me. *"If they weren't, we could all live in perfect harmony. That would be so boring."*

While I would try almost anything to save Marisol, I'd never intended to harm anyone else in the process. She wouldn't have wanted that.

Etienne gave me a long, searching look. "No, I don't have to risk it." His eyes softened even more. So did his voice. "I can't say . . ."

He couldn't say. I could have found a million words right then. I could ask him why he wanted to risk his life for me. I could ask if he loved me, if he wanted me to stay with him. But a man, a man like Etienne given to great times of silence, would not so easily express some things. At least not in a semipublic situation. He stood there, offering to take a deadly gamble. That offering meant as much as any word in any language. But in the back of my mind the thought remained, if he had just told me, brought me here, it might have been different, too.

I stepped away from him to face those who might offer harm. "I can protect you from Aiakós and Laudine. I don't know about Dervick. He's not what he seems to be."

Dervick chuckled. Again I heard the flames. "I want nothing that is here in this building, little sister. Play your game. I'll observe. I've been bored for a very long time." As if to emphasize his neutrality, he stepped back.

Etienne drew a deep breath. And as easily as a hot knife passing through ice cream, he stepped through the alien spell. It shimmered for a moment. Then shattered. Not explosively, but in tiny fragments that puffed like mist in a breeze. Only Laudine and I could feel that dissolution. The event, gentle as it seemed, was not without consequences. Magic from another world had suddenly been freed and collided with earth magic that rushed in. The spell caster was not here to collect and control it.

The building shuddered. The cement under our feet shook like an earthquake struck, like some giant malicious hand tore at it. Hairline cracks appeared in the floor and inched their way up the walls.

Etienne hadn't stopped. He hurried to Marisol. Protection spells are usually feeble, requiring little power. When he touched it, it dissipated and she dropped, still unconscious, into his arms. He whirled and shouted two words. *"Bomb. Run!"*

He raced for the exit. I didn't hesitate. I charged after him. I did glance back once before we made a turn. Laudine hadn't run. She'd gone to the bones of her daughter and knelt beside them. I didn't see Dervick or Aiakós.

Etienne set a good pace. No wasted motion. And we

were running downhill. Had he not been hampered by Marisol in his arms, he might already be outside and away from this death trap. We reached the third level and kept on going. The building shuddered and the sound of concrete cracking came loud and close.

Second level. More cracking noises and the floor dropped a couple of inches. We entered the first level and ran into the darkness.

Etienne slowed. He couldn't see.

"Keep going," I shouted. "It's clear."

He picked up his pace. Running blind, trusting my words.

The building had shuddered when the spell broke. Now it actually shook and thundered. In my mind I saw it collapsing down, one floor at a time. Five, four, three ... The bright light of the opening appeared ahead, seeming so close and yet so far. The floor shifted and Etienne stumbled. He recovered and raced on.

The ceiling groaned. It swayed, bulging down. Tons of concrete cracked and steel folded—and it all fell down.

chapter 32

Etienne dropped to his knees. I ran into him and landed on my butt. In a desperate reaction I drew upon the magic and built a shield over and around us. It could not hold. And yet it did. By luck or the grace of the Great Master of the Universe, a concrete column caught on a slab of pavement above, creating a pocket of space the size of a small car directly over us. All I had to do was keep our minuscule cavern from filling with dust and smaller chunks as the structure came down.

The structure still roared, popped, and snapped like a giant stone beast on a rampage. Every time I thought it might settle, another barrage of thundering sound pounded my frail bubble. The bedlam continued, one volley after another, like cannonballs lobbed at the great stone walls of a medieval castle. Finally, the hideous, bone-jarring reverberation of falling rock eased to an intermittent grumble.

As a witch, I'm given to some mysticism. Luck or fate had created the tiny space that helped save our lives—for the moment. There might be many little holes such as this in the dense pile of rubble, but this was ours. Our little piece of hell at the bottom of a five-story building.

"Nyx?" Etienne shouted over the din of the still-shaking building.

He couldn't see, of course. No light penetrated our grim prison.

"I'm here." I touched his shoulder. "Are you hurt? Marisol?"

He still held her clutched to his chest, face against him. His breath came in ragged gasps. He had some cuts, but I would be no better. The first desperate inclination was to seek a way out. That gave way to rising terror when the floor shifted under us. We might yet be crushed. I might hold it at bay a while, but eventually my strength would give out.

I give Etienne credit. He hadn't given in to panic.

"Are you . . ." He stopped and drew deep breaths.

"Am I holding the building up? No. I'm keeping our tomb from filling up with dust and small rocks." Remembering that he couldn't see, I set a small spell, a tiny flicker of flame on the wall.

He stared around the small space. "Damn!"

"Yeah, we're kind of screwed." I agreed with his assessment. He shifted Marisol to a more comfortable position for both of them. I grabbed at her, feeling her warmth, laying my head against her chest. Her heart gave a trembling beat. She'd slowed it while in her trance. She drew a single breath. Alive. Thank the Mother.

She might not be much longer. The building still made ominous noise around us, groaning and snapping, threatening more destruction.

"Can we get out?" Etienne asked.

"I don't know."

"There you go again with the *don't know*s. What kind of witch are you?"

"One who would have warned people of a bomb before it blew up in her face. Shouting *everybody run* isn't a very good way to broadcast urgent, critical notifications."

It helped to bitch, in spite of our precarious position. We were alive, albeit trapped under a collapsed multistory building with little hope of rescue.

"Darrow will come eventually, looking for us," Etienne said. "But not because a building came down. That happens every day in the ruins. And I doubt he could find us."

"Maybe Marisol will wake up. She can talk to other witches across the magic. I can't. Maybe she could contact Abigail." I offered that small bit of optimism. Maybe if the Earth Mother saw what happened, she'd send someone, anyone, who would rescue us. More likely she'd leave survival up to me. If she actually had a plan, I'd say it was to get rid of those dangerous artifacts. Bitch. Anger at her was better than claustrophobia and pure hysteria.

Marisol remained unconscious in Etienne's arms while the building still groaned and snapped like a living being in its ultimate death throes. Would it never be still?

He stared at my tiny flame that kept complete darkness away. "Does that take much . . . magic?"

"Just a tiny bit."

I laid my hand on Marisol's cheek. I wanted to try to wake her. I didn't dare. I had to concentrate on keeping us alive. The sound of destruction continued to echo around us. Not as loud, not with the thunder of minutes ago, but the building remained unstable. A single chunk of concrete dropped and cracked on the floor. It shattered in multiple pieces so fast I didn't have time to protect us. One chunk hit me on the leg. It hurt, but worse was the feeling that my shield wasn't holding and our little sanctuary would fill with debris. I usually have more control, but truthfully, I was scared. Stunned and scared.

"I have to think about this." I closed my eyes.

"Take your time, witch. We have some of that." He drew a breath, held it, then released in a sigh. "I'm sorry, Nyx. None of this is your fault. Or your sisters'."

I didn't know what to say, so I concentrated on the immediate problem. What could I do? Could I lift an entire building? I didn't know. It never occurred to me to try. I'd tested my telekinesis ability with things like automobiles. I'd even shoved a big troop truck chasing us off the road once. The problem here involved the incredible number of pieces. I could lift the concrete column protecting us, but if I lifted only that, the rest might come crashing down.

The building groaned and shifted again. Another few inches and the column we'd taken refuge under might come down. Cement dust filled the air and particles shone in the small flame I'd created to give him the comfort of light.

More stuff rained down. Pebbles, dust, I should have been able to hold that. I knew it was useless, but I tried to reinforce my protection. I simply didn't have enough power to save us. If it was something I could burn . . . but I couldn't. The fire that came so easily to me was not an option. In order to survive, I needed to take some drastic action. I had an idea. It might not work.

Etienne shifted Marisol again and brushed a bit of dust from her face. "She doesn't look like you."

"She looks like our mother. We have different fathers. Etienne? You want to live?"

"It would be nice."

"There's a price for everything. Are you willing to pay?"

"Don't play games, Nyx. I tired of those long ago." His voice rasped and he coughed at the dust. "I'm well aware of who the guilty one is here. I'll say it. Abigail warned me that night we went to her house. She said you were straightforward and honest. That I could trust you. I refused to accept that. If I had . . ."

If he had accepted me, trusted me, he would have told me, brought me here. My gift from the Earth Mother. A sacrifice would be made to get us out of here. There was no indecisiveness in me on my plan.

I moved closer and laid both hands on his cheeks. We had formed a subtle and intimate relationship, one that bordered on love but could not climb over the wall of mistrust.

"Etienne, you and I are each going to make a sacrifice. You will probably hate me forever if we survive. If I release a beast you will have to live with."

"Beast?" He frowned. His eyes widened and his jaw locked tight. "What are you up to now? I won't be able to rescue you this time if you screw up."

I kissed him slowly and sweetly on the mouth, a mouth dry as our tomb. Then I moved Marisol out of his arms and onto the floor. I could feel his reluctance as he released her. She'd been a shield of sorts, I suppose. Etienne frowned. Suspicion formed in his eyes. This time, he had good reason for that mistrust.

I slid my hands down to his forearms and onto the tattoos. They moved under my fingers like writhing snakes, guarding their nest. I needed power and he held the key to a resource I didn't quite understand and might not be able to control. I had no idea what form of earth magic I would be releasing into the world. And I was going to do it without his consent. Perhaps even the Mother herself would not forgive me. Or she would send the Sisters to destroy both of us. I would die for breaking the rules and he for being too dangerous to live with a power he had not been trained to rule.

I gathered all my remaining strength into a protection ball surrounding the three of us. Then I did the thing he feared most. I took control of him. I held his mind and body tight.

Oh, he fought. Wild, insane. The terror of that control, of me, grew until it broke my heart. He couldn't escape. I focused my attention on the dark bindings locked upon him as a child. One by one, I tore them off. I met no resistance. Whatever power resided in him wanted to be free. It pushed furiously against its magical cage. Whoever bound it hadn't done a good job, or had perhaps planned to return later to remove and use it. I had to hold his great magic, keep it tight until I was ready.

I removed the one last binding. Etienne was gasping, struggled desperately to break free of my control. I held him still. His magic was earth magic, no doubt. But it moved in ways I didn't understand. It also moved at my command. When it met my own . . . Great Mother. They matched. Not the same, male and female, but it swirled together and . . . I could move the world. The fire remained in me, but it stood apart. Why? I had no idea.

He'd stopped struggling and stared at me. I had some idea of what he felt. Something was happening to him, changing him. I remember what it was like the first time the magic quickened in me. But I had my loving grandmother to explain.

"Okay, buddy, here we go. I'd say I'd be gentle with you, but we don't have time."

Using his seemingly endless magic, I did two things. I built a better shield around us. It hurt. This earth magic went far deeper than mine. It brushed across things I didn't understand. Even unconscious, Marisol felt it. She moaned.

Witches use circles and spells for protection. They do

it to keep too much magic from burning their souls away. I had none of that. I stood helpless, preparing to use something I did not understand.

I formed the rest of the magic into a giant fist, one that lay heavy in my gut. It seared my mind, my will, with its power. With everything I had in me, I gave the ceiling a massive sucker punch of earth magic.

Once, in Africa, we came under heavy fire from some regular army troops. A misunderstanding, but deadly all the same. An artillery round landed so close . . . the noise, sheer intensity of the blast . . . it was nothing compared to this. The shield protected us from the blast itself, but it was like being inside a bomb. A big bomb, bigger than the one that had dropped a building on us. A big bomb that again hammered us with the sound of tons of concrete being blasted into the sky. Immense pressure made my ears pop.

Marisol jerked. Her eyes blinked open. I tightened our shield. Some of the wreckage I'd punched out did fall back in, but it was minimal. To my amazement, a large swath of blue sky appeared above us. We sat in a twenty-foot-deep hole, but we would be able to climb out. If we could climb. My shield dissipated. I had nothing left in me to hold it. I'd need days of rest and a massive amount of food to recover. I plopped to the floor.

Marisol struggled and reached for me. She grabbed my hand. She didn't speak. Etienne sat staring at his arms. The tattoos were gone. He looked to me, complete confusion in his eyes. I wanted out, but had to explain.

I struggled to sit. I reached out to take his hand. "I know you don't understand. I don't know how to tell you to deal with it. Maybe Abigail can. Those tattoos on your arms were a ward, a binding. You're a warlock. The male version of a witch. Someone recognized your power as a child and decided to keep you away from it. I removed the wards and used your power and mine to free us."

He jerked his hands away. He would not bear my touch. He stared at his arms. Did he hear what I said?

"I feel . . . ," he whispered. "You . . ."

"You probably feel a lot of things. I don't know what they might be. I know how much you hate magic, but if you'd been trained as you should have been, Oonagh would never have taken you down. Whoever put those tattoos on you put you in a cage far greater than the one she built for you."

He backed farther away, shaking his head. Denial was taking hold.

"Let's get out of here," I said. "There's a lot of loose concrete around us. We can talk later."

A huge gob of slobber plopped on my head.

"Herschel?"

More trash tumbled down. Nothing big, it wasn't comfortable. In my face this time, since I was staring up. As I finished spitting out cement, I looked up again. Herschel stood on the rim of the crater my blast had created.

Marisol clung to me, but she hadn't spoken.

Twenty feet is a long way to climb on unstable rubble. Weakened, I could barely walk. Etienne had recovered enough to help me with Marisol. Surprising since I'd drawn a massive amount of magic from him.

We finally struggled to the top. We were on top of a massive pile of steel and concrete that a person would never guess was a parking garage unless they'd seen it before. I stared back into the hole that could have been our tomb. I searched the area for the wreckage of the truck with the gold and artifacts, praying I wouldn't find it. Praying the blast completely destroyed it. I didn't see anything but more concrete.

"You did all this? The hole?" Etienne stared down. He slid an arm around Marisol when she swayed.

"We did that, Etienne. You and I."

"No!" He spoke the word through clenched teeth.

More rock shifted. We had to get down.

The climb down was worse than climbing out of the hole. Every treacherous step we made threatened more disaster. Dust and more dust billowed and swirled in the breeze. The building rubble moved and shook as if some great creature was under it and trying to dig out after us. The small caverns like the one that had saved us were still collapsing. We were almost there when a large chunk gave way under my foot and I fell. I went crashing across four feet of rubble. I landed on my back, staring up at the sky. At least I hadn't hit my head again.

Then the pain hit. I screamed in surprise. Pain, throbbed with every heartbeat. It knifed through me. My shoulder. I couldn't move my arm. Herschel appeared over me. He breathed in my face. His breath wasn't foul, but warm and comfortable. Fire, my friend. It was temperate and it soothed. The pain didn't go away, but it dulled.

Then Etienne was there, standing over me. He was not careful. He gripped me under the arms and dragged me away across street and sidewalk. I howled the entire way. The ground rumbled again. I lay there on my back, gasping and fighting pain.

"Other buildings are collapsing around us," Etienne said. He felt of me. He was, at least, gentle this time. "Damn, witch, you really did it this time."

Okay, he wanted to reject his part of it and play his *blame the witch* game. Fine. He had to deal the best he could. "I did it? Who planted the explosives? Witch, witch, witch. Pot calling the kettle, buddy."

Marisol hovered over me. She looked years older. Her eyes drooped and her skin sagged. Her spell to keep her alive worked, but it had taken too much of her.

"How did you know?" I choked out the words. "That I would come for you. You left spells."

"I didn't actually know." Marisol's voice rasped. There was none of the musical tone I knew. "The whole situation seemed so dangerous I felt it was prudent to take precautions. I did know that if I was in trouble, if anything happened to me, you were the one Gran would send to help me. You, big sister, were the one who would care the most. The one who could express her caring by kicking ass when necessary."

I closed my eyes.

As I had been taught, as I believed, I thanked the Great Master of the Universe for my life and the Earth Mother for her guidance through the world of her magic. Then I prayed for the pain to ease.

chapter 33

I'd like to think that most everything in life and the world was at least marginally planned by someone. That would speak to some sort of order in a chaotic universe. Foolish of me, I know. Oh, there was planning, but results were not guaranteed to turn out the way the planner intended. And sometimes it came down to simple luck. Good luck and bad luck that I had tripped over my own feet so close to safety.

"Help me sit up," I said.

"No. You're hurt." Marisol laid a cool hand on my forehead. "You have a broken collarbone, shoulder, and some ribs, too, I think. Lie still."

Something was building in me. The knowledge that it wasn't over. The catastrophe begun when I found the truck was still in progress, still happening. "Help me sit up. I have to see."

I struggled. Marisol gave a great sigh, but she helped me. Through sheets of pain, she managed to get me in a sitting position against a building wall. Bone ground against bone in my shoulder. I opened my mouth to scream again, but dust filled my throat and I choked. Would the damned stuff never settle? Why couldn't we have a simple breeze? Finally, she had me sitting against a wall. I gasped for breath, trying not to pass out from the pain.

"I'm too weak to use the magic now, Nyx. Please forgive me. I can't ease your pain."

Herschel came to me and gave me a great wet kiss. I didn't object. I loved the big slob—or at least I would until he had gas again.

Etienne had returned. He carried a first aid kit. He probably had the SUV parked nearby. Hope nothing fell on it.

"Darrow is coming," he said. He made a sling to support my arm so the collarbone wouldn't grind so much. His face was tight, maybe with his own pain or maybe with sympathy for me. He also brought bottles of water. Marisol held mine so I could drink.

"How do you feel?" I asked.

Etienne stared at me. No anger, no fear, simply neutral as always. "Like I have a big worm crawling in my belly, through my veins."

"I'm sorry, Etienne. I had to. To get us out. And I had to hold you still while I did. I know I did the same thing she did. Abigail can teach you, though. Show you how to protect yourself from me, from the whole world." I reached for him.

He leaned away, avoiding my touch.

"Okay. You won't ever forgive me, but we're all alive. We survived. Think about it when you have time."

He looked over at the building rubble.

"What the hell was in that truck?" I asked. "Besides that loot."

"Stuff that makes a big boom. I'm surprised that it was still viable. It's been there since I parked the truck. I wanted to be sure Oonagh never got to use that gold. I set it to go off if she moved the truck."

"What if you were with her when she did?"

"Then it would happen."

I saw him coming. I was right. Our big climax wasn't over.

Aiakós marched toward us. And he was pissed. I knew because of the snarl on his face, his red glowing eyes, and the extended claws on his fingers. His clothes were torn, but otherwise he appeared unharmed.

He stopped and stared down. "Etienne and I will now discuss his forgetting to inform me of the truck's location before I spent years searching for it. And this immunity to magic . . ." He reached out and grabbed Etienne by the upper arms and hoisted him off his feet. The claws tore through flesh. Blood streamed down and dripped off his elbows. Etienne struggled but didn't make a sound. I reached beyond pain for the magic. It slipped away from me.

Aiakós released one arm, but still held Etienne dangling. He held the up-clawed, blood-smeared hand. "I am going to tear your face off. I'll leave your tongue so I can hear you scream."

"No, you are not." The surprising voice interrupted his act of violence.

I had to turn to look toward the sound. That sent another round of pain coursing through my body. No matter. It was worth it.

Sisters of Justice, three of them, the same three who had captured me and brought me back to the Georgia swamp, stood fifteen feet from us. And they were ready to rumble. One carried a fierce automatic rifle and one carried a sword. The third had an old-fashioned double-edged battle-ax she kept shifting from one hand to the other. "Now look what we have here," the one with the gun said. "A Drow. It's been ten years since I've had one to kill."

"Longer than that," the one with the sword said.

I had no idea what a Drow was. I didn't care. The Sisters served the Mother and they didn't like Aiakós. That was okay by me.

Aiakós, suddenly realizing that he had a real threat on his hands, dropped Etienne. Etienne collapsed beside me, struggling but still silent. His face twisted in pain.

Aiakós glared at the trio, the Triad, obviously assessing his chances. I didn't know about his actual strength, though I presumed it was formidable. I'd say the odds were even. He'd go down, but he'd take them with him.

"The Barrows is mine," he snarled.

"Maybe," the one with the gun said. "But we claim the witches. They're ours. Always have been. And the man. We'll take him, too. I'm not particularly interested in him, but I have instructions."

Aiakós relaxed a fraction. "Instructions? And do those instructions include killing me?"

Obviously he knew the Sisters took orders from the Earth Mother. He had to be uncertain. Had she withdrawn her protection of him?

"Killing is an option," the Sister said. "I certainly prefer that one. But only if you don't behave. Go back to your pretty palace, Drow. This day is not yours. Here in this place *you* serve the Mother, too. Whether you accept it or not."

Aiakós glared at them, then down at me, Etienne, and Marisol. I did hear the sound of approaching vehicles. He'd soon be vastly outnumbered.

"This isn't finished." Aiakós turned sharply and walked away.

The Sister with the gun approached. "Now, *that* was truly disappointing. I had hoped . . . No one likes a good fight anymore."

She gave a great sigh and turned her attention to Etienne. "You have certain items that belong to us, man. Will you surrender them, willingly?"

Etienne had managed to sit up. Blood seeped from holes punched by Aiakós's claws, but it didn't seem critical.

The Sisters referred to the Solaire and Morié, of course. The Morié was in his sheath and the Solaire remained around his neck. Why didn't they have him screaming in pain the minute I released his magic? I hadn't thought of that. Did they only work on women? That was possible since there were so few men who could use earth magic.

Etienne was smart enough to know he'd never win with them. He slowly drew the Morié blade from the sheath at his side and tossed it toward the Sisters. A very short toss, since he was bleeding from punctures in his arms. He removed the Solaire and tossed it to the blade. That cost him more, since he had to lift his arms.

The Sister picked them up and stared at them. "These things are more trouble than they're worth." She grinned at me. "Unnecessary, dangerous trinkets. You witches aren't as tough as you think you are. But that's just my opinion."

The trio left us there, but they didn't go far. They stood in the shadow of a building and then left when the shouts of Etienne's men came close. I presume to make sure Aiakós didn't return.

Next thing I knew, Darrow was beside me. He looked at me a long time, then at the parking garage. "Did you do that?"

"Not me, buddy. I already learned my lesson. Setting

off explosives while still inside a building makes bad juju."

Etienne was on his feet now. Rocky held him steady when he swayed.

Darrow held me by the waist and lifted me, but I couldn't stand. "Bring a stretcher," he shouted. I felt really light-headed, which was a good thing. The pain wasn't so bad like that. I wasn't totally there when they lifted me onto a stretcher. I did see Rocky with Marisol in his arms. About that time I remembered Herschel. I shouted his name, only it came out more of a squeak. A single bark answered. Since I was already lying on my back, I looked up to see him on a ten-foot pile of rubble. He barked again.

"He can't get down." I don't know why I said that. I heard Darrow tell someone to go help the dog. They didn't need to. Herschel could go anywhere he wanted when he wanted. He must have been bored and wanted to play.

"Take them to Abigail," Etienne said. Going to Abigail sounded like a good idea. A lot better than going to the hospital like I did last time. Besides, I wanted to deliver a blistering, obscene message to the Earth Mother and that seemed a good way. *Make Etienne trust you. Your gift.* Gift my ass. It was all a game. A game played by a goddess with less compassion than a rat crawling through the Barrows' ruins. She might not be omniscient, but she could try to have a little more empathy.

They strapped me down to the stretcher, put me in the back of a van. Rocky sat beside me with Marisol still in his arms. His expression was one of great curiosity. "Oh, I bet little Nicky has a story to tell. When you get back, I want to hear it. Every word. Especially since you selfishly refused to share the action with us."

I sighed. Yes, I would have a tale to tell.

When they hauled us into Abigail's house, Abigail simply shook her head when she saw me. "You're as bad as Cassandra," she said.

"Sorry, it went boom before I could get away," I apologized. "Take care of Marisol first."

"I'm okay," Marisol said. "Just tired. Not injured." I couldn't see her, but her voice was still strained.

Abigail opened her cabinet, picked out a small bottle. She popped a cork from it, waved it under my nose, and said, "Breathe deep."

"Wait. Abigail, you have to go see Etienne."

"Is he hurt?"

"No. Yes, some. The building collapsed on us. I had to remove the bindings on him, take and use his magic with mine to get us out. I had to hold him still. I had to control and direct the power."

Abigail's eyes widened and the shock spread across her face. "And that worked? *You?* You removed those bindings? I couldn't do that. They were too powerful. You were able to use both your magics? Male, female, together?"

"Yeah. But now he's pissed. Don't blame him. Now he's got this stuff inside of him and he doesn't understand."

Abigail shook her head. The expression on her face said I'd probably rendered her speechless.

I breathed in and the world faded away. When I opened my eyes again, the pain was gone and Marisol was sitting in a chair beside me.

chapter 34

"About time," Marisol said.

I hadn't seen her in ten years, but she'd recovered from her ordeal and seemed young and pretty as ever. Powerful witches live a long time and she hadn't aged a day. She wore a white knit top and a flowered skirt, the kind of feminine outfit she had always favored. I was, of course, the jeans-wearing rogue of the family. She had her dark hair drawn back and clipped at the nape of her neck.

I stretched. "Were you hurt?"

"A few nicks and bruises. Mostly just tired. Depleted. I didn't need healing like you did. I'm told you've been accident-prone lately."

"I guess." I chuckled. "I've been hurt more since I came here to the Barrows than I have in the last ten years. Even in an African war zone."

"Oh, yes. I want to hear about all your adventures, foreign and domestic. Your friends Darrow and Rocky have come to check on you every day. They've been keeping me amused with their own versions of some pretty tall tales."

"I'll bet." I tried to rise. I fell back. Marisol stepped in to help me.

When I could finally sit straight, I asked, "Has Etienne . . . no, I guess he hasn't."

"Abigail told me his story, how he was once trapped by a witch. I went and talked to him. I tried to explain that we children of the Earth Mother do what we can to survive her . . . plans, schemes, whatever. He was very cold. But polite. Abigail went, too, later. She told me what you did with him and magic. That is unbelievable."

"Marisol, I had to. It was the worst thing I could do in his eyes, control him like that, but otherwise we'd be dead. And to show him the magic, the magic he never knew about. Now he has to live with it." In spite of all he'd done, Etienne had withheld some important information, information that put lives in danger, including his. I couldn't say it was *all* my fault.

"You've changed his life forever, Nyx. He will come to understand, I think. Nevertheless, I'm happy to be alive. When I found myself trapped with dwindling power, I had to make a decision. Did I use it to fight or wait to be rescued? I'm glad I waited."

"I doubt that Laudine made it out of the garage," I said. "I saw. She didn't run."

Abigail came to stand in the doorway. "I've been informed that Laudine has rejoined the Mother. I wish her well in another life."

"So do I," Marisol spoke, and I heard genuine sympathy in her voice.

"Not me." I felt sick. "She burned two men to death striking out at me. One was a close friend. I won't forgive that easily."

Marisol nodded. "I understand. She was . . . unbalanced. I felt her sorrow, her guilt. It was she who sent her daughter to find that truck, and the daughter was trapped. Laudine couldn't help her. Couldn't free her."

I shook my head. "But she refused to go to the High Witch. To seek help elsewhere when she didn't have enough power. I'm sure she thought herself noble, believing that Abigail would give the contents of the truck to Aiakós, but to let her daughter die . . . ?" I sighed. I truly didn't understand that. "And then, Marisol, to compound her error, Laudine sent you into the same trap. And she would have sent Gran, had Gran not summoned me."

Marisol grabbed my hand. "My getting trapped was not Laudine's fault. It was my vanity. I accept responsibility for my own stupidity and will not put it on her."

It irritated me that Marisol could be so compassionate. I suppose it gave her a maturity I would never have. I threw back the covers and stretched again. "Which doesn't explain, my little witch sister, *how* you actually managed to get trapped. I'm the one who usually ends up in trouble."

Marisol's pale skin flushed, most likely with embarrassment. "I was careless. Curiosity caught me. I saw that strange magic, not earth magic, and got a little too close. It kind of sucked me in. I wanted to see what was in the truck, but I decided to save my strength and set my protection spell while I prayed to the Mother for you to find me."

I nodded. "If you had explored inside, that thing might have blown right then." I looked at Abigail. "The artifacts in that truck were powerful. I'm pretty sure they're gold dust circling in the atmosphere right now, along with everything else. Is the Mother angry?"

"I doubt it," Abigail said. "She can always make more if she needs them. Besides, they're too dangerous. Etienne told me of them and gave me the list. The fact that Oonagh was able to collect so many of them is proof of the danger." She smiled. "Get out of bed. You need to eat now."

My stomach growled. "Food would be good."

Marisol handed me jeans and a shirt. Darrow must have brought them from the compound. The Dragon's Tears had apparently remained on my arm while Abigail performed her healing. I tried again to slip it off, but it remained stuck like I smeared it with super adhesive. When I touched it with my fingers, though, I could still hear the fire.

Abigail fed me until my stomach filled to inhuman capacity. When I finished, I had questions for the High Witch. "You seemed surprised that I could remove Etienne's bindings and use his magic. Why?"

Abigail set a cake on the table and carefully cut slices. Her placid face scrunched into a worried frown. "I'm a bit perturbed. At my age, and it is considerable, I occasionally feel as if someone is changing all the rules. Male magic, female magic, both are earth magic, but they are far different. They are not opposed, but do not mix. I get no answers from the Mother on the matter."

She placed a saucer with a significant slice of chocolate cake in front of me. Mention of the Mother pissed me off so much I almost pushed it away. Almost. I picked up my fork. "I have issues with her, too. You think I'll get any answers if I ask?"

"I don't know," Abigail said. "I do have some thoughts that might explain you, Etienne, and magic. The Mother's plans, her . . . and yes, I will say it . . . her schemes are incredibly complex. Time, to her, is not the issue it is with mortals. Life and death are often the same to her. I asked Marisol to do some research for me yesterday."

Marisol grinned. I shoveled in another mouthful of chocolate. I might need seconds on dessert to get through this.

"It wasn't easy, but I did talk to your friend Karen in

San Francisco. She called your cell phone. She's wonderful. She helped with the research. You and Etienne were born on the same day and same time, right to the minute. Years apart, but when Abigail studied the moon, the alignment of the constellations, they were exactly the same."

Abigail and Marisol fell silent, waiting for my reaction, which was essentially . . .

"Bullshit. You're saying that Etienne and I were born to be together?" I laughed. It was as if a carnival fortune-teller had read my palm. Outrageous, preposterous, absurd, and get me a thesaurus so I could find more words.

They waited out my laughter. "Okay, you know what? I'm going to walk away from that one. Just forget why anything happens with Etienne, me, and magic. And I'm not even going to waste any more time or energy on being angry with the Mother for her schemes and plans."

Marisol frowned. "Don't you care?"

"No."

Abigail sighed. "I think you've made a very wise decision, Nyx. Knowing the details of something just complicates life."

"Good." I grinned hopefully at her. "Could I have more cake?"

Marisol, always the curious one about all things magic, grumbled. I'd bet she wouldn't stop digging into things. I didn't care.

"Go out back into the garden," Abigail said after I finished my chocolate binge. "Since you are going to put aside your negative feelings, you'll find there is much healing magic there. Help you regain your strength."

Abigail's garden was a bit of acreage with the diversity of an old-growth virgin forest. Once Marisol and I were under the cool shade of the trees, magic filled me like thirsty ground soaked up the rain. We followed a path and it led us to the river. Sitting on rocks, we sat and watched the water flow. It ran slow here, deep and dark.

"I met Chalice," I said. Since I was sure it was an accident. I didn't say the water dragon almost killed me.

"Isn't she lovely? She told me what happened with the case containing my Grimoire. She is very sorry you were injured. She's gone now. She went to join Penrod. I hope the Mother protects her on her journey."

"Penrod might be happy to see her."

Marisol laughed. "Maybe. He's been a bachelor for a long time."

My stomach cramped, but I'm sure it was the vast amount of food and not the picture of baby water dragons swimming in the swamp that formed in my mind.

"What are you going to do now?" Marisol asked.

"I don't know." I thought about Dervick calling me sister. "Marisol, you know your father. Do you know about mine? Did Gran ever tell you? Would she tell me if I asked her?"

Marisol grasped my hand like we were kids again. "No, not exactly. I did ask her once why you had to leave us. I missed you so much. The only thing Gran said was that you had a very different heritage. She said your wilder half, your birthright, would always call you."

"I'm surprised she said that."

"She was almost asleep. Otherwise, I believe she wouldn't have said anything at all." She shifted on her rock, trying to find a more comfortable spot if one existed. "What about Etienne? Are you in love with him?"

"I don't know. He kept telling me how untrustworthy

witches were, how we were all evil. Then he went out of his way to protect me a couple of times. He took a hell of a chance when he walked through the ward to get you. But he knew where you were, where that truck was, all the time. He didn't tell me. But when we made love, he seemed so different. Now I seem to have validated my untrustworthiness by doing what I did."

"So, the answer is yes, you are in love." Marisol sounded so smug.

"The Earth Mother told me—"

Her eyes popped open. "The Mother spoke to you? You talked to ... her? I never ..."

I had to laugh at her dismay. "Well, you're probably doing everything right. You haven't screwed up like I have. There was no need for her to speak. At least you did everything right until you got caught in that spell. Hang around long enough, screw up enough, and she might come and lecture you. All I got from her was cryptic words that confused more than they helped."

"Really? I hope so. I plan to stay here for a while. Abigail asked if she could mentor me. How great is that? Having the High Witch for a mentor. And there is Aiakós."

My absolute horror must have shown on my face.

"He's dangerous, I know. But, Nyx, what would someone who had been to other worlds be able to teach me?"

Her interest in Aiakós terrified me to the depths of my heart. "Marisol, stay away from him. The Barrows interests me, too, but I've seen an evil side you haven't. Part of me wants to stay here, too. Wants Etienne. I really wanted him to be a good guy—or at least an acceptable one."

"Then go see him. I understand. He had a choice in his actions. You did not. Let go of your anger. Forgive him. Or at least talk to him. What's done is done. And don't worry about Gran. I got in touch with her. She's on her way here."

"What? She'd leaving the swamp? She's lived there a hundred years."

"She's old, not senile. When she learned more about the Barrows, she wanted to see for herself."

I frowned and shook my head. "When I left her, she was talking about dying."

Marisol laughed. "You just don't know. She's been talking like that for the last ten years."

"One thing, little sister, those messages. The guide spells you left me were spectacular witchcraft. Subtle, not ham-fisted like I would do."

"Would you believe Laudine taught me those spells?" She smiled at my obvious surprise. "She wasn't a powerful witch, ever, but she did a great service to many in this city. Her small spells, her healing potions, relieved much suffering. Abigail is trying to find someone to replace her. Someone willing to live outside the Barrows." Marisol stared straight into my eyes so long I thought she might be trying to spell me. Finally she shook her head.

I had to ask. "Have you become an oracle now? This is something new. I think you were just peering into my soul. What did you see, little sister?"

"More things than I can understand. When I first realized I could see inside witches' hearts, I was horrified. Gran taught me to control it, though. I accept it now. And you're my sister. I have a right to be nosy. What do I see in you? I see fire. I see a great holocaust of flame. Flame that I don't understand. But it is you. I see your man. Etienne. Earth magic has tied you to him—and him to you. I could see that long before I researched your birth connections. I suggest you go get him before he does something stupid."

Laughter came from the woods, from the leaves and the light wind circling us. I could see Marisol didn't hear it. I still wondered if the Mother's blessing was equal to her plans and scheming.

chapter 35

The cab I called dropped me off on River Street and I walked through the Barrows to Etienne's compound. He and I had lived through a night of incredible sex and harrowing events that came close to killing us. And there was his betrayal and what he would perceive as mine.

I understood the concept of the greater good, keeping magical artifacts away from Aiakós. I understood his fear of earth magic. I'd felt it at one time. I had the blessing of a strong witch standing behind me to guide me through those fears. If I stayed with him, would I have to take on that role? Did I want to stay? Accept that responsibility? I barely knew myself. I figured I'd know when I saw him. All I could do was hope for a solution to the problems we faced.

I had talked to Abigail more about Etienne and me, and why his magic was bound in the first place. She advised me to let the reasons for the original binding placement alone. "Occasionally," she said, "someone is born with power that should not use it. Perhaps in this case, he was bound until the time came for *you* to use it. I suspect this event is the fruition of some scheme for which the mother laid the foundation many years ago."

"The Mother came to me in a dream." I wanted her take on that. I gave her the details of my encounter.

Abigail gathered my hands in hers. "I'm used to her cryptic language. Occasionally I can even decipher it. When you saw her, you saw her as a woman, a humanlike mother who is benign and loves her children. I have devoted my life to her and I believe she does love us. What you have learned about her is something most witches will, thankfully, never know, because she does not speak directly to them. She is a goddess, a goddess in charge of our world. From the tiny innocent child to the chilling evil of the psychopath, she rules us. And uses us. And should it strike her fancy, she could cleanse the land of us and start over."

When Abigail said that, I simply decided to leave the conversation be and go on with my life.

The warehouse buildings at the compound remained as they had, tall, silent, and seemingly abandoned. The facade worked to discourage the occasional person walking or driving among them—if there were any persons who actually did that. I knew how the equipment was hidden, but how did he keep things so quiet? Probably truckloads of insulation, since all buildings had AC and heat.

As I approached the building that housed the office and Etienne's apartment, Michael walked out, followed by Etienne.

Michael gave me a brilliant smile. Etienne didn't. I saw it in his eyes. The uncertainty. I was still a witch and he'd given up his protection. A witch he'd betrayed by withholding information on someone she loved. A loved one who might have died had I not been so persistent.

Michael spoke first. "I understand there have been problems, Nyx. I'm happy you weren't injured." Easy enough to compare his voice to Aiakós's. I seriously wondered if he could morph into the beast that wanted to tear Etienne's face off in the ruins. It seemed likely that he could.

"Thanks." I gave him a carefully neutral smile.

Michael nodded pleasantly and walked to a Jaguar parked not far away. That left me alone with Etienne. Bandages wrapped around his upper arms, and he had dark circles under his eyes. An ache settled in my gut as I recognized the wariness, the tension in his body. Okay, so I still wanted him. If some desire for me remained in his heart, I'd take a chance on him.

"You get some antibiotics for those punctures?" I asked.

"Yes."

That single word was followed by an awkward silence.

In an effort to break it, I said, "I'd like to get my clothes and car."

At the same time he said, "Did Abigail heal you?"

Talk about clumsy. More silence.

"Can we go in and talk?" I asked. Maybe I could relieve some of the stress if we weren't on display. I could see no one, but I knew perfectly well someone watched.

He nodded and I followed him up the stairs to the apartment. The first thing he did was go to the kitchen and pour himself a drink. He tossed it down and poured another. I sat on the couch and he came to sit there, too, only being careful not to get too close.

"You're angry at me." He made it a statement, not a question.

"Yeah." I leaned back and tried to relax, or at least give the appearance that I was relaxed. "Maybe more confused than angry. I guess I'd say disappointed, too. So much of this didn't have to happen. If you'd just told me."

He leaned back and sighed. "I made a mistake. I'm sorry."

"And you're angry at me. I'm sorry you're angry, but not sorry for what I did."

"Logically, you're right. It was what you had to do. I guess."

I knew that, being a man, he wasn't going to give me much else. There would be no deep discussions—unless we made love again. I was lucky he admitted a mistake and apologized. What he told me about Oonagh after we made love came only because we were in an intimate situation and he'd let his guard down. That might never happen again. But it might, if we tried. If we could learn to trust each other.

"Is Aiakós after you?" I changed the subject. "I know he's pissed."

He gave a brief shake of his head. "Oh, yes. He's pissed. But Michael's intervened. Michael pays the bills and he wants everything to stay the same. I think I'll avoid the Zombie for a while if I can. But if dangerous things come through, I'll go fight."

"How are you dealing with . . . ?" Now, how did I talk about that?

"With what?"

"With the bindings being gone." I raised my hand to touch his forearm but drew back before actual contact. I was afraid he would get the idea that I had some fiendishly conceived plan to overcome him.

"I don't feel anything. Now. It was like indigestion for a while. Like something boiling in my body and . . . my brain. Abigail did something."

"Oh."

If she masked his power, it might show up at inappropriate times and places. I silently groaned. Unless she expected *me* to deal with it. The implications of that situation for an inadequate witch like me were mind-boggling. Not to mention he would probably be more powerful than me if punching a hole up through twenty feet of concrete was any indication. How would I handle the deplorable prospect of him having more power than me?

"Okay, so what happens now?" I truly didn't know.

He drained the glass and stared at it for a moment. Then he said, "I'd like you to stay here. Stay with me. I don't blame you if you want to leave, though. What do you want, Nyx?"

"I'd like to stay. If you can be honest with me. We really haven't had a chance, have we?"

"I'll work on it." His lips twitched, as if he wanted to smile. He would not leave himself vulnerable yet.

"You better work really hard," I told him. "Because the first deception and I'm out of here."

We both sat silent for a while; then he rose and went back to the kitchen. He lifted the bottle he'd left on the counter and poured another. I frowned. Why was he drinking so much? I suddenly realized I had something he had not received. Healing. Yes, he had meds, probably painkillers, but Aiakós had punched holes in him, not to mention the battering he'd taken in the collapse of the garage.

"You're in pain," I said. "If I get something from Abigail to help, will you accept it? It's better than drinking yourself into oblivion."

He glanced at the glass, then at me. "Yes."

It didn't take me long to get my car, then go to Abigail's and back. Abigail had no problem giving me a pain potion for him. When I brought it back to him, Etienne tossed it down like the glasses of whiskey and immediately became sleepy.

While he rested, I made the necessary calls to Single-Eye in San Francisco. Karen bubbled for twenty minutes about how wonderful my sister was and how she so wanted to meet her in person. Karen also became a highly paid manager and personal assistant. She could deal with my business and personal things in her usual competent manner. She could handle Harold, too. I'd miss it. I might have to fly out there occasionally, but this was the electronic age. Or Karen could bring things to me. She was ecstatic at the idea. Most business could be taken care of from Missouri.

I went in search of Darrow and found him in a gym. Men and women worked out on the floor, sweating and grunting like it really hurt. I plopped down beside him.

"Exercise at its best," I said. "Watching someone else do it."

Darrow chuckled. "Absolutely."

I sat close so I could lean against him. I'd leaned on him so many times in past years it seemed right. Once, for a few brief weeks before I left him to go him, he and I had been lovers. Not in love, or at least I wasn't, but very close. It wouldn't have happened before I was ready to leave, but once I'd made the decision, he'd asked and been received in my bed. Only once, at that final moment before departure, had he said "I love you." I did love him, but not like he loved me. It was a good memory, though, and one I cherished.

"You gonna hang around?" he asked.

"For a while."

"That's good. Boss man really likes you. Needs you. This place? You belong here. It fits you."

"Seems that way." I grinned. "Etienne might change his mind about having me around when he realizes I won't do everything he says."

"Nicky, if he doesn't know that by now, he's not as smart as I thought he was."

The prospect of facing unknown problems and agony daunted me a bit, but life was full of those. Except they had a tendency to be magnified here in this place of magic and a door to other worlds.

Darrow nodded. "Dark moon is coming. That's when crazy things happen. And other things have a tendency to come through the Zombie. We might get to fight. I kind of miss that."

"Have you seen Herschel?" I knew he could take care of himself, but needed to check on him. I hadn't seen him since we'd left the crush in the Barrows.

"Try the kitchen. He and the chef have become best friends. Chef says the dog is the only one who appreciates his culinary skill. Chef says they have an agreement. Big dog doesn't pass gas or drool in the kitchen and chef feeds him all he wants." Darrow laughed out loud with true amusement. "Etienne hasn't seen the bill yet."

Herschel was indeed lying by the wall in the kitchen. I sat beside him and laid my hand on his head. I wanted to thank him and tell him that I loved him, but it didn't seem necessary. "I guess we've come a long way from the swamp, buddy. Lot of mystery around you. Maybe I'll figure it out someday."

Herschel sighed. I took that as an agreement of sorts.

I left Herschel, talked with Rocky a while, and went back to the apartment. I found Etienne sitting on the couch.

"How is it?" I asked.

"Still hurts, but it's better." His face had lost that pinched look and I didn't see the bottle or a glass anywhere.

I sat beside him and he didn't pull away. "Have you seen Dervick around?"

"No. I haven't been out much."

"I need to find him."

"We can try where he was before. I'll take you." He hesitated. "If you don't mind."

Etienne showed me the way, but I had to drive. Though the pain in his arm had abated, he remained weak. We went to the place where I met Dervick the first time. The Bastinados were gone, so I couldn't be sure he was there. I walked into the abandoned building. Etienne followed me.

"Dervick?" My voice echoed.

"Yes, sister." He entered from another room. I thought he might take on the aspect of the first Dervick I saw, but he did not. He remained as I saw him in the parking garage, strong and fit. He gave me a warm smile and his eyes flickered with a tiny light. He was dressed more casually this time, jeans and a shirt.

"Will you tell me . . ." What did I ask him? What was it I wanted to know? How we were related and who—or what—he was. That would do to start.

"Of course. You and I, Nyx, have the same father by two very different witches."

"And our father is . . . ?"

"Someone who lived upon the skin of this world in the days of early man. One of the Earth Mother's children who is banished beneath her now. But those Hidden Ones are eternal and have been promised freedom in the future when man's time is finished. Our father walks here at times. He is able to assume a human form. He is ancient and the most powerful of his kind. He said our mothers found him and asked him to give them a child. He did so." He bared his arm to show me a bracelet much like the one I wore on mine. "Father gave us these, so we could speak to him if we wished. And to show our kinship with the fire. His fire. I've had mine all my life. You must be new to yours." He held out his hand. "Let me show you."

I stared at the hand of my supposed brother. Did I dare? Information on my father was something I really didn't need. In childhood I'd been curious, but if my father had never shown any interest in me, why should I care now?

"Nyx?" Etienne expressed his concern.

"I understand, but I have to learn what this is about," I said.

I wrapped my fingers in Dervick's.

The world dissolved in flame. It burned high with light, but with no heat. Below me I saw rivers of molten lava. Above there was no sky, only more flame. I understood that it was a vision, since I could still feel Dervick's fingers. A single word came, wreathed in fire.

"Daughter."

I turned and saw . . . it could not be. Of all the impossible and improbable things. Enormous, bright as the finest gold ever forged and polished by man.

Dragon.

chapter 36

I don't know how long I stared. Time had ceased. My mind suddenly seemed too small to absorb the presentation of such an amazing thing. Of course I'd seen water dragons, Penrod and Chalice. This dragon was on a scale so massive it would dwarf them like Herschel would dwarf a flea. And it had wings.

"Isn't he magnificent?" I heard Dervick's words, but *magnificent* seemed too trivial.

The dragon turned its head and stared at me — saw me.

"No!" I couldn't get my jumbled thoughts to wrap around it. I jerked my hand out of Dervick's and the fire ceased. I stood not in the flames but in a decrepit hollowed-out building somewhere in Missouri. And it was cold. So cold I thought I would freeze. My teeth chattered. Etienne came and wrapped an arm around me and dragged me away from Dervick. He held the gun in his other hand, pointed straight at Dervick. I relaxed against him.

"Are you hurt?" Etienne asked. He didn't look at me, but kept his eyes and gun on the possible danger.

Dervick himself stood watching us, silent and patient. I got the feeling that the bullets Etienne might send his way were of no concern to him. He'd told me as much. I wasn't bulletproof. How could he be?

By the time my teeth stopped chattering, anger had risen to an astronomical level. I stood straight, ready for battle. And there was nothing to fight.

"What kind of illusion was that?" I demanded. It had to be a trick. I knew magic, but . . . was I so sure that my knowledge was complete?

"Illusion? You don't believe?" He sighed. His mouth turned down and his shoulders slumped. "I wish I could be like him. I can't. Neither can you." He looked away so I couldn't see his face. I heard deep sadness in those last words. Had he actually wanted to be able to change shape? To become like our supposed father?

"No. No. There are no . . . they don't exist." I crossed my arms and shook my head. Denial. I would remain in denial. I couldn't make myself say the word.

Dervick gave a loud laugh, seeming truly amused by my rejection. "I understand. I was only a child when I received the revelation of my parentage. And in some ways, you are right." His voice tightened and I heard the frustration there, too. "It might as well be an illusion for all the good it will do you or me. There are none of his kind here in this time and place, and will be none for the foreseeable future. At least not in that particular form. If we could only be . . ."

"Be what, Dervick? Beasts men would fear and try to destroy?"

"Perhaps." His smile turned smug. "But now you know. Every time you use your magic and call upon the fire, you will hear his voice. And you will understand."

"Why are you here?"

"My mother was an earth witch like yours. I can create some small illusions, as you saw when you first met me. I have built myself a rather luxurious nest I'll show you someday. But I am different in ways you cannot see. I can do other things. I've tried to live, but I have no place in the world but here." He held out his arms, palms up in a grand gesture. "This is where the magic lies. This place is a haven and a source. It called me." He grinned. He'd turned boyish again. "And I have had some legal disputes with the authorities in Miami."

"Get me out of here," I said to Etienne.

"I am not your enemy," Dervick called as we walked out of the building.

I heard a bit of a plea in his words, and loneliness. I turned back to him. Nest? Did he actually say nest? "We'll talk again, Dervick."

He laughed. "Anton. My name is Anton."

"Okay, Anton. I don't want to be your enemy, either."

I didn't speak as Etienne led me to the SUV and drove us back to the compound. When he parked the car, he asked the inevitable question. "Are you okay?"

Was I? I shuddered. "Yeah, I'm okay." Dragons? Or bullshit and illusions. I'd added another problem to my list. Anton Dervick and his pronouncements of his heritage and my own would come right after dealing with my feelings for Etienne and keeping Marisol away from Aiakós. What Dervick had shown me might be—or might not. A dragon? It was certainly improbable.

I already knew two dragons. Both were very real. The thought of them taking on a human shape and fathering or bearing a half-witch child seemed ludicrous. But if I believed Dervick and the vision he'd given me, while I remained the Earth Mother's child, I was not entirely human. I didn't like that.

The Earth Mother had done something rare when she spoke to me directly in my dream, so rare even Marisol was jealous. Now I'd have to find a way to ask her about dragons. Etienne distracted me by sliding his hand in mine. I moved closer and kissed him as gently as I could.

He frowned. "Visions . . . dreams . . . nightmares. They're not real. They can be lies. *Talk* about magic is basically all lies. The magic itself is real, but it injures everyone it touches. Now it's in me. Like a . . . disease."

Ah, yes. Get away from my problems and back to his. I wasn't the only one dealing with revelation in my life. "I guess I understand. When I was a kid, magic was a plaything. Then I had to grow up and it became a weapon. It was never a way of life. I didn't want what others wanted. To live with it every day, to let the study and practice consume me."

"But it does, Nyx. It's consumed you since you came to the Barrows. You may not study, but have you ever used magic on a day-to-day basis before you came here?"

"No, but it was always there. Not a way of life, but a part of me. And you have a lot to learn about magic." To be safe, he would have to learn.

He held me tighter. "I love you, Nyx. From the minute I first saw you sitting at Laudine's. When you came outside with me, it was all I could do not to grab you and take you away from her. And that's something I never thought I'd say to a witch—or a woman."

"I'm here, Etienne." Did I love him? Probably. It wasn't perfect. I simply couldn't bring myself to say the words. But I thought I would someday. I kissed him to show him how I really meant it.

ABOUT THE AUTHOR

Lee Roland lives in Florida. She received an RWA Golden Heart nomination in 2008. To learn more about the world of *Vicious Moon*, please visit www.leeroland .com.

See how it all started in
the first Earth Witches novel
by Lee Roland,

VIPER MOON

Available now in print and e-book
from Signet Eclipse.

Mama wanted me to be a veterinarian. She'd probably have settled for a nurse, teacher, or grocery store clerk. She never came right out and said, "Cassandra, you disappointed me" or "Cassandra, you have so much potential," but I knew I'd let her down.

The idea of me running down a slimy storm sewer in the desolate, abandoned ruins of the Barrows section of Duivel, Missouri, probably never crossed her mind. The unconscious five-year-old boy strapped to my back and the angry monster with fangs and claws snapping at my heels were just part of my job. Maybe Mama was right— I'd made the wrong career choice.

I'm in good shape, but I'd run, crawled, and slogged through the sewer for over an hour. My chest heaved in the moldy, moisture-laden air by the time I finally reached my escape hatch. The glow from phosphorescent lichen gave me enough light to see the manhole shaft leading out of this little section of hell. Claws clattered right behind me and the tunnel echoed with slobbering grunts. This particular monster was an apelike brute with porcupine quills running down its spine and glowing green eyes.

Up into the manhole cylinder, two rungs, three ... Roars bounced off the tight walls ... Almost there—a claw snagged my slime-covered boot.

I jerked away and heaved myself out onto the deserted street.

Not good.

Clouds covered the full moon's silver face, so my vile pursuer might actually take a chance and follow me. The Earth Mother has no power here in the Barrows, save her daughter's light in the midnight sky. Maiden, mother, and crone, signifying the progression of life from cradle to grave, that ancient pagan female entity had called me to her service years ago. Now, in her name, I ran for my life. In her name, I carried this innocent child away from evil.

I'd managed to get off two shots and my bronze bullets hurt the ugly sucker, but a kill required a hit in a critical area like an eye. I could stop and aim or run like hell. I ran.

Its claws gouged out the asphalt as it dragged itself after me.

Under usual circumstances, I wouldn't have gone below the street. I'm good at kick the door down, grab the kid, and run. This time a bit of stealth was required since the door guards carried significant firepower. I was definitely outgunned.

Most things living in the storm sewers were prey. The small creatures ran from me. This time I'd crossed paths with a larger predator determined to make me a midnight snack.

I'd parked my car on the next block, so I sprinted toward a dark, shadowed alley that cut between the three-story brick buildings. Derelict vehicles and broken furniture made my path an obstacle course as I threaded my way through the debris toward the pitiful yellow light of a rare streetlamp at the alley's far end.

A coughlike snarl came from behind. The creature would leap over things I had to go around. I wouldn't make it, and if I did, those claws would tear the metal off my little car like I would peel an orange. I'd have to turn and fight soon. I hoped I could take the thing down before it overwhelmed me.

Halfway down the alley, a door suddenly opened in the building to my left. A Bastinado in full gang regalia, including weapons, stepped out. Though technically human, Bastinados are filthy, sadistic bastards whose myriad hobbies include rape, robbery, and murder.

I had nothing to lose as terror nipped at my heels and gave me momentum. I rammed the Bastinado with my shoulder, knocked him down, and rushed inside. Drug paraphernalia and naked gang members lay scattered around the room. I'd crashed their party and brought a monster as my date. The Bastinado at the door certainly hadn't stopped it.

The creature roared louder than the boom box thumping the walls with teeth-rattling bass. The Bastinados grabbed their weapons. They barely glanced at me as I crossed the room at a dead run. Two guards stood at the front door, but they had their eyes on the monster, too. I shoved my way past the guards. Screams and gunshots filled the night. Throw the door bolt and I emerged onto the sidewalk.

I raced down the street. I hadn't gone far when the ground suddenly heaved and shuddered under my feet. The whole block thundered with a massive explosion. A vast wind howled, furious and red, and surged down the street in battering waves.

Tornados of brilliant orange fire blasted out the windows of the building I'd escaped, and washed over the street like an outrageous, misguided sunrise. A hot hand of air picked me up and slammed me to the broken concrete. I twisted and landed face-first to protect the boy strapped to my back, then rolled to my side with my body between him and the inferno. I covered my face with my arms. More explosions followed and the doomed building's front facade crumbled into the street while burning debris rained from the sky.

What in the Earth Mother's name had been in there?

When the fury abated a bit, I forced myself to my feet and headed for the car. Was the pavement moving or was it me staggering?

The sound of the explosion still hammered my eardrums. I opened the back door, peeled away the straps and protective covering holding the boy secure against my body. I laid him across the backseat. He didn't seem injured, and he still slept from the sedative I'd given him to keep him calm.

It wasn't until I climbed in the driver's seat and fumbled for my key that I noticed the blood—my blood—too much blood. Slick wet crimson streaked down the side of my face and soaked half my shirt. Shards of glass protruded like rough diamonds from my forearm's blistered skin. It didn't hurt—yet. Pain would come soon enough.

I turned the key in the ignition. Nothing happened.

Another deeper blast rumbled under the street, shaking the car.

Sirens sounded in the distance, police, fire trucks, ambulances, rushing to the scene. They rarely entered the Barrows, but the magnitude of the blast I'd lived through couldn't be ignored.

I turned the key again. And again.

Last month I'd had to make a choice. Fix the car's starter or buy special hand-loaded bronze bullets. I'd chosen bullets.

The fourth time I twisted the key, the engine jerked to life. It sputtered twice, then smoothed. I popped it into gear and rolled forward, away from the fiery beast still raging behind.

Symptoms of shock crept in and pain found me. It rose by increments, increasing in intensity with every passing moment. My heart raced at a frantic pace and my arms shook so I could barely hold the wheel. Sweat formed an icy second skin as my body temperature took a nosedive. Sweet Mother, it hurt. The street blurred and shifted in my vision. Worse, though, was the feeling of pursuit. My little car chased through the deserted streets by some invisible, unimaginable horror. With considerable will, I kept my foot from mashing down the gas pedal.

Clouds drifted away from the cold, exquisite full moon.

"Follow," a soft voice whispered and urged me on. The white orb in the sky suddenly filled the windshield, rising to a brilliant mass of pure, clear light. I drove toward the radiance, navigating well-known streets as if dreaming of driving. North, keep moving north. A stop sign? Okay. Don't run that red light. If a cop stopped me, they'd call an ambulance, take me to the hospital, and I'd die. I was already beyond the skill of modern medicine's healing.

The child in the backseat moaned, as if in a nightmare. I had to stay conscious long enough to get him to safety. I wouldn't go down for nothing.

The guiding brilliance faded as I reached my destination. Control of the automobile eluded me, however, and the mailbox loomed. Before I could hit the brakes, I'd rolled over the box and the small sign that marked the home and business of Madam Abigail. The sign offered psychic readings, but gave not a hint of the true power and grace of the woman who dwelled and worked there.

I plowed through the flowered yard. Abby was going to be seriously pissed at me. Two feet from the front porch, the car jerked to a halt. Abby would find me. Abby would care for me as she always had. Luminous moonlight filled the night again, then faded, leaving only sweet-smelling flowers that lured me into painless darkness.